# 3 Nights in Thailand

*"One man's dream can be (*

Based on

By

Trevor Whitehead

*"Be careful what you wish for."*

The author's imagination inspires this story.. The names of all the characters in this book are fictional.

**Please note that this book contains adult content that may be disturbing to some readers.**

All rights of distribution, including via film. Radio and television, photomechanical reproduction, audio storage media, electronic data storage media, and the reprinting of portions of the text are reserved.

The author is responsible for the content and corrections.

I dedicate this book to my wife, my son and my daughter.

*By the same author:*

*The Curry Affect*

*The Investigator's Part 1*

*The Investigator's Part 2*

*The Investigator's Part 3*

*The Investigator's Part 4*

*Pattaya Dangerous*

*More Laughter, Sweat & Fears*

*Housemates*

*The Bomb hoax*

*July 13$^{th}$*

*Birdie or Bust*

*Pattaya Pete: Friends Reunited*

*Arthur Ascot's Greatest Cases*

*Night Manager*

*Pattaya Calling*

## Chapter 1

### 2008

It was always going to be a strange morning for Bob Bates. It was a morning he wasn't looking forward to. He had shared the journey to and from work with his dear friend Tony Fellows for over twenty-five years. This was Tony's last day at work after being made redundant, and Bob didn't want to admit to himself how much he was going to miss his best friend and work colleague. The two of them had worked at the forklift truck manufacturing plant since the mid-seventies. Tony and Bob became friends after Bob started going out with Tony's wife's sister. They remained good friends even after Tony's bitter divorce from Susan two years previously. After giving up his stake in the matrimonial home in exchange for him keeping all his company pension, Tony had moved into a very smart rented flat. Bob insisted they continue to travel to work together, even though he had to do an extra five miles in the wrong direction when it was his turn to drive. As with any other morning, Tony was standing waiting at the entrance to the flats as Bob pulled up.
'Morning, Bob.' Tony called out as he climbed into the car.
'Here he is, old golden bollocks.' Bob loved to wind his friend up.
'I'd hardly call myself that. Chucked on the scrap heap at fifty-four.'
'Scrap heap? You'll be alright, a little lump sum and a pension, the world is your oyster.'
'Well, I'm not going to argue about the little lump sum. Little being the operative word. You know full well, mate, my pension is crap. I've lost nearly half of it because of my age.'
'Come on, Tone, you'll soon get another job, add that to your pension, you'll be quid's in.'
'Where on earth do you think I'm going to get another job that pays like this one in Ipswich?'
'I heard B&Q are hiring.'
'Oh, that's alright then. Maybe I'll get that sought-after position of meet and greet the customers.' That statement from Tony made Bob laugh.

'What, with your colourful language and a short fuse, you wouldn't last a day.'
'Precisely, Bob. Anyway, I've booked a holiday, so I'm not going to worry about looking for another job until I get back.'
'You never said you were going on holiday? Janice and I were going to ask you if you wanted to rent a villa with us in Greece for a couple of weeks next May.'
'That's very thoughtful of you, Bob, and to be fair, May is a long way away, so who knows? I loved all our holidays over the years, but to be honest, I'd feel a bit of a gooseberry. Plus, the fact that Janice is still in contact with Susan, and she'll be asking what I get up to.'
'Well, they are sister's Tone. I wouldn't worry, Susan is remarried now, and I'm sure she's not bothered by what you get up to.
'Yes, funny how you can be married to someone for thirty years, but you never really know them.'
'That's why I've never tied the knot, if it goes tits up, I can just walk away.'
'You're as good as married, how long have you been together now?'
'I don't know, about twenty-seven years. Listen, Tone, I know it's still painful, but you will meet someone else, I'm sure of it.' Bob did his best to cheer his friend up.
'Well, I've not had a lot of success so far. That internet dating has been a disaster.'
'Don't say I didn't tell you, it's dangerous, Tone, you don't know who you're going to meet on those types of sites.'
'You're not wrong there. The last one had a wooden leg!' Bob tried not to laugh.
'You should try meeting someone in the pub or a club.'
'I've tried Bob, I'm too old, it's a young man's game, not for an old fart like me.'
'What about those gingerbread clubs? I've heard you can get some nice women there.'
'I went to one meeting. Upstairs in the Crown. Bloody disaster. Full of old and fat rejects.'
'Whoa, that's a bit harsh, Tone.'
'Yes, sorry. Let's just say it wasn't for me.'
'Okay, well maybe you'll meet someone on holiday, where are you going?'

'Thailand.'
'Thailand … You, lucky bugger. That's the top of my wish list. I've always wanted to go there, without Janice, mind.'
'To be honest, it's never been a place I've given much thought to, but the temperature is good for October, and I got a good deal on the internet last night.'
'What? You've not gone through a travel agent?'
'Travel agent? Old hat, Bob. You can get better deals on the internet.'
'I don't know what you find to do on the internet for hours on end?'
'You need to get with the times, Bob. I spoke to Carol for a couple of hours last night on Skype.'
'Christ, how much did that cost you?'
'Nothing, it's free.'
'You spoke to your sister for two hours in Australia for free?'
'Yes, and it was a video chat, so we could see each other. It was just like I was sitting in her lounge.'
'Unbelievable. I'm going to look into getting a computer. Janice isn't keen, she thinks I'll be checking out the porn.'
'Well, she won't be wrong, Bob.'

After parking the car, the two men swiped in through the security gate.
'You didn't hear this from me, but they are having a presentation for you at lunchtime.'
'Really? What, that clown of a manager is going to present me with a miniature forklift truck mounted on a plinth and say what a wonderful worker I've been for the past thirty-eight years, but has, unfortunately, had to let me go? He can just f*** off.'
'The lads have had a good whip round, Tone. You were a popular guy here.'
'Not popular with the management, though?'
'No, well, you ruffled a lot of feathers in your time as a union rep.'
'Yes, and now I'm paying the ultimate price. Oh well, roll on four-thirty and I can get out of here for good.'
'Alright, Tone, I'll see you at lunchtime.' Bob wandered off towards the production line, and Tony headed off to the maintenance area.
Standing, waiting for him were a few of his colleagues and his long-time foreman, Geoff Smith.
'Pop in the office once you've changed, Tony.'

'Alright, Geoff.' The foreman walked off, and the young apprentice, Dave, bought a mug of tea over.

'Here you are, Tony. Last morning cuppa from me.'

'Well, young David, in three years you've not learnt a lot, but your tea has improved tenfold.'

'I'm coming to your drink up tonight.'

'Are you now? Do you want me to write a note to your mother, asking if you can stay out late?'

'No, but you can write to my girlfriend if you like, she'll be the one waiting for me to come home.'

'Remind me, how old are you?'

'Nineteen.'

'Take a bit of advice from an old man. Once you've finished your apprenticeship, get out of here and see some of the world. If you don't, the years will pass by and before you know it, it will be you standing here on your last day.' David looked around at the group of middle-aged men.

'I will, Tony. Thanks for the advice.'

'Right lads, let's get busy.' The man Tony wouldn't miss came bowling in. Steve Sherwood, senior shop steward and the man who took over from Tony after he'd resigned from the position because of the stress of his sudden divorce.

'Not you, of course, Tony. I'm surprised you're working today. You could have just come in for the presentation and then just f***** off.'

'Two things, Steve. One, you're not management, so don't come in here shouting the odds, secondly, I wouldn't give these c**** the satisfaction of thinking they're doing me any favours.'

'Alright, Tony, calm down. I was just saying, that's all.'

'Well, say it somewhere else, you prick.' Steve Sherwood stood and stared for a minute, then sloped off.

'Nice one, Tony. I love the way you talk to him; I'm going to miss you being here.'

'Thank you, young man, I'm going to miss your tea. Right, let's see what our Geoff wants.' After getting changed into his overalls, Tony headed to Geoff Smith's office.

'Come in, Tony, shut the door, mate.' Tony closed the door and sat down opposite Geoff's cluttered desk.

'End of an era, Tony.'

'It is Geoff.'
'Listen, I'm gutted to be losing you today, and I wanted to tell you to your face that I fought tooth and nail to keep you. You're one of, if not the best, fitters we have here. Bloody madness to let you go, I can sacrifice at least ten guys before you.'
'Thanks, Geoff, I appreciate your kind words, but I think we both know why my name came up. It's payback time. That c*** Wheeler is getting his revenge. As soon as I heard there was going to be a reduction in the headcount in the factory, I knew I would be the first on the hit list, or should I say his hit list.'
'Unfortunately, and off the record, you're right, Tony. Makes a whole mockery of the system, I have guys older than you who are desperate for early retirement, there's you, eleven years away from retirement, being pushed out.'
'Oh well, what goes around comes around, hopefully. Let's hope Wheeler gets his comeuppance. Listen, Geoff, you will pop in for a beer at the club tonight?'
'Absolutely. Oh, I nearly forgot why I called you in here.' Geoff opened a drawer and pulled out a small wrapped gift and a card.
'Just a little something from June and me.'
'Thanks, Geoff. Right, I'd better do something, even if it is my last day.'
'All the best, Tony.' The two men shook hands, this was one of the people Tony would miss once he left the factory.
As lunchtime approached Tony and a few of his colleagues made their way to the works canteen. Halfway through his meal, he spotted his manager, Peter Wheeler, come into the canteen with a few other staff employees.
'Here we go, Tony. Looks like old Wheeler is going to present you with your little fork truck.'
'Yes, followed by a kick up the arse,' joked Dave the apprentice.
'Hello lads, mind if I sit here?'
'Sit down, Bob.' Gestured Tony. Bob Bates sat down with Tony and the other maintenance men.
'So, Bob. Losing your brother-in-law and travelling companion after all these years? What on earth are you going to do without him?' Asked electrician Peter Stubb.
'Use your blow-up doll, Bob. Stick some clothes on her and put her on the front seat.'

'Stupid boy.' Remarked Bob.
'I am going to miss him, Pete. I'm sad to see him go.'
'So, Tony, have you thought of what you're going to do?'
'Not really, Pete. I've booked a holiday, so I'm not going to worry about anything until I come back.'
'Where are you going?' Inquired the electrician.
'Thailand.'
'Lovely, I've been there, beautiful country. When are you going?'
'Next Friday.'
'Take plenty of sun cream, it can be very hot, even in October.'
'Whereabouts did you stay in Thailand, Peter?'
'A beautiful island called Koh Chang. It was a bit of a trek from the airport, but so worth it. Where are you staying?'
'Somewhere near Pattaya, can't remember the name.'
'Jomtien?'
'Yes, that sounds like it. About an hour on the bus from the airport, according to what I've read up about it.'
'Get a taxi, Tony. It will only be about twenty pounds, and save all the hassle of the bus ride. Remember, you'll still have to get a taxi from the bus station to your hotel.'
'Twenty pounds, you sure?'
'Positive, just make sure you agree on the price with the driver first. You'll have the time of your life, Tony. It's a single man's paradise. You don't fancy it then, Bob?'
'I do, it's on the top of my wishlist, but the boss wouldn't travel that far.'
'That, and she wouldn't like all the Thai women chasing after you.'
'Don't, I'm jealous enough as it is.'
'Ladies and gentlemen, if I could have your attention. As you all most probably know, we have four of our employees leaving us today. So, if the four in question would like to make their way over here, I'd like to say a few words and present you with a miniature replica of our bestselling forklift truck. Cyril will take some photographs to record the event, and you'll all get a keepsake photo.' Tony strolled up and joined the other three. One by one, they walked up and had their presentation and photograph. Eventually, Tony reluctantly shook hands with Peter Wheeler and accepted the plinth with a little fork truck sitting on it and a brass plate inscribed with, "Presented to

Anthony Fellows for 38 years loyal service at Hystar fork truck company." Doing his best to smile for the photo, he then went to walk away.
'All the best for the future, Tony.' Not saying a word, Tony turned to go back to his colleagues; however, Bob was standing in the way.
'One moment, Tone. On behalf of all your friends who are here, and not forgetting the nightshift who have also contributed, I would like to give you this Marks & Spencer voucher as a goodbye gift from us all.' Tony took the voucher and smiled.
'Well, what can I say? Just that it's been an absolute pleasure working and knowing you guys, thank you very much for this generous gift. I shall use this to kit myself out for my forthcoming holiday.' Tony shook Bob's hand.
'Thanks, Bob. Oh, and don't forget I'm having a leaving do at the rugby club tonight, free food and I've put some money behind the bar, you're all welcome.' That bit of news produced a loud cheer.

Four-thirty on the dot, Tony swiped out for the very last time. Walking through the large car park, he couldn't help but take a final look at the factory he'd worked at for nearly forty years.
'Come on, Tone, never look back.' Bob called over and unlocked the car.
'It will seem strange on Monday; I'd better remember not to set the alarm.'
'You can always run me to work if you want.'
'No, you're alright, mate.' The journey home was fairly quiet. Bob wasn't quite sure what to say to his friend that would make him feel better.
'That was a good collection for you, Tone.'
'It was, Bob. I'm guessing you organised that.'
'Guilty as charged. It was easy, Tone. A lot of people are grateful for what you did for them when you were our union rep.'
'Well, had I not resigned a couple of years ago, I'd still be the union rep and I'd still have a job. Another thing I can thank Susan for.'
'Hindsight is a lovely thing, Tone. Listen, mate, you can't change anything now. A whole new life is beckoning. Tell you what, when we get to yours, you can show me your computer and where you're going on holiday.'

'It's a laptop, Bob. Yes, come in and have a beer. We should celebrate the last drive home. You're not driving tonight, are you?'
'No way, Janice can pick me up. How are you getting home?'
'Taxi most probably.'
'We'll take you home, Tone.'
'But it's miles out of your way, and Janice won't be happy.'
'I'll tell her we're going to pop into yours for a nightcap, you know she's been dying to see your flat for the past two years. Curiosity killed the cat, and all that. She'll take you home, no problem.'

Inside the flat, Tony was sorting out the drinks.
'You want a glass, Bob?'
'No, bottles fine thanks.' Tony walked from his small kitchen into the lounge where Bob had made himself comfortable on the sofa.
'Cheers.' The two men clinked bottles.
'All the best, Tone. Right, make me jealous and show me where you're going, then?' Tony played around with his laptop and eventually, a nice hotel popped up on the screen.
'Here we go, that's my hotel. Right opposite the beach.'
'Bloody hell, Tone, that looks nice. I bet that wasn't cheap.'
'It was actually, works out at twenty-five pounds a night with a buffet breakfast.'
'What's wrong with it?'
'Nothing, they're all around that price for a 4-star.'
'How much for the flight?'
'Now, that wasn't cheap, six hundred pounds. I could have got it a bit cheaper if I was willing to change flights, but it's a twelve-hour journey, so I'd rather pay a bit extra and have a direct flight, rather than add hours to the journey.'
'I don't blame you. Christ, twelve hours, the longest I've done is four and a half to the Canaries. So, you've booked everything on here?'
'Yes, there are a few sites that offer deals on hotels, you just put in where you want to go. Once I saw the hotel was available on those dates, I just checked the flights. Once I was happy, I booked and paid for them both.'
'How did you pay?'
'On my credit card.'

'Credit card, are you mad? I've read about some real horror stories about people putting their credit card details on the computer.'
'It's safe, Bob. I'm telling you, this is the future; the days of using a travel agent are numbered.'
'But how do you get your ticket?'
'You get a confirmation number. I need to get a few things printed off, but I can do that in town on Monday. I'm half thinking about buying my own printer, it would come in handy for sure.'
'Can you bring up anything about the town where you're staying?'
'Yes, I had a look last night and put it in my favourites. Apparently, I'm only a ten-minute bus ride from Pattaya.'
'I've heard of that place.'
'Who hasn't? Now, don't go getting all excited when I show you this site.' Tony clicked on to a Pattaya website he'd saved, and Bob's eyes lit up.
'You, lucky sod, Tone.'
'Let's have a look at that island, Peter was on about?'
'Did he say Koy Change?'
'No, you Muppet, Koh Chang.' Laughed Bob.
'That's the one.' Tony typed the island's name in and he went into one of the websites.
'Wow, welcome to paradise.'
'It certainly looks beautiful, is it anywhere near where you're staying?'
'I don't know, but I might enquire while I'm there, I want to see a bit of the country.'
'This laptop is great, Tone.'
'I told you, try checking out a few holiday sites before you go throwing your money at a travel agent again. I'm sure you'll save yourself a few quid.'
'Good thinking, Tone. Here, I might use that ploy to convince Janice to let me buy a computer. Long term, the money saved on holidays it will pay for itself.'
'Remind me, who wears the trousers in your house?'
'Alright, I hear what you're saying, and you are right. I'm going to go out this weekend and buy one, sod her.'
'Careful, Bob. You don't want to be sleeping in the spare bedroom again, do you?'
'I'll have you know that bed is really comfortable.'

'Well, you sleep in there often enough. Right, while I think of it, hang on to my spare key.'
'What for?'
'I don't know, in case of an emergency or something.'
'What? Do you think something is going to happen to you?'
'No, I just think you should look after my spare key. You never know, I might lock myself out or lose my keys.'
'Alright. Just take care over there, Tone. Strange country and you'll be on your own.'
'Don't worry, Bob, I'll be fine. Right, I'll find the spare keys, then I'd better get myself ready. I want to get to the club early to make sure the food is all there.'
'Okay, I'll leave you to it.'
'Listen, Bob. Thanks for everything, mate. If it wasn't for you, well, I don't know how I would have coped once Susan announced she wanted a divorce. You've been a very good friend to me, and I want you to know that.'
'You'd have done the same for me, Tone.' The two men shook hands. 'I'll see you tonight.'
'You most certainly will.' Tony handed the spare keys to his flat over and walked Bob to the door. Waving him off, he went back into the lounge. Even after two years, he still felt the loneliness.

Opening his rucksack, he pulled out the little retirement plaque and placed it on the TV cabinet. The Marks and Spencer voucher for five hundred pounds he put on the coffee table. Pulling out the wrapped gift from his foreman, Geoff, he unwrapped it and inside was a five-year diary. After opening and reading the card, he put it on the other side of the TV cabinet. "Merry Christmas," he mumbled to himself as he went to get ready.

At six thirty on the dot, Tony arrived at the rugby club. After paying the taxi driver, he strolled in, and even though he told people that he would be there anytime after seven, he was surprised to see young David standing at the bar sipping a pint.
'You old enough to be drinking that?'
'Don't you start, Tony? The bloody barman has already asked me for ID?'

'Well, it's that baby face of yours. You ready for another?'
'I never turn down a pint, Tony.'
'Pint? I was going to get you a half. Two lagers, please. Sid.'
The barman strolled over.
'The food is all laid out in the function room, Tony. Just needs unwrapping when you're ready. Two lagers you say?'
'Please, Sid. Stick them on the tab.'
'Will do.'
'Food? Pushing the boat out a bit, aren't you?'
'You only retire once, David. Anyway, I can't expect everybody to stand in that room and not feed them.'
'So, you're off to Thailand next week.'
'I am, this time next week I should be there.'
'Get them in then.' Tony turned around to see Bob heading towards them.'
'Bloody hell, I said any time after seven.'
'It's the free bar, Tony. Old Bob wants to make sure he's not missing out on anything.'
'Cheeky git, you old enough to be drinking beer.'
'Oh, like I've not heard that one before.'
'Alright, you two, that's enough. It's not a free bar, I've put some money behind and once it's gone, it's gone and you'll have to buy your own.'
'I rest my case.' David winked at Tony and went over to the fruit machine.
'I've got some news. When I got home, I told Janice I'm buying a computer. She said it was a good idea, so we're off into town tomorrow to get one.'
'That's a change of heart then?'
'Yes, but I'm not going to knock it.'
'I'm no expert on computers, Bob. But I'd go for a laptop. You can pack it away when you're not using it, plus it's portable. I'm taking mine to Thailand.'
'Really? Whatever for.'
'In case I want to check things out. I can still call my sister and watch a DVD if I want to.'
'You'll be able to call me, Tone. Once I'm set up, we can be Skype friends. You can call me from Thailand.'

'If I get time, Bob. Look, here come a few of the others. I'd better start to mingle.'

After a boozy session, Tony, slightly worse for wear, was thanking his ex-sister-in-law for picking him and Bob up.
'Thanks ever so much for the lift home, Janice.' Tony was sitting in the front of Janice's car, and Bob was lying across the backseat, drunk and asleep.
'I don't mind, Tony. So, this early retirement came out of the blue then?'
'It did, and about five years too early.'
'Yes, Bob said you weren't happy about it.'
'It's the pension, Janice. It won't be enough to live on. It doesn't even pay the rent on my flat.'
'You'll find another job, I'm sure of it.'
'Yes, but it's not going to be easy at my age. I'll start looking when I come back from my holiday. Bob told me you're getting a computer?'
'Yes, I've moaned at him for ages about getting one. You know what he's like when it comes to spending money. But as soon as I said I'd pay half, he wants to get one.'
'Really?'
That wasn't the story Bob had been telling Tony, but he thought it best not to mention anything.
'How long have you been in this flat now, Tony?'
'It will be two years on the 1st of December.'
'Blimey, that's gone quick. It's a nice area, mind. You think you will stay here?'
'I doubt it, I most probably will have to find something a bit cheaper. My lease renewal is coming up, so I'll have to give it some serious thought soon.'

Janice pulled up outside the posh-looking flats.
'Thanks ever so much for the lift home, Janice.'
'That's okay. Can I be cheeky and use your toilet?' Tony knew this was just an excuse to have a look at your flat.
'Yes, of course, you can.' Tony wasn't surprised Janice asked. He also guessed this would filter back to his ex-wife.
'I'll leave sleeping beauty in the car.'

'Will you wake him up when you get home?'
'No way. I'll chuck a blanket on him and leave him in the car.'
Tony led the way and opened the main door that led to the flats.
'Security cameras?' Janice pointed above the door.
'Yes, on all the floors, it's very safe here.'
'No lift?'
'No, mind you, there are only four floors. Luckily, I'm on the second.'
When they reached Tony's flat, Janice was panting a bit.
'Glad you're not on the top floor, Tony.'
Smiling, Tony unlocked the door and let Janice in.
'Wow, it's very nice, Tony.' Janice had a quick peek around.
'A real bachelor pad.'
'Yes, the guy didn't scrimp when it came to kitting it out. He bought it as an investment. I'm the first person to live in it. I just wanted somewhere where I'd feel comfortable for a while. You know, it all happened so quickly, and as I was feeling so low, well, I just wanted to treat myself.'
'Yes, I can understand that. Listen, Tony, I never knew anything about Susan carrying on. I was absolutely horrified when she told me. I know she's my sister, but I've never taken sides.'
Tony had never spoken to Janice about the breakup and divorce before.
'Thanks, Janice. It nearly broke me, you know. If it weren't for Bob, I'm not sure I would have made it through. He was like a rock for me.'
'Oh, he has his moments, but he has a good heart. He told me right at the beginning that you were his best friend and nothing would change that. I know you think I only wanted to come up here to check out your flat so I can tell Susan. But I won't. She will ask, but I will tell her it's not her business. She's rushed into marriage with this Frank; I can only think she had some form of midlife crisis. After Emily got married, I guess that affected her. Do you hear from her?'
'We speak on the phone maybe three times a week. She was really worried about me. But she has her life, I know she's busy at work. I think she feels in the middle of what's gone on and doesn't want to take sides.'
'Well, if it's any consolation, and you didn't hear this from me, she hardly contacts her mother. Right, I'd better go.'
'What about the toilet?'

'I think I can hold it, to be honest. Come round for dinner Sunday, Tony.'
'You sure?'
'I wouldn't ask you if I wasn't sure. You take care.'
Janice gave him a quick hug.
'Come at about 1 pm. See you.' Tony watched her go down the stairs and then walked over to his lounge window so he could see Janice walk to the car. She turned and gave him a wave. Climbed in and drove off.

Tony hadn't had dinner at Bob's house since the divorce. He'd bought a nice bottle of wine to take with him. Pulling up on the driveway, Bob was already waiting by the door.
'Hello, Tone. You found us then?' He joked.
'Well, I wasn't quite sure, I had to stop and ask a couple of people.'
'Come in, I want to show you our new toy.'
'Something smells nice.' Tony couldn't remember when he'd last eaten a home-cooked Sunday roast.
'Hello Tony, hope you're hungry.' Janice appeared at the kitchen door.
'I am, this is for you.' Tony handed the wine over.
'This is my favourite, thank you.'
'I remembered you liked that one.'
'That's very kind of you. Bob, get Tony a beer out of the fridge. Dinner will be about thirty minutes.'
'Yes, boss.' Bob gave a comical salute.
'Go up to the spare room, Tony, I'll bring the beers up.'
'Spare room?'
'Yes, Tony. Bob wants to show off our latest acquisition.'
Tony went upstairs and opened the door to the spare bedroom. On a nice computer table was a shiny new laptop. Bob came into the room carrying two beers.
'What do you think? We have broadband and everything.'
'Very nice, Bob.'
'Here, I'll put your beer over here on the window ledge, can't be too careful. Take a seat and have a go on it, I think you'll be impressed.'
Tony sat down and brought up the internet.
'Yes, it's quick, a lot quicker than mine. Have you used it much?'
'I was on it until 4 am this morning.'

'Says a man who questioned me the other day about what I find to do on the computer all that time.'

Tony clicked on the history tab, and a long list of porn sites sprang up.

'Whoa, Bob, you need to clear your history, mate, if Janice sees this, she'll go mad.'

'How do you clear the history, Tone?' Asked an embarrassed Bob.

'Look, click on that icon, then history, then this one, clear history. See, all gone.'

'Thanks, Tone. What about this Skype, how do we become friends?'

Tony played about on the laptop for a minute. After setting up Skype, he turned to Bob.

'There, I've sent a contact request to me. When I get home, I'll accept, then we should be able to video call.'

'Thanks, Tone. Do you think it's worth having a few computer lessons?'

'I don't know, it depends on what you want to do. You know how to start it up and shut it down. I think you can teach yourself. I didn't have a clue to start with, but I soon found out how to send emails and attachments. You can put all your photos on here for storage, download music, and surf the net. Just play around with it, Bob. If you get stuck, I'll always help you.'

'Cheers, Tone, I appreciate that. Well, I don't know about you, but I'm ready for my dinner.'

'Me too, my stomach is rumbling.'

After sliding his dinner plate to one side, feeling bloated, Tony thanked the cook.

'That was superb, thank you, Janice.'

'You're more than welcome, Tony. It's been way too long since you came here for dinner. So, Bob tells me you're getting ready for this trip of a lifetime?'

'Getting there. I have to go into town tomorrow, I need to get a bit of printing done. Then, I'll have a browse around Marks and Spencer, and get a few bits for the holiday. From what I've been reading up on, it sounds like a vest, shorts and flip flops type of place.'

'You'll only need a small case, then.' Remarked Janice.

'Don't forget your king-sized pack of condoms.' Called out Bob, forgetting where he was for a second. There was an embarrassing silence for a few seconds until Janice started giggling, followed by rapturous laughing from the two men. Eventually, they did their best to compose themselves.

'Bob, what a thing to say at the dinner table.'

'Sorry, Jan. It was the old Boy Scout coming out in me.'

'Be prepared,' called out Tony, starting them off again. The laughter stopped when the doorbell rang.

'See who that is, Bob. Tell them you're in the middle of dinner. Right, I'll clear this away, and I have a nice apple pie for dessert.' Bob stood up and headed for the front door.

'Pour some more wine out, Tony.' Grabbing the bottle, Tony topped Janice's glass up.

'I'd better not have any more, I've got the car. When I return from my holiday and am settled, you and Bob can come over one night. I'll order us in a takeaway, I'd forgotten what good company you two are.' Janice walked over and put her hand on his shoulder.

'That's a lovely thing to say, Tony.' Bob walked into the dining room like he'd seen a ghost.

'What is it, Bob?'

'Err …. We have a visitor.'

'What did I say to you? Tell them we're having dinner. Who is it?'

'I don't want to say; she's sitting in the lounge?'

'For goodness' sake, Bob, who?'

'Your sister.'

'I don't believe it. Why didn't she ring first?'

'She's upset, Jan. Apparently, Frank has left her.'

'Sorry, Tony. I'd better go and see what's happened.' Tony went to stand up.

'No, you're our guest. Stay here with Bob. I'll see to Susan.'

'Here you are, you sure you don't want a drop more wine or a beer?'

'No thanks, Bob, tea is fine. Any idea what's happening out there?' Tony spoke in a lowered voice.

'Tears. As predicted, I might add. We said it would end in tears, and here we are two years down the road and her toyboy has left her.'

'I've never seen the bloke, Emily mentioned he was a bit younger.'

'A bit? About fifteen years, Tony, he's only in his late thirties.'

A flustered Janice came into the dining room.

'I'm so sorry about this, Tony. Can I give Susan a glass of that wine?'

'You don't have to ask, of course, you can, take the bottle.'
'Thanks. Bob, can you take that I told you so look off your face and dish up the apple pie? There's ice cream in the freezer.'

Thirty minutes later, Tony was helping Bob with the washing up.
'This takes me back, Bob'
'What does?'
'Washing up. I've not had to wash up for two years.'
'I forgot you've got a dishwasher in your flat, you lucky bugger.'
'Should invest in one, Bob. '
'Janice thinks they're a waste of money.' Tony wondered if it was Janice or was it Bob using that excuse not to spend money again. On cue, Janice walked into the kitchen.
'What are we like, getting our guest to wash up?'
'Not a problem, Janice, it might be a good experience for my next job, chief washer-upper.'
'Say no if you want to, but Susan wants to talk to you.'
'Really?'
'Yes. Listen, don't feel obliged, the way she treated you, well, I think you know our feelings on the matter. I don't mind telling her you don't want to.'
'What does she want?'
'Make the peace, I would imagine.' Tony hadn't spoken to his ex-wife since he'd moved out of their home nearly two years previously.
'Okay, I'll see what she wants. Tony went to walk through to the lounge when Janice called out.'
'Try not to gloat too much, she is still my sister after all.'
'I'll try my best.' Tony winked at Janice and walked into the lounge. Susan was sitting there, still an attractive woman at fifty-one. Red-eyed and holding a glass of wine, she smiled at her ex-husband.
'Hello, Tony. My God, you've lost some weight.'
'Yes, I lost a couple of stone. Started going to the gym again and took up squash.'
'Well, it suits you. I'm sorry to spoil your dinner, Jan said It's the first time you've been around since the divorce.'
'No problem, you didn't put me off my pudding.' Tony tried not to sound too sarcastic.
'I heard about you losing your job. What are you going to do?'

'Oh, I don't know, I have a few options,' he lied.
'I'm sorry, Tony. I never did apologise to you for what I did.'
'It's a bit late for that, Susan. Look, I'm sorry to hear about your troubles. Really, I am. But you made your bed, and well, you know the old saying.'
'Yes, I know. I've been a fool.'
'Well, if it's any consolation, you're still an attractive woman, you'll meet someone else.'
Janice walked in carrying a tray of teas.
'Bob's gone out to the garage to find the boxing gloves.'
'Not funny, Jan.'
'I'm joking, he's gone to the loo. You had enough to eat, Tony?'
'I'm stuffed, Janice. I'm not used to these big dinners.'
'Well, I'll cut up a bit of apple pie for you to take home.'
'Thank you.' Janice stood up and looked out of the lounge window. 'Where's your car, Susan?'
'I got a taxi, I'd already had a couple of glasses of wine at home.'
'Well, drink that tea, you've polished off that bottle.' Bob walked in and sat down.
'Well. This is nice, just like old times.' Janice gave Bob an "If looks could kill" stare.
'What?' He asked. After an uneasy silence, Tony broke the ice.
'Well, I'll have this tea and make a move.'
'You don't have to rush off on my behalf, Tony.'
'No, it's not that, Susan. I have a few things I need to get on with.'
'Tone's off to Thailand on Friday, aren't you, mate?'
'Yes, I've not had a holiday since … Well, since we all went to Minorca.'
'Thailand? That's a long way to go for a holiday, Tony.' Susan's remark was in a voice that had a slight growl to it.
'Single man's paradise, Susan.' Bob once again got a stare from Janice, but he didn't care. He'd never been over-keen on her sister, even more so after her behaviour that had a deep effect on his best friend.
'So, I've heard. Do you think you could drop me off at home, please, Tony?'
'I'd rather not, sorry. You know the old saying, Never go back to the scene of a crime.' There was no way Tony would entertain taking his ex-wife home.

'Oh, I see.' Another uneasy silence came, only broken when Tony said his goodbyes.
'Right, well, I'd better hit the road. Once again, Janice, thanks for a lovely meal.'
'You're more than welcome, Tony. Enjoy your holiday.'
'I will. Bye for now.' Tony didn't make eye contact with Susan.
'Come on, Tone, I'll see you out.' Bob led Tony out into the hallway.
'You played a blinder there, mate.'
'One thing I've learnt in those two year's Bob, something you reminded me of on Friday in the car park, never look back.'
'True, Tone. Listen, did you say your flight was Friday night?'
'Yes, ten-thirty, I need to be there by seven-thirty latest.'
'Okay, I'll run you to the airport.'
'You sure? I was going to get the train.'
'Of course, I'm sure. The train will take you all afternoon. I'll finish work a bit earlier, pick you up at four, that will give us plenty of time to get you to Heathrow.'
'Thanks, Bob, I appreciate that.'
'No problem. I'll pop in one night after work, I'll ring you first, make sure you're in.' The two men shook hands.
'Okay, Bob. Take care, mate.'
'You too.' Bob watched his best friend drive away and shut the front door. Walking into the lounge, he could see the two sisters in full gossip mode.
'I'm going up to play on the computer.' He went upstairs and left the women to it.

After getting home, Tony started on a list of things he had to do before his holiday. He'd decided to crack on with everything tomorrow morning. Tuesday, he'd dedicate to getting his holiday clothes sorted. He was looking forward to a spend up in Marks and Spencer. After showering, he climbed on top of the bed and started to watch some late-night football highlights. He had plugged his mobile phone into the charger, and the ringtone blasting out made him jump. Looking at his watch, it was nearly midnight. Picking the phone up, he could see Bob Bates name flashing at him.
'Alright, Bob. A bit late to be calling.'
'Sorry, Tone.' Came the reply.

'I can hardly hear you, Bob. Why are you whispering?'
'I don't want Janice to hear. Can you tell me how to erase the history again? I've forgotten?'
'What are you like, Robert Bates? You'll go blind.'

The next few days flew by for Tony. What with buying a printer and setting it up. A whole day spent summer clothes shopping. After a visit to the job centre and a couple of letting agents, he felt like he'd had a productive couple of days. Late Wednesday afternoon the entrance door buzzed. Tony could see Bob's face on his little screen.
'Come up, mate.' Tony pressed the door release button and could see Bob disappear through the door. Tony opened the door to the flat and waited for Bob to come into view.
'Bloody hell, Bob. You want to start doing some exercise, you sound like an old locomotive coming up those stairs.'
'I get enough exercise on that production line, Tone.'
'True, well come in. What do you want, a cup of tea or a beer?'
'I wouldn't mind a beer, cheers, Tone.'
'Sit down, I'll bring a couple through.' Bob sat down and then spotted Tony's new printer.
'Been splashing out?' Tony came through carrying two glasses of beer.
'Yes, and to be honest, I think it will be money well spent. It was reduced from eighty pounds to fifty-nine. I've done all my own printing, it is so easy.'
'Might be to you, but as you know, I'm not really computer literate.'
'Yes, I've noticed. Sorted out how to remove the history yet?'
'Yes. Steve at work showed me on his laptop how to remove just the sites I need to hide from Janice. He said if I keep removing all the history, then Janice will become suspicious.'
'Very true.'
'So, what else have you been up to?'
'Well, I registered at the job centre. As predicted, there isn't much going on. However, I had a phone call from Ronnie Taylor. He has a job coming up next month at the power plant and said he can give me at least three to four months of work. Good money too.'
'Do I know, Ronnie Taylor?'
'Not sure, he's a contractor who comes into the factory now and again, and does a lot of the overhead steel work.'

'I know the guy. That's a result, Tone.'

'Yes, it will help me out for a while. I've been to a couple of letting agents, and I've decided to move when the lease runs out in November.'

'That's a shame, it's lovely this flat.'

'It is, mate. But to be honest, I'm paying way too much. Here, take a look at these, tell me what you think?' Tony passed Bob some information on flats that had taken his fancy.

Bob flicked through them as he sipped his beer.

'How much are you paying a month here, Tone?'

'Seven hundred. Plus, all the utility bills, and trust me when I tell you, these night storage heaters are expensive and crap. They start going cold in the evening when you want some heat.'

'Blimey, these are all nice, and half the price of what you're paying here.'

'Yes, I know. I'll see what's about when I get back from my holiday. Talking about holidays, I've been busy. I've booked three nights in a lovely hotel in Koh Chang. I can get a minibus to the port, then a thirty-minute crossing to the island.'

'What about the hotel you're staying at?'

'Well, I'll just have to bite the bullet on that. I'm there for three weeks, so I've booked Koh Chang right in the middle.'

'Three weeks? You never said you were going for three weeks?'

'Didn't I? Well, it's a long way to go, Bob. Plus, the fact I have nothing to rush back for, do I?'

'Fair point. So, you did all this on the internet?'

'Yes, I got some advice from a forum I joined.'

'Forum? What's a forum, Tone?'

'Hard to explain, really. I just found it by chance. It's people who have links to Thailand. A bit like a club, I suppose. I joined, and you can ask questions related to Thailand. I asked about Koh Chang and how far it was from Pattaya. I got loads of answers and advice. So, I booked and paid for the three nights.'

'I take my hat off to you, Tone. I don't think I have the confidence to do what you're doing.'

'It's not rocket science, mate.'

No, you're right. I said to Jan yesterday, we'll book our next holiday online. I was looking last night, and there are some real bargains. Only one problem with me waiting to book a holiday so late.'
'What's that? Normally, it works in your favour to hang on.'
'Jan's insisting, Susan, comes with us.'
'Oh … That's a bummer, Bob.'
'She's got me over a barrel, I'd mentioned a while back about asking you to come with us next year, so it sort of takes my argument away.'
'Does a bit. What's the latest there?'
'Well, the latest is she has moved into the other bedroom. Jan said she doesn't want her to be on her own?'
'Any chance she can patch things up with this, Frank?'
'No chance, Tone. I'm not getting told a lot, but what I have gathered is this: Frank has moved in with a younger model, and get this. Apparently, Frank wants half the house.'
'Surely he's not entitled to that?'
'I don't know, Tone. Susan went to a solicitor today about it. I'll most probably hear something when I get home.'
'What a stupid woman, all those years I worked to get a nice home, and she's most probably going to have to sell it now because she fell for a chancer.'
'You've hit the nail on the head there, mate.'
'So, you have a lodger. The extra money will come in handy.
'You think Jan would take money off her sister? Of course, she won't, and not being funny, Tone. It makes my home life a tad uncomfortable. I can't waltz around in my pants, and I have to be careful letting out a fart.'
'Yes, I can see that would make your life uncomfortable.'
'Anyway, let's change the subject. You all packed and ready to go?'
'Just about, Bob. I feel I'm taking a lot of clothes, but I'm there for three weeks, so need plenty of t-shirts and shorts.'
'What's the time difference when you get there?'
'Thailand is six hours in front of us.'
'That might make Skype calling a bit difficult.'
'Listen, Bob, I'm on holiday, I'll call you if I get a chance, okay.'
'Yes, of course, Tone.'
'I have a pizza in the freezer, you want to stay for a bite to eat?'
'Go on then, thanks. I'll just ring the boss; tell her I'm dining out.'

Ten minutes later, Bob eventually came off the phone.

'Christ, Bob, what was all that about?'

'Janice just gave me an update on Susan. It sounds like it's going from bad to worse. Young Frankie has filed for divorce and wants half of everything. Listen to this, his grounds for divorce are that Susan and he never consummated the marriage.'

'Never.'

'Honestly, that's what Janice has just told me. She said Susan might ask you to help. Sort of a character witness.'

'Trust me, she doesn't want me getting up on the witness stand. In the last ten years of marriage, I can count on one hand the number of times we had sex. I just put it down to her menopause.'

'You too?'

'What?'

'Must run in the family, our sex life dried up years ago.'

'No wonder you're always on those bloody porn sites,' laughed Tony.

Friday afternoon, and Tony was going through his check-off list. Ticking off one by one all the items, he checked his watch. Bob was due in an hour. Time for a cup of tea and a sandwich. He knew how expensive the airport food was, so he would eat now and then, hang on until he got some food on the plane.

Just as he sat down and took a bite of a cheese sandwich, his door buzzed. Thinking it was Bob being early, he ambled over and pressed the button to release the entrance door downstairs. Opening the flat's door, he went and sat back down on his sofa. A few seconds later, a light tapping on the door made Tony call out.

'Come in, Bob. The kettles just boiled if you want to make yourself a cuppa. We've got time, you're a bit early.'

'Hello, Tony.'

Tony jumped up and turned around. Susan stood there.

'Have I got to make my own tea?'

'Oh, sorry, I thought it was Bob.'

'So, I gathered. Listen, I know you are off shortly, so I just wanted a word before you do. Sorry to turn up just like this.'

'No problem. Take a seat, do you want a coffee or something?'

'No, I'm fine. I suppose Bob has filled you in on the latest?'

'Well, he told me you are in danger of losing the house.'

'Yes, that, and I'm being accused of not consummating the marriage?'

'Really. Well, I guess he has to make some excuse to make grounds for a divorce.' Tony tried to be diplomatic.

'It's a lie, Tony. Of course, we've had sex since we've been married. He's just a bastard and a liar.'

'Look, Susan, if you've come here looking for sympathy, well, you've come to the wrong place. I told you the other day, I'm sorry for your predicament, but it's got nothing to do with me.'

'Yes, I know. I'm sorry, I shouldn't have come here.'

'How you're feeling at this moment is exactly how I was feeling two years ago. Cast aside without a second thought for a younger model. Having to lose your home. Oh yes, been there and got the T-shirt. Trust me when I tell you, Susan. That hurt will never go away. It will get easier, but the hurt will remain in the background.'

'I've been a bloody fool.'

'Yes, you have.' Tony looked at his ex-wife and, for the first time since she told him she didn't love him anymore, he felt slightly sorry for her. 'Bob's not due for a little while yet, have a coffee and tell me what your hot-shot solicitor has told you.'

'She was only doing her job, Tony.'

'Yes, and took me to the cleaners along the way. Hang on, I'll boil the kettle.'

Tony went into the kitchen and made Susan a coffee. When he returned, she was browsing through the letting agent's property brochures.

'You moving, Tony?'

'Yes, most probably. It's a bit extravagant, this place. I like it here, but the rent is high for a one-bedroom flat. I could rent a three-bedroom house in town for the same price. Those flats you're looking at are more in my price range.'

'They look okay.'

'Yes, once I get back from Thailand, I'll start looking. So, what did your solicitor have to say?'

'You most probably already know, Tony. In a nutshell, we put all our assets in the pot and split it down the middle. So, Frank's total assets are about three hundred pounds in the bank and a ten-year-old BMW. So, he's going to get about a hundred and twenty thousand pounds out

of the house after it's sold and all the costs are taken out, and it looks like another couple of thousand because of the difference in the value of his car to mine.'
'Jesus Christ, Susan. Why didn't you protect yourself? Get some sort of prenuptial agreement?'
'Because when I mentioned that he flew off the handle, he said he couldn't marry me because I didn't trust him. So, I didn't. Look, Tony, say what you want, you won't make me feel any worse than what I do now.' Susan pulled a tissue out of the box on the coffee table and wiped her eyes.
'I'm not promising anything, but I'll see what I can do to help you when I get back.'
'You will?'
'Yes. I'm not a cold person, Susan. I don't know what can be done, but don't give up hope just yet.'
'Thanks, Tony.' The conversation ended when the entrance door buzzed.
'That will be Bob's taxi service.'
'I'd better go.'
'No rush, he's early. Drink your coffee first.' Tony pressed the door release button and opened the door to the flat. After a few seconds, Bob came marching in.
'Here, that looks like Susan's car downstairs … Oh, hello Sue.'
'Sit down a minute, Bob. I'll just get everything ready.' Tony went into the bedroom.
'You okay, Sue?'
'Yes … No. Oh, I don't know, Bob. I just needed a shoulder to cry on.'
'I understand, it's a tough time for you.' Bob did his best to sound sympathetic.
'Yes. Thanks for putting me up, Bob. I know I've just sort of landed on you, but I can't face being on my own at night at the moment.'
'Not a problem, Sue. You can stay as long as you like.' Bob tried to sound genuine but meant the opposite. Tony came out of the bedroom carrying a suitcase and a laptop case.
'Okay, let's just rinse these cups, and we'd better make a move.' Susan stood up.
'I'll get going. Thanks for the coffee and listening to my woes, Tony. Have a nice holiday and maybe we can meet up when you get back.'

'For sure, Susan. You take care and try not to worry about things. You know your sister and Bob will look after you.'
'I know.' Susan walked over and gave Tony a hug and a quick kiss on the cheek. She then walked out of the flat without looking back. Tony and Bob stood in silence for a few seconds.
'Right, Tone. You got everything?'
'Suitcase, laptop, tickets, passport and money. Let's roll.'

It was a good hour into the journey before Bob broached the subject of Susan.
'Well, that was a surprise seeing Sue at your flat when I arrived. Had she been there long?'
'About twenty minutes. She just turned up out of the blue.'
'Janice must have told her your address.'
'I guess I've mellowed a bit towards her. You know Bob, it's funny, but for the past two years had Susan asked me to come back I would have jumped at the chance. But today, I realized that if she asked me now, I'd say no.'
'Well, she caused you a lot of heartbreak, Tone.'
'She ruined my life, Bob. Had we still been together I could have retired and not have to get another job. What with the house being paid off and Susan on a reasonable wage? I could have been spending my time on the golf course and taking it easy.'
'True, but you're doing alright. I mean, I can't afford to swan off to Thailand for three weeks.'
'Yes, but in three weeks I'll be back to face reality.'
'Don't think about that, go and enjoy yourself.'
'I will, thanks, mate.'
'I bet you're not looking forward to that twelve-hour flight?'
'No, I can't imagine being on a plane that long.'
'Have a couple of beers before you take off, it's a night flight, so hopefully, you'll sleep most of the way.'
'Yes, it will seem strange losing six hours because of the time difference. So, when it's midnight tomorrow, my body will think it's only 6 pm.'
'That will feel odd. Jet lag, I've often wondered what that feels like.'
'Well, I'll be able to tell you when I get back.'

'I'll be at the airport waiting, Tone. I have the flight number, so I'll be waiting in the arrivals lounge for you.'
'Thanks, Bob, I appreciate all this.'
'You're welcome. Look, Heathrow, twenty miles.'
For the first time Tony could remember, he felt a slight sensation of butterflies in his stomach.

Bob backed into a space in the short-term car park.
'You could have dropped me at the departure gate, Bob.'
'I don't mind, I love the hustle and bustle of the airport. I'll come with you to the check-in desk, then leave you to it.'
'Here, take this towards the petrol.' Tony offered up a twenty-pound note.
'Put it away, Tone. You never know when I might need a lift to the airport one day.'
'Well, you only have to ask.'
'Do you want a trolley?'
'No, my case has wheels. If you could carry my hand luggage and laptop, that would help.'
The two men lifted the bags out of the boot of the car and headed into the airport.
Looking up at one of the big information screens, Tony spotted his flight number.
'There it is, Eva Air, 22.30. Book in at desk twenty-seven.'
'This way,' called Bob as he marched along, leaving Tony struggling with his suitcase, trying to keep up.
'This is it, Tone.' Tony joined the back of the queue.
'Well, thanks again for the lift, Bob.'
'No problem, I'll wait until you've checked your case in, then leave you to it.' Tony wondered why his friend wanted to stay until he spotted who was standing in front of him. A beautiful Thai girl was smiling back at Bob.
'Hello, looks like you on same flight as me?' Bob stood there speechless.
'No, my friend is not on this flight; he has just come to see me off.'
'Oh, sorry,' laughed the girl.'
'Have you been to the UK for a holiday?' Asked Bob, now over the shock of this beautiful girl speaking to him.

'No, I live here in the UK. I go home to see my family with my husband.'
'Oh, I see,' said Bob, trying to hide the disappointment of the girl being married.
'Where is your husband?'
'He go toilet, here he come now.' Bob and Tony looked back and could see a man of about sixty-five coming towards them.
'That's your husband? Asked Bob.
'Yes.'
'That's better, that beer has gone right through me.' Said the husband without taking any notice of Bob or Tony.
'Lift the suitcases on, sweetheart, you know I can't risk my back.'
The two men watched in amazement as the young girl lifted two heavy cases onto the rollers next to the check-in desk as her husband stood idly by.

After Tony had booked in, he went to say goodbye to his friend.
'Well, this is it, Bob. I'll see you in three weeks.'
'Here, what did you make of that couple? He was old enough to be her grandad?'
'What I've read up on, it's quite a common practice for a Thai woman to marry an older Western man.'
'Really? Well, don't you go bringing one back with you then, two, yes, not one?' Joked Bob.
'Yes, I'm sure Janice won't mind.'
'Well, I can dream, can't I?'
'You can, Bob.' The two men shook hands and did a bit of a man hug.
'For God's sake, be careful, Tone.'
'I will.' Tony took the laptop case and hand luggage from Bob and headed towards the customs area.

An hour later, after a brief look through a few of the shops, Tony settled down with a pint. He could see a big screen from where he sat and watched for his flight to be called.
'Do you mind if I sit here, mate?'
'Not at all.' A man of a similar age to Tony sat down.
'Where are you heading?' Asked the man.
'Thailand.' Answered Tony.

'Oh, me too. Eva air?'
'Yes.'
'I'm George.' The man offered his hand.
'Hello George, I'm Tony.'
'Nice to meet you, Tony. So, you a seasoned traveller to Thailand?'
'Me, no. First time.'
'I see, well, you're in for a trip of a lifetime, my friend.'
'I hope so.' Smiled Tony.
'Where are you staying?'
'Near Pattaya, Jomtien.'
'Fantastic, good place to start. Been there many times, I'm off to Phuket, down south.'
'Any tips, George?'
'Only one, try not to fall in love with the first girl you meet.'
'Don't worry, I won't.' Laughed Tony.
'Famous last words. You want another beer, Tony?'
'That's kind of you, do we have time?'
'Yes, we have about another thirty minutes before our flight gets called.'
George went off and returned with two beers.
'Cheers.'
'Cheers, George. So, have you been to Thailand often?'
'I've lost count. I go twice a year, usually for Songkran and again around this time.'
'Songkran?'
'Yes, it's the Thai New Year in April, you get hammered with water and powder for a week, it's all good fun.'
'Sounds it.'
'You're single, I take it?'
'Yes, dumped for a younger model.'
'Well, you're going to a single man's paradise, Tony.'
'So, I've heard.'
'Hang on, better drink up, it looks like our flight is boarding.'
'Not looking forward to twelve hours on the plane.'
'Have a couple of drinks, and once you've had your meal, recline your seat and you'll sleep for a good half of the flight.'
'I hope so. Thanks for the drink and advice, George.'
'My pleasure. Next stop, Bangkok.'

## Chapter 2

Tony had never been on a plane so immense in size, and he cursed his luck. He couldn't have been placed in a worse seat. Stuck in the middle of a row of five. Undeterred, he sorted out what he needed from his hand luggage and, unfortunately, had to disturb two people who had already sat down to get into his seat.
'Sorry about this.' Tony apologised to the two men.
'That's okay, mate, not the easiest of seats to get to.' Replied one of the men.
Sorting out his seat belt, he made himself as comfortable as he could. Another man and a Thai-looking woman came and sat down on the other side of him. He was glad he'd used the toilet before he boarded; however, he knew that at some point during the flight, he'd have to go again. The guy who'd already spoken to him gave him some advice as if he had read his mind.
'Best bet, mate. Wait until we've had our food, then go to the toilet. Then we can all settle down for a few hours.'
'Sounds like a plan.' Answered Tony.
'My mate here has a weak bladder, that's why he has to have an aisle seat, he'll be up and down like a fiddler's elbow.'
'I'm not that bad,' answered his friend.
'I'm Barry, and this is Alan.'
'Nice to meet you, I'm Tony.' The three men shook hands.
'Whereabouts are you staying in Thailand, Tony?' Asked Alan.
'Jomtien. What about you guys?'
'Pattaya.'
'Right, I believe that's not far from me then. This is my first trip to Thailand.'
'We're about ten minutes up the road from Jomtien. First visit? Well, Tony, we won't spoil it for you, but you're about to have a holiday of a lifetime.'
'So, I keep being told. Do you mind if I ask how you get to Pattaya from the airport?'
'Taxi. Listen, if you want, you can share a taxi with Alan and me.'
'That would be great, thank you.' Tony was relieved to have some company on the final leg of his journey.
'No problem.' The plane started to move backwards.

'Not long now, Alan, you'd better nip to the loo.'
'I've only just been. I'll be okay.'
Tony wasn't listening to his new acquaintances; he was too busy worrying about how this monster of a plane was going to get airborne.

An hour into the flight and sipping a plastic cup of red wine, Tony was beginning to feel a bit better. He was a nervous passenger at the best of times, and being stuck in the middle of this huge plane did nothing to help calm his nerves. Luckily, Alan and Barry were good company, which helped take his mind off the flight.
'Here comes the food, Alan.'
'You and your stomach, Barry. You ate a huge pizza before we boarded.'
'That was hours ago.'
'Well, I'm ready for it,' announced Tony.
'I had half a cheese sandwich about three o'clock this afternoon.'
'I get a headache if I don't eat regularly, Tony.'
'Yeah, and you give me a headache when you keep moaning, you're hungry.' Remarked Alan. Everyone in that row of seats put their trays down in anticipation of the food arriving.
'I should have nipped to the loo before the food came.' Remarked, Alan.
'Well, it's too late now. You'll have to hold it; we don't need you holding up the food chain.'
'It's no good, I won't enjoy my dinner.' Alan stood up and caused havoc trying to get past the food trolley.
'See what I mean. He waits until the food is here, then decides to go.' Tony decided not to mention to Barry that he wanted to go. He'd wait until they'd finished eating before making a move.
'So, where do you hail from, Tony?'
'Ipswich, born and bred. What about you?'
'Alan and I live in Eastbourne.'
'Nice part of the country.'
'Yes, it's okay. A bit grim in the winter, like most coastal places.' The food arrived, and Barry had to put Alan's tray on top of his.
'He's a pain in the arse.'
'Here he comes, he's stuck behind the food trolley.' Tony spoke as he peeled the lid off his hot food.

'Looks like cottage pie.' Tony took a forkful.
'Not bad.'
Barry couldn't wait any longer and put Alan's tray on the empty seat.
'We'll be finished by the time he gets here, serves him right.'
'Yes, his timing is a bit out. Mind you, when you've got to go, you've got to go.' Tony laid the ground for his sooner-than-expected need for the toilet. Having wolfed his food down, he had to disturb Barry, who was tucking into the cottage pie.
'Bloody hell, Tony, were you hungry?'
'Yes, that and the need for the toilet, sorry.'
'You need to go now?'
'Yes, sorry. I had a couple of pints before I boarded.' Barry sighed and then placed his tray on top of Alan's. He then squeezed out into the aisle. Tony stood up, holding his tray, then put it on his seat and made his way past the standing Barry.
'Take your time,' smiled Barry as he went back into his seat.
Halfway along the aisle, he squeezed past the returning Alan.
'I bet you were popular, disturbing his feeding time,' laughed Alan.
'I don't think he was amused. I won't rush back, I want to try and stretch my legs a bit.'
'He'll be alright once he's eaten. See you in a minute.' Alan continued his quest to get back to his seat as Tony edged himself towards the toilets.
This was one time Tony didn't mind there being a bit of a queue to use the toilet. He wasn't desperate, and he wanted to stand up for a while before heading back to his seat. In the end, he let a couple of people jump in front of him, and he eventually made his way back to his seat after a good twenty minutes.
'Alan was just about to send out a search party,' joked Barry as he let Tony get back into his seat.
'I wanted to stretch my legs, to be honest.'
'I know the feeling, not ideal these seats. Anyway, let's settle down for a while. They'll dim the lights soon. You need the toilet?' Barry asked his friend.
'No, I'm alright.' Replied Alan.
Tony reclined his seat slightly, kicked off his shoes and plugged his earphones in. He'd seen the movie that was being shown, but knew if he watched it for a while, he would soon be nodding off.

'I think I'd better go,' announced Alan, much to Barry's annoyance.

Tony checked his watch, he couldn't believe it was just gone 07.30 am. He estimated he'd slept for a good six hours. Barry was still asleep. Tony looked at him; he could tell he was a seasoned traveller as he had an eye mask on and one of those blow-up neck collars. Alan's seat was empty, and Tony didn't need to guess where he was. After a couple of minutes, Alan returned.
'Morning,' he said softly.
'I need the loo,' Tony whispered back.
'No problem,' Alan replied as he poked Barry in the ribs. Barry lifted the eye mask.
'What,' he croaked.
'Don't be so selfish, Tony here wants to use the loo.'
'What time is it?'
'Getting on for eight. Now shift your arse and let Tony out.'
'I need to go as well.' Alan stood to one side, and Barry, followed by Tony, climbed out of the seats and headed for the toilets.
'Better change the time on my watch.' Barry unstrapped his watch.
'What's the time in Thailand now, Barry?'
'Well, it's 7.40 am in the UK, so it's 1.40 pm in Thailand.'
'What time are we due to land?'
'About 4.30 pm.'
'Less than three hours to go, then?'
'That's right. Breakfast must be due soon, I'm starving.' Barry felt his stomach as he slipped into the vacant cubicle.
'I might be a while, Tony. Safer to use one of the other cubicles.'
'Do you want a newspaper?' Joked, Tony. Much to his surprise, Barry pulled a rolled-up newspaper from the back of his jeans.
'Need to finish the crossword.' Barry laughed as he squeezed into the cubicle.

After a typical airline breakfast, the stewardess handed out a departure card to be filled out and handed into immigration at the airport.
'Not long now, Tony.' Barry started to fish for his seat belt.
'That's the trouble with these middle seats, you can't see a lot.' The captain informed his passengers that he expected to land in twenty minutes, and the temperature in Bangkok was 36 degrees.

'Shit, that's hot,' announced Tony.
'Yes, just a tad. Let's hope we don't get held up for too long at the airport.'
'Stop being so gloomy, Barry. It was your fault we got held up last time.'
'Why was that?' Asked Tony.
'They found fifty Viagra pills in his suitcase.'
'Fifty? How long were you staying in Thailand?'
'A month.'
'Alright, Alan, let's not go there again.' Barry looked embarrassed at Alan's revelations.
'Luckily, I don't think I need them yet, I've not had sex for about three years.' Alan and Barry looked at Tony.
'You've not had sex for three years,' called out Barry in a loud voice, causing the lady on the other end of their row of seats to stare at Tony.
'Easy, Barry. I'm just saying that's all. I've been through a divorce and I've not got a girlfriend.' Tony replied in a soft voice.
'God help the first girl you tug then,' joked Alan. The seatbelt sign came on, and the three of them prepared for landing.

Ninety minutes later, Tony and Alan were seated at a bar having a beer in the arrivals lounge. Barry was still being questioned by the Thai immigration.
'Well, he never learns that man, does he?'
'Be fair, Alan, he did cut back, only thirty pills this time, I believe.'
'Thirty too many. I'm sorry about the hold-up, Tony. Listen, if you want to get going, I don't mind. I'd better stay, but you don't have to wait.'
'Don't worry, Alan. I'd rather share a taxi with you guys, I'm in no rush.' Tony looked out of one of the large windows.
'It looks like it's getting dark outside.'
'Yes, unfortunately, you don't get the light evenings here. Doesn't move much all year round, be around 6.30 pm this time of year.'
'Looks like I'll have to wait until tomorrow to see the beach.'
'I'm afraid so. Hang on, look over there, here he comes.' Both men watched a forlorn Barry, pushing a trolley as he made his way towards them.
'How'd you get on, Barry?' Asked Tony.

'Bloody confiscated them again, and a warning this time.'
'I don't know why you do it. You can buy them out here?'
'Well, I like to get them from the UK. That way I know they're genuine. Now, let's leave it at that. Right, let me have a beer, then we'll get a taxi. I suppose you two want another?'
'Too bloody right, we're on holiday, aren't we, Tony?'
'Yes, we most certainly are.'

After downing the beers, the trio headed towards the exit doors to sort out a taxi to take them to Pattaya. As they went out of the air-conditioned airport and into the elements outside, Tony was shocked by his first encounter with the brutal Thai heat.
'Jesus Christ. How warm is it? And it's dark.'
'You'll get used to it, Tony.' By the time they'd negotiated a price with a taxi driver, the three of them were soaked in sweat.

Thirty minutes later, they were settled in the cool air/con taxi and heading for Jomtien. Tony sat in the back with Barry. Fishing in his wallet, he pulled out the equivalent of ten pounds, a 500 baht note.
'Take this towards the fare, Alan.'
'Cheers, Tony. We'll drop you off first, then we'll head off to our condo.'
'You not staying in a hotel?'
'No, we have a friend who owns a few condos in Pattaya. Cheaper than a hotel.'
'But no room service?' Moaned, Barry.
'We can pay a girl to come in once a week, change the bedding and have a clean-up for 500 baht.'
'Cheap enough.'
'It is.'
'Where are you staying, Tony?'
'Hotel called the Grand.'
'Nice, how much did that set you back? Asked a curious Barry.
'Just over five hundred pounds for twenty-one nights.'
'That's not bad, do you get breakfast?'
'Yes, buffet allegedly. What did you guys pay?'
'Four hundred for twenty-eight nights. He charges us a hundred pounds a week.'

'That's cheap.'
'Yes, it's not a bad price for a month. If you stay longer, you can get a great deal. Our friend, Tom, lives in one of the condos. He pays around two hundred pounds a month for a year's contract, doesn't he, Alan?
'Yes, something like that.'
'Really? Sounds good. What are these condos like?'
'They're nice. One-bedroom, nice little kitchen area and lounge. Balcony and two TVs and two air-cons.'
'Are they far from the beach?'
'About a ten-minute walk. Or two minutes on a scooter. The complex has a small gym and a nice swimming pool.'
'Have you got one of the cards, Barry?'
'Yes, in my wallet, I think.' Barry pulled his wallet out and hunted for a business card.
'Here we go, this is our friend who owns the condos. Alan and I always chill around the pool late afternoons. If you want to come and take a look, we'll be glad to show you around the place.'
'Thanks, I will. I think the first thing I'm going to do when I get to the hotel is to find somewhere to eat.'
'I know the feeling,' agreed Barry.
'Alan, see if the driver will stop at the next services, I'm sure it has a Kentucky at that one.'
'You don't eat the Thai food, then, Barry?'
'I can eat it, but it doesn't agree with me. I ended up locked in the bog most of the next day. Alan, tell the driver we'll bung him a good tip if he stops and waits for us at Kentucky.'
'Why do you keep asking me to ask him?'
'Your Thai is better than mine.'
Alan reluctantly turned to the driver.
'Khun driver. Stop at the next service, my friend wants to eat. He give you a big tip.' Alan held his wallet up.
'See, Tony. Alan's just about fluent.'

As the taxi approached Tony's hotel, He marvelled at the nightlife.
'Christ looks busy.'
'Jomtien is quiet compared to Pattaya, Tony. Don't forget to look us up.'
'Yes, I will, I'll give it a few days, then I'll come to your complex.'

'Just get a motorbike taxi over, won't cost much. Just tell him the name of the complex that's written on the business card, and he'll know where it is.'

'Thanks, lads, and thanks for sharing a cab with me. It's been very entertaining.' The taxi pulled up outside the very smart-looking hotel.

'Looks very nice, Tony. Remember, pace yourself.'

'I will, Alan.' Tony shook hands with the two men as the taxi driver lifted his case out of the boot. As he stepped out of the taxi, he was again shocked by the sheer volume of heat.

'Christ, it's hot, what's it going to be like during the day?'

'Hotter,' smiled Barry.

'I'll see you in a few days.' Tony waved the taxi off, and a porter had already put his case on a trolley and was pushing it inside the hotel's lobby. The receptionist took Tony's booking confirmation and passport. She spoke good English.

'There you are, sir, room 703. Here's your door entry card. You can pick up your passport tomorrow. Breakfast is served between 7.30 am to 10.30 am. You must check out before midday on the day of your departure. There is an information pack in your room. The porter will take your bags.' Tony smiled at the pleasant girl who gave a prayer-type gesture in return.

'Thank you,' he turned and started to follow the porter to the lifts. Once on the seventh floor, Tony again followed the fast-walking porter to room 703. Holding his hand out, Tony handed him the door entry card. After a quick swipe, the door opened, and the porter slipped the card into a small holder just inside the door. Tony realised you needed to place the card inside the holder to turn the electricity on. The porter picked up the air/con remote and pressed the on button.

The man stopped and did a little hand-together prayer-type motion the same as the receptionist had done to him. Tony pulled a 100 baht note out of his wallet, and the porter gave a beaming smile.

'Khob Khun khab,' he said as he prayer motioned again and left the room.

Tony had a quick look out of the balcony and could see he was going to have a nice view of the beach during the day. Stepping back inside, he could already feel the benefit of the air conditioning. The actual room was very nice, and Tony went to the fridge and checked the items inside. Pulling out a can of beer, he opened it and took a swig.

"Heaven," he smiled to himself. Checking the large bathroom, he felt satisfied he'd chosen a good hotel. He decided to unpack, get showered and maybe venture out and sample the nightlife. After working out how to set up the safe, he put all his valuables inside. Alan and Barry had warned him about walking around with his gold chain around his neck, so he put that in the safe along with the majority of his cash and his bank cards.

Opening another beer, he stripped off and took a nice long shower. Walking back into the bedroom, he climbed onto the bed and checked out the TV channels and found a live football match between two Thai teams. Flicking through the information pack it was full of excursions and hotel rules. Checking his watch, it was 9 pm. He felt extremely comfortable on the bed and decided to work out how to connect his laptop to the hotel's Wi-Fi before getting dressed and heading out. After a bit of hit-and-miss, he got connected. Checking his emails, there was nothing of interest. He lay back and felt tiredness coming over him. Time for a quick power nap, he thought to himself.

It was one of those rare times when Tony woke up and didn't have a clue where he was or what day of the week he was waking up to. Opening his eyes, the room was cold and dark. Slowly realising he was in a hotel in Thailand brought a smile to his face. Carefully climbing out of bed, he walked over to the curtains and opened them. It was light, but the sun was behind the hotel, so his balcony was in the shade. Sliding open the door, he again felt the heat hit him. Looking out onto the Beach Road, he could see quite a bit of activity with deckchair vendors sorting out their plots and a fair sprinkling of the keep-fit brigade either jogging or walking along. Going back inside, he shivered. Finding the air/con remote, he checked the temperature setting. Seeing it was set at 18 degrees, he guessed that was a bit too low, so he knocked it up to 24. Picking up his watch, he could see it was coming up to 8.30 am. Feeling hungry, he decided to have a quick shower, get dressed and find out where the breakfast buffet was located.

After a cool shower, Tony wasn't sure what to wear. Bob had mentioned that as it was a 4-star hotel, there would most probably be a dress code for dining. So, he settled for smart jeans, a polo shirt and sandals. Hiding his laptop under some clothes in a drawer and picking

up his mobile phone, he took the keycard out of the holder, shut the door and headed to the lifts. Once down in the reception area, he followed a couple who he guessed were also heading for breakfast. Going into the large dining room, Tony immediately felt overdressed. All the men he could see were only in shorts, t-shirts or vests.
'Room number, please.' Tony turned, and a beautiful Thai girl stood by a lectern.
'703.'
'Okay, sir. Sit anywhere you want and help yourself. There are tables outside if you would prefer the fresh air.
'Thank you. A tad too warm outside for me. I'll find somewhere in here.' The girl did the prayer motion and a small bow. Tony had read in the information pack that this was called a wai. So, he did a wai back to the girl.
Pouring out a cool orange juice, Tony put it on a small table and he headed off to explore the morning's culinary delights.

After breakfast, Tony went back to his room and slipped on a pair of shorts and a vest. Rubbing in some sun cream, he felt like a day on the beach was in order. It was far too hot to be exploring; he would leave that until the evenings. Taking the equivalent of forty pounds with him, he headed across the road. Within seconds, a man had steered Tony to a nice front-row sun lounger, with a shade, table and bin.
'How much?' He asked the man.
'One hundred baht. You have all day.'
'Okay, that's good.' Tony quickly worked out that it was about two pounds. He'd been used to paying six to seven Euros in Spain, so he knew this was very cheap. Pulling out some money, the man stopped him.
'Pay at end, mister. You want a beer?' Tony checked his watch. 10.30 am.
'Go on then, I am on holiday.'
'What beer? Chang, Leo or Singh?' Tony remembered he'd drunk a couple of cans of Leo in his room, so he went for that.
The man returned with a large, ice-cold bottle of Leo, held in a sleeve that was used to help keep the beer cold. Tony couldn't believe that he was sitting on a beach in October, drinking beer at 10.30 in the morning. A few other tourists were sitting around and Tony watched

as people went into the sea. It looked very inviting, but he guessed the sea would be like every other holiday resort he'd been to; it would be cold.

After knocking back the beer, he decided to brave it and dip his toes. 'Hiding his money in his baseball cap and rolling it into his towel, he took off his vest and walked down for his first dip in the ocean.

"Holy shit," he said to himself as he walked into the beautiful, warm sea. He couldn't believe how warm the water felt, he waddled out until it was waist deep, then dived under. Surfacing, he smiled and called out not for the first time since he arrived, "Heaven."

Back on the beach, Tony was persuaded to have another beer. Different beach vendors came along, and Tony ended up with another baseball cap and a pair of sunglasses. A pretty lady asked him if he'd like a massage.

'Oh, I don't know,' he replied.

'Be good for you, mister, you lie in the shade on this mat. Make you feel very relaxed.'

'How much?'

'Two hundred baht.' Realising this was about four pounds, Tony was tempted.

'One-hour, mister, full body massage.'

'Okay, what's your name?'

'My name is Beer.'

'Beer? Well, I like your name, so where do you want me?'

Tony enjoyed the massage immensely. Beer was very good, and she spoke reasonable English. Now and again, she'd ask him if he was okay.

'It's fantastic, Beer.'

After the massage, which cost Tony 300 baht, because he gave a 100-baht tip, he was starting to feel peckish. As if reading his mind, the deckchair vendor suddenly appeared with a menu.

'Food very good, mister.' Tony browsed through the pages and eventually settled for chicken with cashew nuts and rice.

Twenty minutes later, the food arrived, along with another beer.

'This is the life,' he told the German couple who were sitting close to him.

By mid-afternoon, Tony decided he'd had enough of the beach and wanted to try out the hotel swimming pool. Signalling to the deckchair vendor, the man came over with a piece of paper. The bill came to 600 baht. Tony smiled, the sun lounger, 3 beers, 2 bottles of water and his lunch came to about twelve pounds. Tony gave the man a 1000 baht note and waited for his change. After giving the man a 50 baht tip, Tony strolled back across the Beach Road towards his hotel. A scooter hire shop caught his eye. Sat outside were half a dozen sparkling scooters.

'You want scooter, mister?' A pretty girl had zoomed in as soon as he stopped to look. Tony took a liking to a very nice red Yamaha. He had ridden motorbikes for years and was a proud owner of a Suzuki Bandit back in the UK.

'How much?'

'150 baht a day. 700 for a week, or 1.200 baht for 2 weeks. Good price, mister and bike very new.'

'What do I need to rent one?'

'Just a copy of your passport, mister, and where you are staying.'

'Okay, I will come back. I need to collect my passport.' The girl looked disappointed; she'd heard that saying many times. Tony strolled back to the hotel and straight to the swimming pool area. He couldn't believe how quiet it was with many sun loungers sitting empty. Tony put his towel and bag on one in the shade. Spotting the showers, he walked over and got the sand off him. Diving in, he again marvelled at the temperature. After a couple of lengths, he climbed out and dried himself. An elderly man had arrived and was sitting next to Tony's sunbed.

'Hi,' Tony wasn't sure if the man was English.

'Hello young man, the pool is lovely, isn't it?'

'It certainly is. Are you going in?'

'Yes, in a while. I've only just got up.'

Tony looked at his watch; it was nearly 4 pm.

'Blimey, you like a lay-in?'

'Well, I don't think I got to sleep until about 8 am. I bought two girls back to my room last night, or should I say this morning.'

'Two? What was it, buy one get one free?' Laughed Tony.

'Yes, something like that,' the man laughed back.

'I'm Tony.'
'Pleased to meet you, Tony. I'm Albert, but you can call me Bert.' Tony offered his hand.
'Nice to meet you, Bert.' As the men shook hands, a waitress appeared and put a large bottle of beer and a glass on the table.
'What will you have, Tony?'
'Well, I wouldn't mind a Leo.'
'Nung, Leo, nung gaow, Nam kang, khab.' Called out Bert. The waitress smiled and walked off.
'You speak a bit of Thai, then Bert?'
'Just the basics, Tony. I asked for one Leo beer and one glass and ice.'
'Very good.'
'To be honest, you don't need to know much in the tourist areas, comes in handy if you venture out into the country, mind. So, you just got here, I take it?'
Tony looked down at his white torso.
'Yes, arrived last night.'
'You ventured into the bars yet?'
'No, I'm afraid to say that I fell asleep last night and didn't wake up until this morning. I've had a nice day on the beach, though.'
'You here on your own?'
'Yes, and this is my first time in Thailand.'
'Really? Well, if you want, you can come with me tonight. I know a lovely little restaurant that does a fabulous fish and chips, we can get a baht bus into Pattaya, and I can show you the ropes. Only if you fancy it?'
'That's very kind of you, Bert. I'd love to tag along.'
'That's settled then, meet you in the reception bar, say 7.30?
'Suits me.' Tony finished his beer.
'Want one for the road, Bert?'
'Be rude, not too.'

It was getting on for 6 pm by the time Tony had made it back to his room. By the time he'd finished his shower, the room had cooled down nicely. Remembering the scooter, he wrote himself a reminder on a piece of paper. Pick up passport and rent a scooter. Having just over an hour to kill, Tony fired up his laptop and connected to the hotel's wi-fi. Going into Skype, he could see Bob was online. It was lunchtime in

the UK, so Tony called his best friend. After a couple of rings, he got connected. Bob's red face came into shot.
'Bloody hell, Bob, sit back a bit, you're scaring me.'
'Can you hear me if I sit back?'
'Of course, I can. Why is your face so red? You watching porn again?'
'Guilty as charged,' laughed Bob
'How are you, Tone?'
'Great, the place and the people are fantastic. I ended up sitting with a couple of lads from Eastbourne on the flight over. They were a bit of a double act, I shared a taxi from the airport with them.'
'That was handy. What's the hotel like?'
'Very nice, I have a fantastic sea view, hang on, I'm not sure you will see anything as it's getting dark.' Tony unplugged the laptop and went out on the balcony.
'Can you see?'
'Just about, Tone.' Tony went back into the comfort of the cool room.
'I'll tell you something, Bob. I've never experienced heat like it. Even the time we went to Turkey, it's nothing compared to the heat here. It doesn't cool down much at night. One bonus, the sea is like getting into a warm bath.'
'Sounds great, Tone. So, what's the nightlife like?'
'Don't laugh, but I fell asleep last night, so I've not sampled it yet.'
'Fell asleep? What are you like?'
'Don't worry, I'm going out with a guy I met around the pool this afternoon. Bert, he's a right old character. He had two women in his room all night.'
'The lucky bastard. Two? I don't think I could manage two at my age.'
'At your age, this Bert's seventy-five.'
'Never.'
'He is. Anyway, you have two women in your house.' Tony couldn't help but laugh at Bob's recent predicament.
'What, the sisters glum. Don't remind me, they've gone out for the day, shopping.'
'No wonder you're watching porn then.'
'Err, yes. Anyway, enough about me. So, you're off out with this stud, Bert, tonight?'
'Yes, he has been coming here for years. We're going for something to eat and then get a thing called a baht bus into Pattaya.'

'Pattaya? You're going to Pattaya tonight?'
'Yes, apparently it takes about fifteen minutes on the bus. Here, listen to this. It only costs ten baht to get there, that's twenty pence.'
'What's the cost of beer and food like, Tone?'
'It's a lot cheaper than Spain, mate. I had a massage on the beach for an hour; it was heaven. And guess what, it only cost four pounds. Two pounds for a sun lounger and an umbrella. I had a nice lunch, three big beers, a couple of bottles of water and with the price of the sun lounger included, it came to twelve quid.'
'That is cheap, Tone. When Jan and I went to Majorca last year, they wanted eight euros for a bloody sunbed. Two euros for an umbrella. I'm sure a small beer was about two euros too.'
'Yes, I thought it was cheap when I paid the bill. Listen, Bob, I know you want to get back to the porn, so I'll give you a call in a few days.'
'Cheeky git. Alright, Tone, thanks for calling. Enjoy yourself tonight, I'm not jealous.'
'Alright, Bob, take care, mate.' Tony disconnected the call and started to get ready. He picked the thinnest material polo shirt he had and a smart pair of lightweight shorts. He realised a lot of the T-shirts he'd bought with him were too thick for this climate. Grabbing a pen, he wrote, "get some thin t-shirts" on his list of things to do.

Tony was sitting in the reception bar and halfway through a beer when Bert came walking in.
'Alright, Bert. You want a beer?'
'No thanks, Tony. I'm pacing myself, long night ahead.'
'Okay, give me a minute to neck this and we can get going.'
'Take your time. Here, I've got something for you.' Bert dug in his pocket and produced a small foil-wrapped card with four light green pills attached.
'Get one of them down you.' Smiled Bert.
'What are they?' Asked an inquisitive Tony.
'Magic pills, lad. Don't worry, they're herbal. I've been taking them for years.'
'What are they, a sort of pick-me-up?'
'Yes, you could say that. Let's just say it won't matter how much you have to drink tonight, you'll be able to perform like a twenty-year-old.'
'Herbal, you say?'

'Yes, they are safe. Trust your old mate, Bert.'
'Oh well, I'm on holiday, why not?' Tony pushed one of the pills out and stuck it in his mouth. Swallowing it down with the aid of an ice-cold beer.
'Here you are,' Tony went to hand the pills back.
'Keep the pack, Tony. Only take one a day, mind. If you like them, I'll take you to a place that sells them cheap here.'
'Thanks, Bert. I feel like a stallion already, let's go.'

Walking across the road from the hotel, Bert waved a baht bus down. Tony had seen the converted pick-ups, but this was his first time sitting in the back of one.
'Only ten baht, Tony. All the way to Pattaya.'
'I know, it's so cheap. Funny, took me a while to realise they were not tooting at me.'
'You'll get used to it, they are tooting at potential customers.' As they drove along, the pick-up kept stopping to let people on. He was amazed at the number of people who clung to the back of the pick-up. He couldn't believe it when he counted sixteen people jammed in the back. As they approached Pattaya, Bert hit the buzzer and the pick-up pulled up.
'This is us, Tony.' Bert led the way and Tony squeezed past people to get out. By the time he'd done so, Bert had paid the driver and was heading into a small restaurant.
'In here, Tony.' Walking into the small restaurant, two women came over and started making a fuss of Bert.
'Put me down, you two. This is my friend, Tony.'
'Sawadee ka,' said the older woman.
'Just say Sawadee khab, Tony.'
'Sawadee khab,' repeated Tony.
'Right, Mai, I'll have the small fish and chips, with mushy peas, and a nam soda. What do you fancy, Tony?'
'Can I have a large fish and chips? What's that drink you ordered, Bert?'
'Sparkling water.'
'Go on then, I'll have one of them too.' Tony sat down opposite Bert.
'So, how did you find this place then, Bert?'

'Mai, the owner, was married to a mate of mine, Terry. He died a couple of years ago. He had a couple of fish and chip shops in Essex. Eventually, he retired out here and bought this place.' The young girl came over with the drinks.
'This is Ong, Terry's daughter.'
'Sawadee khab, Ong.' Tony was trying out the welcome.
'Sawadee ka,' replied the girl with an infectious smile.
'So, Bert. Where are we going from here?'
'Well, young man, about a three-minute stroll from here is a little side alley that will take us through to Walking Street. Have you heard of it?'
'Oh yes, I certainly have.' Smiled Tony.
'Just remember to pace yourself, and don't go off with the first woman you meet.'
'I won't, Bert, don't worry.'

The sound of a door slamming brought Tony out of a drunken sleep. Unsticking his eyes, he had the same feeling he had the morning before, apart from this time, he felt badly hungover. Where the hell was he? Sliding his feet over, he sat on the edge of the bed and looked around this strange room. A slight moaning sound came from under the sheet. Tony turned around and could see a mass of black hair poking out. He walked over to a small fridge and was relieved to see two bottles of water inside. Opening one, he knocked the bottle back in one go. Opening a curtain slightly, he checked his watch; it was coming up to 10 am. He had a vague recollection of being in a bar with Bert; after that, it was all a bit hazy. Going into a basic bathroom, he took a quick cold shower and started to get dressed. He wasn't sure what to do about the sleeping girl. To save any embarrassment, he decided to leave her asleep. He couldn't remember her or how he got to the hotel he found himself in. He didn't have a clue where he was. He felt nauseous and uncomfortable, he just wanted to get out of the room as soon as possible. Getting his wallet out he checked what money he had left. He counted 2,500 baht. He'd gone out with 6,000 baht in his wallet; he felt he'd spent a lot in one night, considering how cheap it had been up to that point. Pulling out 1,000 baht, he left it under the girl's handbag. Creeping over to the door, curiosity started to get the better of him. He wanted to see the girl's face to see if he could remember her. He slowly pulled the sheet down, and he smiled

at the beautiful girl who was fast asleep. As Tony went to leave, the girl groaned and kicked off the sheet in her half-sleep. Lying face down, Tony marvelled at the beautiful olive-skinned body and perky backside. "Beautiful," he whispered to himself. As he opened the door, the girl rolled over, and Tony's worst nightmare stared right back at him. A pair of silicone breasts and a small penis that looked like it was waving at him.
'Shit,' he cried as he fled the hotel.
Spotting a motorbike taxi, he waved him down.
'Jomtien, please.'

Back in the safety of his hotel, Tony took another shower and doubled-dosed the mouthwash. Drinking two bottles of water, he started to feel slightly better. After slipping into some shorts and a vest, he vowed not to drink like that again. Looking at his reminder list, he went to the safe, got some more money out and headed down to the reception to collect his passport. Once he'd done that he strolled over to the shop where he saw the scooters for hire. The same pretty girl was sitting inside the shop.
'Hello, mister, you come back?'
'Yes, I said I would. I see you still have that red Yamaha for rent, so I'll take that one if it's available.'
'Okay, how long you want to rent?'
'Just under three weeks. What price can you do?'
'Three weeks, I can do 1,700 baht.' Tony worked that out to be around thirty-five pounds. He felt it was a bargain at that price.
'Okay, can you supply a safety helmet in the price?'
'Yes, of course, mister. You have passport?'
'Yes.' Tony handed it over. The girl photocopied the passport and handed it back. She filled out a form and got Tony to sign.
'You have accident, you pay first 5000 baht, okay?'
'Yes, sounds fair.'
'You ride bike before?'
'Yes, I have a bike back in the UK.'
'Okay, I not fit stabiliser for you.'
'No, I do not need a stabiliser.' Tony looked at the girl and could see she was laughing.

'I joke, mister. Here, try this?' The girl passed over a safety helmet. Tony tried it on, but it was too small.
'You have big head, mister, try this one.' The girl passed another helmet over. This one fitted Tony.
'Perfect. Right then, is that it?'
'Okay, mister, here the key. Be careful, many bad drivers.' The girl led Tony outside and put the key in the red scooter.
'Hold brake and press button to start, mister.'
'My name is Tony.'
'Okay, Tony, my name is Pooki.'
'Nice to meet you, Pooki. You are very beautiful, your husband is a lucky man.'
'I not marry.'
'Oh, well, your boyfriend is very lucky.'
'I not have boyfriend, I too old.' Tony looked at this beautiful girl whom he thought was in her early twenties, in amazement.
'Too old? How old are you?'
'I'm thirty.'
'Wow, well, you look much younger, and hey, you're not too old for me.' Tony laughed.
'I not go out with tourists, they have their fun, make promises, and I not see again. You bring bike back with full tank, okay.' The girl walked back inside the shop, leaving Tony feeling a tad sorry for the girl.

After taking his passport back to his safe, Tony decided to venture into Pattaya and get some lightweight shorts and t-shirts. He loved the freedom of the bike and venturing into new places. As he rode into Pattaya, he spotted the hotel where he'd spent the night with the ladyboy. "I won't be going back there again," he thought to himself as he rode past. Realising he hadn't eaten anything that morning and it was now lunchtime, his first port of call would be to get something to eat. Spotting a McDonald's, he went for a quick hunger fix.

After a spicy burger, Tony continued to ride around Pattaya. He stopped and parked when he came across a huge outdoor market. The next hour he spent buying vests, t-shirts and a couple of lightweight combat shorts. A new pair of brief swimming shorts and some designer underwear. On his way out, he saw a vest, perfect for Bob. Written on the front was "Good guys go to heaven; the rest go to Pattaya." 100 baht well spent, he thought to himself as he put the vest in a bag. Riding along Pattaya Beach Road, he eventually headed back to Jomtien.

Dumping all his purchases on his bed, Tony slipped on his new brief swimming shorts and put a longer pair of shorts over the top. Putting a new vest on, Tony grabbed a towel and his book and headed down for an afternoon chill out around the swimming pool. Finding a nice shaded area to lie out, Tony, who was still feeling slightly fragile, plonked himself on a sun lounger and picked up his book.
'Song Leo, song Gaow and nam kang, khob khun khab.' Tony looked up and saw Bet standing in front of him.
'Surprised to see you up and about so early, young man.'
'I'm hardly a young man, Bert, I'm in my mid-fifties. I've been up a long time, hired a scooter, been to Pattaya, done some shopping.'
'Yes, you youngsters have so much energy. Here, where did you get to last night? I didn't see you go?'
'Oh, you know, I sampled the delights of Pattaya.'
'Well, I have to say, that ladyboy was very attractive, not my scene, but I can understand the attraction. How was the magic pill?'
'Err ...' Tony stopped talking as a waitress came over and put two beers on the table next to him.
'Get this down, you, it will make you feel better.'
'I need to ease up on the beer, I haven't a clue what happened last night.'
'So, you don't know if you pumped him or not?' Tony started laughing at Bert's direct approach.
'Do you have to say that, Bert? I'm not gay, I'm into women.' Pleaded Tony.
'Listen, son. What you do, and who with, is not any of my business. I enjoy your company. I'm just going to stroll down to a few local bars tonight, not going to drink too much. Come with me if you like?'
'Go on then. Are you eating out?'
'Yes, just around the corner from the hotel is a nice little restaurant that does Thai and Western food. Come and join me if you like?'
'Sounds good, I will, cheers, Bert'

The next few days, Tony spent a lot of time touring around Jomtien and Pattaya. He soon found his way around and enjoyed the area immensely. His evenings were spent accompanying Bert to various locations and waking up with different women. On his way back from Pattaya one afternoon, the front brake on the scooter stopped working. Tony guessed it was the brake cable, so he rode back to the hire shop. The girl was sitting by the door in the shade. Parking up, Tony took his safety hat off.
'Sawadee khab, Pooki.'
'Sawadee ka, mister.'
'It's Tony. I think the front brake cable is broken?'
'You break my scooter, Khun Tony?' Pooki was smiling, so Tony knew she was joking. Pooki called out to a man a couple of shops down. She spoke to the man in rapid Thai.
'Ten minutes, he fix. You can get a nice ice coffee next door while you wait.'
'I've not tried the iced coffee; do you want one?'
'Khob Khun ka.' Tony knew that meant thank you. Walking into the shop, he ordered two ice coffees.

Returning with the drinks, Pooki called him inside the scooter hire shop.
'Come sit in here, Khun Tony, scooter won't be long.' Tony walked in and passed one of the coffees over.
'Khob Khun ka,' Pooki fiddled with the fan so Tony could feel the breeze.
'That's nice. So why do you call me Khun Tony?'
'It polite way of saying your name.'
'I see, so Pooki, how long have you worked here?'
'Three year. I come Pattaya five year ago, I work in massage shop for two year, but very quiet in low season. My friend own this business, she live in Germany now, so I run shop for her. She very good friend and let me live upstairs for free.'
'You don't have an excuse to be late for work then?'
'No. But no one check.' Pooki smiled. Tony liked this beautiful woman.
'You work in England?'
'I did. My company got rid of me. I'm sort of retired now.'

'Rid? I not understand?'
'It means to push out, you no longer wanted.'
'I understand now. How can you retire? You still young?'
'I'm fifty-four.'
'You younger than my papa, and he still works on farm.'
'Well, it wasn't my choice, I wanted to work six more years, then retire.'
'You like the coffee?'
'Yes, it's very nice.'
'Best coffee shop in Jomtien.'
'Well, I'll certainly be coming back.' Tony thought that would be a good excuse to see Pooki again. A man stuck his head in the shop and spoke to Pooki.
'Scooter fixed, Khun Tony.'
'Oh, right. Well, thanks for the chat.'
'Try not to break scooter again.' Pooki smiled, and Tony reluctantly said goodbye.

Looking at his watch, it had just gone 3.30 pm. Pulling out his wallet, he found the business card Barry had given him. Checking the address and name of the condo complex where Barry and Alan were staying, he thought it was about time he went and said hello. Starting the scooter, he headed back to Pattaya. Stopping and asking a group of taxi motorbike riders, he eventually found the complex. It looked very smart and had a 7-11 convenience store right at the entrance. Parking the scooter, he walked past a security guard who gave him a salute. The complex was L-shaped, and in the middle was a huge swimming pool. The complex looked fairly empty and as Tony looked across, he could see Barry sitting on a sunbed. A Thai woman was massaging his shoulders.
'Hard life.' Tony called out.
'You're not wrong, their mate.' Barry looked up and recognised Tony. 'I was only saying to Alan this morning; I wonder if you'll turn up?'
'And like a bad penny, here I am.' The two men shook hands.
'Alan's having a kip. Yar, go wake Alan up. Tell him a friend come to see him. Then go 7-11, get six bottles of Chang.' Barry passed some money over to the girl, and she went off without a murmur.
'So, how are you finding Thailand?'

'Fantastic, Barry. I'm having the time of my life.' As the two men spoke, a man came over and said hello.
'Alright, Barry. You got a different girl, I see?'
'You know what it's like, Tom.'
'Oh, I certainly do.'
'Tom, this is Tony, we met on the flight over.'
'Hello, Tony, nice to meet you. Where do you come from?'
'Ipswich.'
'Oh, that's not far from me, I used to live in Colchester.'
'I know Colchester well. Nice town.'
'Tom was the guy I was telling you about, Tony. He lives here full time.'
'Really, how long have you been here, Tom?'
'Five years, I got made redundant, took a small pension and live the quiet life out here.'
'Same as me, I've just been let go by my company and getting a small pension.'
'A small pension goes a long way out here, Tony.'
'Tom, why don't you show Tony your apartment while I wait for the beers to come? Tony may be interested in renting one.'
'Yes, no problem.'
'As long as I'm not putting you out, Tom
'Of course, you're not.'
Tony followed Tom inside the complex.
'I'm on the top floor.' Tom pressed the number five in the elevator and the lift quickly went up. Stepping out into a smart corridor, Tom walked over to his door.
'Here we are,' Tom unlocked the door, kicked his flip-flops off and went inside. Tony followed suit.
'These apartments are only small, but for two of you, they're ideal.'
Tony looked at the small kitchen and lounge.
'In here is the bedroom and bathroom.' Tom opened the bedroom door and Tony went in. The bathroom was big with a nice shower at the end.
'Out here is the balcony.' Tom slid open the door and walked out.
'Not huge, but enough for a table and two chairs, and check out the view?' Tony looked out and, in the distance, he could see the sea.
'One thing about living out here, Tony. You don't need all the clutter and clothes you have in the UK. I only have shorts, t-shirts and vests. A

couple of pairs of trainers and two pairs of flip-flops. That's my wardrobe. You don't need anything else. I've not worn a pair of long trousers for five years now.'

'Yes, I guess you wouldn't need them in this climate. I have to say, Tom, it's a lovely apartment. Can I ask what you pay a month?'

'9,000 baht.' Tony worked that out to be about a hundred and eighty pounds.

'Christ, that's cheap'

'It's about the going rate, Tony. That includes the free WI-FI, cable tv and use of the small gym. My electric and water come to around 1,000 baht a month, so yes, about two hundred a month covers it.'

'That's good, Tom.'

'I looked at it like this, Tony. Had I stayed in Colchester, what sort of life would I be living? My pension isn't enough to have a comfortable life, I have another two years before I get my state pension, so I would have had to get another job, not easy at my age. Or, retire and live in Thailand. Doesn't take a lot of working out, does it? There is one key to being happy out here. Find yourself a good woman. Not an easy ask, I can tell you. Took me a few bad experiences before I got lucky. But I met my wife three years ago and never looked back.'

'You married?'

'Yes, that's my wife.' Tom pointed to a large photo on the wall. Tom was dressed in traditional Thai clothes, and his wife looked stunning.

'Your wife is beautiful, Tom.'

'Yes, she is. If you move here, that's what you need to do, Tony. The bar life will quickly make you poor.'

'Yes, I can imagine.'

'If you fancy giving it a go, I know the owners of a few apartments in this complex. They'll do you a good deal for a long contract. I have the keys to two apartments, I'm sort of the caretaker for them.'

'Thanks, Tom. I must admit it's very tempting. You're living the dream.'

'Well, you know where I am, if you want to take a look or want to know anything else, just give me a knock.'

'Thanks, Tom, that's very kind of you. Right, I'd better get back to Barry.'

'I'll leave you to it. Hope to see you again, Tony.'

'I think you will, Tom.'

By the time Tony got back to the swimming pool area, Alan was sitting with Barry and two Thai girls.
'Hi, Alan.' Tony shook hands.
'Well, what did you think of the apartment?'
'Very nice, and bloody cheap.'
'That will be me in another two years, Tony.' Announced Alan.
'What about you, Barry?'
'Can't do until I'm sixty-five, I'm self-employed, I'm paying into a private pension scheme, but it isn't much. Unless my dear old mum pegs out and I can sell her house, I have another seven years before I can retire out to the land of smiles. I'm going to start spending a few months of the winter out here starting next year, so that won't be so bad. What about you, Tony?'
'Well, I'm only just retired. I'm fifty-five in January. My pension isn't that good. About seven hundred a month.'
'Enough to live out here,' stated Alan.
'You think?'
'Yes, it's a different lifestyle if you live here. We're in holiday mode, so it's drinking, women and having a good time. Look at Tom, beautiful wife, lovely apartment. He has a small car and a motorbike and has this beautiful climate to wake up to every morning. His pension is less than yours.'
'Really? But doesn't he get bored?'
'He seems to have a busy life, he goes sea fishing most late afternoons, he goes out on his mountain bike in the mornings, and plays table tennis three times a week. Belongs to a darts team …'
'And a quiz team,' chipped in Barry.
'He does a session in the gym most days, he's very fit for sixty-three.'
'Yes, he looks good for his age,' admitted Tony.
'Here, get one of these down you.' Alan took the top off a bottle of Chang and handed it to Tony.
'Cheers, so where did you meet these ladies?' Tony looked at the two pretty girls.
'We took them from our favourite bar, we'll have these and take a stroll down.'
'I can't drink too much, I came on the scooter.'

'Don't go worrying about that. If you drink too much, get the baht bus home and come back tomorrow and pick the scooter up. It will be safe here.'
'Yeah, you don't want to be riding a scooter around here after a drink. It's bad enough when you're sober,' pointed out Barry. Tony was halfway through his beer when Barry stood up.
'Drink up, Tony, we're leaving.'

The next morning, Tony was picking at his breakfast, nursing yet another hangover, he decided today was going to be a dry day. He had to get back to Pattaya to pick the scooter up and sort out transport to take him to the Island of Koh Chang. He couldn't believe he'd been in Thailand a week already. He kept thinking of his conversation with Tom and the thought of living in Thailand interested him immensely. Any thoughts of returning to a UK winter were making him feel depressed. After breakfast, he strolled outside and started to walk towards Beach Road. He spotted Pooki cleaning one of the scooters and walked over to see her.
'Sawadee khab, Pooki. You want an iced coffee?'
'Kob Khun ka.' Pooki did a wai and smiled. Tony went into the coffee shop and ordered two coffees.

'Here you are,' Tony returned and handed one of the plastic cups to Pooki.
'So, where scooter, Khun Tony?'
'Oh, I left it at a friend's condo complex in Pattaya last night. I had too much to drink, so I came home on the baht bus. I'm going to collect it now.'
'I take you ka,' announced Pooki.
'What about the shop?'
'Boss can look after shop.'
'Boss? I thought you were the boss?'
'Yes, I am the boss, that's Boss.' Pooki pointed to the man at the motorbike repair shop who fixed the brake cable.
'He watch shop for me.' Pooki called out to Boss in Thai. The man came over and Pooki gave him some keys.
'Need to get hat for your big head ka.' Pooki went inside the shop and came back out with a pink safety helmet.'

'Here, this will fit you.'
'Have you any other colour?'
'Mai ka. Only this one.' Pooki passed it over, and Tony put it on. Pooki started to laugh.
'Look good on you.' Walking over to a pickup truck, Pooki climbed in and started it.
'Come on.' Tony walked over and stood next to her.
'Why am I wearing this hat?'
'You look good in pink.' Pooki started to laugh.
'Take it off and leave it on the table.' Tony took the safety hat off and placed it on the table outside the shop. He then climbed into the passenger side of the truck.
'You tell me where to go once we get to Pattaya.' Pooki drove confidently away, and Tony sat back and relaxed.

'You're a good driver, Pooki. Is this your truck?'
'Ka, my truck. I have five years now.'
'It's nice. Here, you might be able to help me. Where can I book transport to Koh Chang?'
'You going to Koh Chang?'
'Yes, next Tuesday, for three nights. Have you been there?'
'Mai ka, it meant to be beautiful.'
'An old work friend said it was worth a look, so I thought I'd check it out.'
'I know a shop that can sort transport for you.'
'Thank you. Where do you go on holiday?' Pooki turned and smiled at Tony.
'I never been on holiday.'
'Really?'
'Ka, I go home to family for one week at Songkran.'
'Where is the family home?'
'Khamphengphet.'
'Is that far from here?'
'Six-hour drive.'
'Oh, quite a way then.'
'Ka, long drive. My friend say I can close shop anytime and have holiday, but I can't afford it. I still pay for this truck. One more year and it finished.'

'Why don't you come to Koh Chang with me?' Tony blurted it out without thinking.
'You take me to Koh Chang with you?'
'Yes. I will try and book a room for you; I don't want you to think I'm taking advantage or anything.'
Pooki smiled and said nothing. After a couple of minutes, she asked Tony where the scooter was parked.
'We're nearly there, take the next road on the right.'
'We call road, soi in Thailand.'
'Okay, this soi on the right, Pooki.' As they turned into the soi, Pooki could see the red Yamaha parked up outside a condo complex.
'You have friend live here?'
'Yes, and I met a guy who has retired here. I must admit I'm tempted to follow suit. I love it here.'
'You should, Khun Tony.' Pooki stopped the truck.
'Well, thanks for bringing me over here.'
'No problem ka.' Tony climbed out. Pooki hadn't mentioned Koh Chang, he guessed she wasn't keen.
'Maybe you can let me know where I can book the transport for Koh Chang later?'
'No need, we can go in truck.' Pooki blew him a kiss and drove off. Tony was smiling like a cat that got the cream.

As Tony unlocked the scooter, his mind was racing. He loved Thailand, and Pooki was lovely. He could see himself living in Thailand. He needed to think it through.
'A penny for them.' Tony turned and Tom was sitting on his mountain bike.
'Hello, Tom. Going out for a ride?'
'Just got back, Tony. Love riding the bike along the beach. I went into your territory today, Jomtien.'
'Blimey, how long did that take you?'
'Not long. About twenty minutes. I rode the whole length of the beach, stopped and had breakfast on my way back. So, I take it you had a session with Laurel and Hardy last night.'
'Yes, you could say that. Do you think I could have a look at those apartments, Tom?'

'Of course, you can. Let me sort my bike out, then come up and have a cup of tea, and I'll show you both of them. You can get a good deal if you want a six-month contract. An even better deal for a year's contract. Follow me.' Tom pushed his bike, and Tony locked the scooter back up and walked with him. After locking his bike up, they headed up to Tom's apartment.

As he opened the door, Tom called out to his wife.
'We have a guest, sweetheart. Come in, Tony.' As he walked in, Tony had his first glimpse of Tom's wife.
'Sawadee Khab.' Tony did a wai.
'Sawadee, ka, what's your name.'
'I'm Tony.'
'Hello, Tony, I'm Suk.'
'Suk works in an early morning market. We get up early, but she finishes at ten-thirty.' Explained Tom.
'I go shower, Tom.' Suk smiled and disappeared into the bedroom.
'Let me make a cuppa and then I'll show you the apartments.'
The next thirty minutes, Tom explained the visa situation, and a lot of the do's and don'ts regarding moving to Thailand. Again, he emphasised the importance of meeting a nice woman. How he kept himself busy and roughly what it cost a month to live in Pattaya. Tony asked some questions about renting a condo.
'There's a lot for rent in Pattaya, Tony. Lots in Jomtien too. It's just a case of finding one that suits you. This complex is in a good position. It's away from the real hustle and bustle, but not that far from the beach. Come on, I'll show you the apartments.' Tom searched through a drawer in the kitchen and pulled out two sets of keys.
'The first one is on this floor,' Tom put on his flip-flops and walked along the corridor.
'I think you'll like this one, it's just been decorated and had some new furniture.' Unlocking the door, Tom ushered Tony inside. He was immediately impressed.
'Wow, it's nice, Tom.'
'This is the better one out of the two.' Tony walked through to the bedroom and could see a new mattress still wrapped on the bed.
'This sofa is new,' remarked Tom. Tony slid the balcony door open and looked at the view.

'Get the shade in the morning, Tony. Just imagine sitting out here having your breakfast.'
'It's perfect, Tom. How much is it a month?'
'10.000, but you could most probably get it for 9,000 if you sign for a year. I'll have to email the owner and ask.'
'I'm so tempted, Tom.'
'I can see. Do you want to look at the other apartment?'
'No, I like this one. Tell you what, if he accepts 9.000, I'll take it.'
'You sure? I don't want to mess the owner around. Why don't you think about it?'
'No, I'm sure, Tom. I can't face going back to the UK now, I've been spoiled. No, this life is for me. Hey, looks like we will be neighbours.'
'Welcome to paradise.' The two men shook hands.

## *Chapter 3*

Not once on the ride back to his hotel did Tony feel any signs of worry or regret. In fact, he was more interested in the logistics of moving to Thailand. He knew he needed to sit down and make a list of things he needed to do. Before any of that, he wanted to share the news with Pooki.

As he pulled up outside her shop, he could see her smiling and waving at him from inside.
'Coffee?' He asked as he walked in.
'Mai ka, khob khun ka. Too much coffee not good for you. I'll have green tea, ka.'
'Sounds interesting, hot or cold?'
'Cold, ka.' Tony went next door and ordered two ice green teas. When the girl passed them over, he sipped through the straw. He liked the taste.

'Here we are, madam,' Tony passed one of the plastic cups over.
'You like?'
'Yes, very nice.'
'I message my friend, she said give shop keys to Boss, he can watch shop when I away next week. What time we go on Tuesday?'
'I don't know, I'm not sure how long it takes to get there?'
'My friend say four hour to harbour. We go to a place called Trat to get ferry.'
'Okay, well perhaps we can leave around 9 am. I'll try and get directions printed out.'
'I know, way, Tony.'
'You do? That's great then. I'll pay for everything and the petrol. I'll try and book you your own room in the hotel.'
Pooki smiled at Tony.
'No need ka, remember I not young girl, I thirty-year-old.'
'Well, you only look twenty, besides I didn't want you to think I'm taking advantage.'
'I not think that, I know you a nice man.'
'Thank you, that's a lovely thing to say. I have some news for you. I remember you telling me you don't like to go out with a tourist, so I

have decided to rent a condo for one year. I'm going to live in Thailand. I'm moving to that complex you took me to earlier.'
'Really? You not joke with me, Khun Tony.'
'No, I do not joke with you. I'm just waiting to hear from my friend who has contacted the owner.' Pooki stood up and came over, and hugged Tony. This was the first physical contact between them.
'I happy, Tony.'
'I'm happy too. Do you want to have dinner with me tonight?'
'Ka, I'd like that.'
'Okay, what time?'
'I close shop at seven tonight. Come at eight.'
'Okay, I'll go now, I have things to organise. I'm excited.' Tony went to leave, and Pooki stretched up and kissed his cheek.'
'See you at eight, don't be late ka.' Pooki smiled, and Tony's heart skipped a beat.

Sitting in the comfort of his air-conditioned room, Tony had switched on his laptop and connected it to the internet. He made a start on a to-do list. He broke it into two groups: the UK and Thailand. In the Thailand column, he wrote about sorting out a Thai bank account and applying for a retirement visa, Tom had told him he knew an agent that could help him with that. As he was writing an e-mail alert pinged up. Going into his emails he could see it was from Tom. Opening it up, there was a brief note.
"Hi, Tony,
The good news is that the owner will accept 9,000 baht a month for the apartment for a one-year contract. You'll need to pay one month's rent and 9,000 deposit before you move in. He has sent me a contract for you to sign. I will just need the date you want to move in.
Cheers, Tom."

Tony opened the calendar on his phone, his flight home was booked for the 26$^{th}$ of October. He sat there pondering what to do. Did he really need to go home? He needed to talk to his best friend. Checking his watch, it was 12.30. He knew it was 6.30 am in the UK. As it was Saturday morning, he wondered if Bob was up and about yet. He checked on Skype and could see Bob was not online. Looking in his travel bag for his diary, he'd written the code to the UK from Thailand.

He entered the code and then Bob's number. After a few seconds, it started to ring. A croaky Bob answered.
'Hello.'
'Morning, Bob, It's Tony.'
'Hang on.' Bob sat up and checked the time.
'Tone, are you okay?'
'Yes mate, listen, I need to talk to you urgently. It's nothing bad, so don't panic. Make yourself a cuppa, then switch your computer on. I'll give you a Skype call in ten minutes.'
'Are you in some sort of trouble, Tone?'
'No, everything is good, it's fantastic. I'll call you in a little while.' Tony hung up.
Going back to his to-do list, he started to make notes of things that needed doing in the UK. He'd already told the letting agent that he wouldn't be renewing his contract on his flat, so that wasn't a problem. He had his car and motorbike, but neither was worth that much. Bob could sell them for him. In fact, he could sell just about everything. Tony smiled to himself. He decided there was no need to fly back. What it would cost in another airfare to come back to Thailand, he could buy a new scooter. All he had to do was convince Bob.
While he waited, he sent Tom a quick reply.

"Hi, Tom,
That's great news about the apartment. To keep things simple, can you make the contract to start on the 24th of October? That will give me a few days to get organised before I move in full-time.
Thank you so much for your help. I'll treat you to a few beers once I'm settled.
Let me know when you want the contract signed, and I will come over and pay the deposit as well.

Kind regards

Tony Fellows."

After sending the email, Tony opened Skype and could see that Bob was online. After a few rings, his best friend answered.

'Bloody hell, Tone. You've got me all worried. I've not heard from you all week.'
'Sorry, mate. With the time difference and all that, it's not easy to catch you online. I checked a few times, but you weren't on.'
Tony hadn't, but he tried to ease the situation.
'I thought you might have. You can leave a message on here.' Pointed out, his friend. Something Tony knew but played dumb.
'Oh, I forgot about that, I'll remember to do that next time.'
'So, what's going on, Tone? It must be important for you to ring me so early.'
'It's nothing bad, Bob. I'm after a favour.'
'Anything, Tone, you know that.'
'I need you to empty my flat.'
'Empty your flat? Why?'
'I'm not coming back, mate.' Bob sat there with a blank look while he absorbed this revelation.
'What do you mean, you're not coming back?'
'What I mean is, I'm going to stay out here for a bit longer.'
'How much longer?'
'I don't know yet, a few months most probably.' Tony decided not to tell Bob about the year's contract he was about to sign.
'What about all your stuff, Tone? You've left it all a bit tight timewise.'
'Yes, sorry, mate. Look, keep all my documents. I'll tell you what to send out to me here. Things like my birth certificate and bank books, a few photos.'
'What about your car and motorbike? I can keep your motorbike in the garage, but I'm not sure where I can keep your car?'
'Sell them both, Bob. Take my golf clubs out of the boot and sell them too.'
'But you won't have anything here when you get back?'
'I can soon buy a runaround car, and the motorbike, well, I hardly use it anyway.'
'What's bought this on, Tone?'
'I don't know, I think it's the thought of returning to a UK winter. I've met a guy who lives out here on a small pension; he has a great lifestyle, Bob. The weather is fantastic, the food is cheap, and you can rent an apartment for less than two hundred pounds a month. In fact, roughly what I pay in council tax each month.'

'Bloody hell, Tone, I don't know what to say. I don't blame you, you're right, another winter is fast approaching. And the price of an apartment, why would you want to come back? Is there a lady involved?'
'No, nothing like that,' Tony didn't want to mention he was smitten with a girl from the scooter hire shop.
'If you can just help me out, Bob, otherwise I'll have to fly back and do it myself.'
'Of course, I'll help you. I haven't anything on, so I'll make a start today. I'll put everything in this room and garage, then you can tell me what you want me to send out.'
'Thanks, Bob. Remember the flat was fully furnished when I moved in, so all the stuff in the kitchen is not mine. Have everything that's in the fridge. All my clothes you can either have or dump.'
'I'll hang on to a few bits, Tone. You'll need some clothes when you come back.'
'Okay, I'll let you know what to keep. Thanks for doing this, Bob.'
'No problem, I just hope you know what you're doing. So, I take it you're having the time of your life?'
'I am, Bob. I'm living the dream.'

Bob closed the computer down and went downstairs to sort out some breakfast. He was surprised to see Janice and Susan already at the kitchen table.
'Tea in the pot, love.' Bob took a mug out of a cupboard. When Janice called him love, he knew she was after something.
'So?'
'What?'
'Don't what me, Bob Bates, what did Tony want? And don't say nothing, he knew what time it was here. He rushed you onto a Skype call, so it must have been something important?'
'Did he say he was staying out there?' Susan asked Bob outright.
'Were you listening at the door?' Bob asked Janice's sister.
'What …. No. I was on my way to use the toilet, and I thought I overheard Tony say he was staying out there?'
'You heard that on the way to the toilet, did you?'
'Yes,' replied a guilty-looking Susan.

'Well, in fact, he is staying out there. He has asked me to clear his flat and sell everything.'
'Sell? How long is he staying out there?' Susan was horrified. Something Bob picked up on.
'A long time I would think, I mean, he wouldn't ask me to sell everything if it was only for a few more weeks. No, I would imagine he's looking long-term.'
'He's gone mad, he's most probably hooked up with some young Thai girl who will bleed him dry. He'll be back within a few months, skint, and nowhere to live, you mark my words.'
'If that's the case, he can stay here until he gets himself sorted.'
'Over my dead body,' called out Susan.
'Can I remind you that this is my house and we have let you stay here, Susan?'
'Of course, she can stay here, she's my sister.' Protested, Janice.
'Yes, and Tony's my best friend, so if he needed somewhere to stay, I'd tell him he can stay here. I'm getting ready and going out.' Bob stood up and headed off upstairs.
'Wow, Hark and Mr Grumpy. Someone got out of bed the wrong side this morning.' Commented Susan.
'Well, he's in shock. He's just lost his best friend.'
'Yes, and I've lost an ex-husband. Hey, do you think we should help Bob clear Tony's flat? He has some nice stuff.'
'Yes, Bob won't have a clue what to keep and what to take, plus he had some really nice bedding, it would go a treat in our bedroom.' The sisters laughed at each other.

The next few days, Tony spent time at Pooki's shop, going to see Tom and signing the contract, and conducting another inspection of the apartment he was about to rent. After making a note of things he needed to buy, it amounted to very little. Bedding and towels were the two main things. The kitchen was well equipped with a large fridge and a washing machine. There was a microwave, toaster and kettle, plenty of dishes and cutlery. He'd bought Pooki to view the apartment.
'So, what do you think?'
'It's very nice. When we get back from Koh Chang, I'll take you to get nice bedding and towels.'
'Thanks, Pooki, I haven't a clue. The bed looks big?'

'King size, too big for one man.'
'Ideal for two,' smiled Tony. He hadn't slept with Pooki, and he was beginning to worry about tomorrow night when they would spend their first night together.
'Yes, good for two.' Pooki squeezed Tony's arm. This show of affection from Pooki made him feel a lot better.
'I'd better get back to shop, you want to come with me?'
'Of course, I'll just give Tom the keys back.'

On the drive back to Jomtien, Tony asked Pooki if she was excited about the trip to Koh Chang.
'Ka, it meant to be beautiful there. We can put scooter in back of truck, then tour the island.'
'Sounds fantastic. I'm so glad you are coming with me, Pooki. I really like you.'
'Why? I just normal lady.'
'Oh, you're are much more than that. You have a nice way about you, you're beautiful and funny, and I just love being with you. You make me very happy, Pooki.'
'Just never lie to me, Tony. I've been hurt before, I not let happen again. If you want to be with me, promise me you never hurt me. I could be a good woman for you, I take good care of you.'
'And I will take care of you. I will never lie or hurt you, Pooki. I have been hurt before as well. I just want a happy life, you make me very happy, I hope you know that.'
'Yes, I know,' Pooki smiled and squeezed Tony's leg.
'See, you rent scooter and you get me as well.' That comment from Pooki had them both laughing.

On Tuesday morning, Tony was up early, had breakfast and was outside the scooter shop at 8 am. Pooki hadn't opened the shop, and Tony sat down and waited patiently.
After fifteen minutes, Pooki opened the door; she only had a towel wrapped around her. Her hair was dripping wet.
'Sorry, I not wake up, come upstairs.' Tony followed Pooki up. He was shocked at how basic the room was. There was a bathroom in the corner, no kitchen of sorts and a mattress on the floor. A long clothes hanger held most of Pooki's clothes. There was an old chest of drawers

and a mirror on the wall. A small TV sat on a table, and there were two wooden chairs.
'Take a seat, I won't be long.' Pooki disappeared into the bathroom and then came out in just a small bra and matching panties. Tony couldn't help but smile at this beautiful woman.
'You're beautiful, Pooki.'
'Thank you, handsome man.' Pooki walked over and planted a kiss on his lips.
'I'm falling in love with you, Pooki.'
'But you hardly know me?'
'I know enough to know I want to be with you forever.'
'Khob Khun ka.' Pooki kissed him again, held his hand and walked him over to the mattress.
'Are you sure?' Tony asked as Pooki helped him off with his shirt.
'Ka, I'm sure.'

An hour later, they started the drive to Trat. With the help of the repairman, Boss, they lifted Tony's hire scooter onto the back of the truck and tied it down. Tony edged a bit closer to Pooki as she drove and rested his hand on her leg.
'Are you hungry?' She asked
'No, I'm okay. I ate something at the hotel.'
'I not eat yet.'
'Stop somewhere, you should have some breakfast.'
'I know nice noodle shop, not far from here.'
'You and your noodles, do you eat anything else?'
'Yes, I like many things, my favourite is chicken feet.'
'Chicken feet, we throw them away in England.'
'Really? Best part of chicken.' Tony wasn't quite sure if Pooki was joking or not.
'You have student?' Tony looked at Pooki, confused.
'Student?'
'Ka, boy or girl?'
'Oh, children.' Tony smiled.
'Yes, I have a daughter called Emily. She is nearly thirty.'
'Same age me?' Tony looked horrified.
'Christ, yes.' Pooki glanced over at Tony.
'You good age for me, Tony. Don't worry, okay.'

'I never thought about our age difference.' Tony was concerned about telling his daughter he was seeing a girl the same age as her. And Susan will have a field day, he thought to himself. Pooki could see the worried look on his face.
'It not a problem, Tony. If you love someone, it not matter how old you are.'
Tony smiled at Pooki. She made him feel good about himself and he had fallen for her in a big way.
'You perfect man for me.'
'And you are the perfect woman for me.' Tony leaned over and kissed Pooki on the cheek.
'Look, noodle shop, I order you chicken feet.'
'Err ... Maybe another time.'
'I joke with you, handsome man.'

Meanwhile, back in Ipswich, Bob was making a start on clearing Tony's flat. He'd emptied the fridge and switched it off. The majority of the contents he'd packed into bags and put in his car. He decided to put everything into bin bags and take them home. He found a briefcase full of Tony's important paperwork, including his birth certificate and divorce papers. He would go through it all with Tony and destroy what he didn't want.
The door buzzer made him jump. Walking over to the small screen, he could see Janice and Susan waiting outside. Pressing the intercom, he asked what they wanted.
'Open the door, Bob. It's cold out here.'
'What do you two want?'
'Open the door, we've come to give you a hand.'
'Be bloody nosey more like.'
'Susan can drive your car back, and you can ride Tony's motorbike home.' The thought of riding the motorbike was too much of a temptation for Bob. He pressed the door release button.
'Blimey, you've not done much?' Observed Janice.
'It's not a race, I've emptied the fridge and freezer, the stuff is in my car already.'
'I'll empty the bedroom,' announced Susan.
'Just the clothes, Sue. I'm not sure about the bedding. It might have come with the flat. I'll ask Tone next time I speak to him.'

'What about this printer?' Asked Janice.
'Yes, we'll take that. Let's empty the kitchen cupboards. Take all the food and bits.'
'Look what I've found hiding in the wardrobe?' Susan stood holding a photo album.
'What is it?' Asked Bob.
'He kept our wedding album, isn't that sweet?'
'Tone will most probably want me to shred that.'
'No way, I'll keep hold of this.'
'Up to you. Tone always said he'd never go back to the scene of a crime, so maybe best you do keep it.' Smiling to himself, Bob disappeared into the kitchen.

Tony and Pooki held hands as the car ferry approached the island of Koh Chang.
'According to this booklet, Koh Chang is 70% rainforest.'
'I want to see hotel, swim in the sea, ride on an elephant, eat on the beach.' Announced, Pooki.
'Yes, we can do all those things.' Passengers started to make their way back to their vehicles, so Tony and Pooki followed suit.

Once the ferry had docked, and after a short delay, Pooki drove off the ferry and followed the cars in front.
'Looks like we turn right and follow the coast road, we need to find White Sand beach.'
'Okay, I think we will have a scary drive, darling.' Tony suddenly saw the huge, steep mountain road they had to negotiate.
'Christ, I didn't know it was so hilly here.' Pooki pulled into a layby.
'You drive, I not good with hill.'
'No problem, you just need to keep in low gear.'
'I should have bought an automatic.'
'Why didn't you?'
'Another 50,000 baht.'
'Okay. Well, the manual is good. That's what I drive at home.'
'Thailand, your home now, darling.' Tony smiled. He liked being called darling.
'Yes, it is my home now.' Tony climbed into the driver's seat. He pulled away and climbed the winding hill to the top in second gear.

'Stop there, I want to take photo.' Tony pulled into an area that had a sign saying viewpoint. Pooki jumped out of the truck and stood by a low fence that stopped you from going any further. Tony walked over and joined her.
'What a fantastic view.'
'Smile, I take our photo.' Pooki cuddled up to Tony and took a photo of them with the sea in the background.
'Come, let's find the hotel.'
'Should be downhill all the way from here.' Tony said hopefully.

Twenty minutes later, and after a scary drive up and down the steepest hills Tony had ever driven on, Pooki spotted a sign for the hotel as they drove along. After parking, they went to the reception of the hotel. After booking in, they were taken to their room by a porter. Tony looked disappointed when they were shown the room.
'Hang on a minute, Pooki. I wanted a room that was on the beach.'
'This is okay, darling.' Had Tony been on his own, he wouldn't have minded. But he wanted it to be special for Pooki.
'Just wait here a moment, I will see if they have a beach room.' Tony shot back to reception and, after a bit of negotiating and an extra 3,000 baht, he got a room that led straight onto the beach. Going back to get Pooki, he smiled at her.
'Bit of luck, they have a room that is next to the beach.' The porter picked up the bags again and led them to the new room.
'This is much better.' Tony could see the beaming smile on Pooki's face as she surveyed the new room.
'I love it, darling. Let's unpack and go for swim. Then we can eat.'
'How do you stay so slim?' Tony looked at Pooki and smiled.

Two hours later, after a long swim in the beautiful warm sea and a very passionate lovemaking session, Tony was helping a security guard get the scooter off the back of the truck. Pooki spoke to the guard, and when the scooter was safely on the ground, Tony handed over a 100-baht tip.
'Security say very nice fish restaurant on the beach about 2 kilometres along the road.'
'Okay, sounds good to me. I'm hungry.'

'You work hard, darling.' Pooki gave one of her cheeky smiles and climbed on the back of the scooter.

Tony surveyed the table. He was full, but Pooki was still munching away.
'Food very good, darling.'
'It certainly is. I can't remember a nicer meal.'
'You want some more?'
'Me, no. I'm absolutely stuffed.'
'Have another beer.'
'I've had three already.'
'You on holiday, I can ride scooter back.' Pooki called the waiter, and he went off to fetch another beer.
'Do you want another drink?'
'No, I'm okay.' Pooki only ever drank water. A waitress walked past with a coconut on a tray.
'That looks nice.'
'Yes, coconut is very good, darling.'
'Why don't you have one?'
'Can I?'
'Of course, you can. You can have anything you want.' As Tony spoke, the waiter came over with a bottle of beer. Pooki spoke to him and ordered the coconut.
'You're on holiday too, sweetheart. Order anything you want.'
'You lovely man, darling. I glad you come to my shop.'
'I'm glad I came to your shop too. You are the perfect woman for me.' Pooki put her hand across the table and held Tony's.
'Would you marry me, darling?' Tony looked at this beautiful woman sitting opposite him. He didn't have to mull over the question.
'Yes, I would love to marry you.' Pooki smiled and had a tear rolling down her cheek.
'I'm so happy.'
'I fell in love with you the first time I saw you. I can tell you now, I rented that condo in the hope you would see I'm serious about you.'
'Thank you for love me, when would you marry me? I not want to wait a year, you may change your mind.'
'I'll never change my mind. I don't know, how about six months, say March or April? Give us a bit of time to get to know each other better.'

'Okay. You will have to come and meet my family. You will have to give my mama and papa some money. It's tradition in Thailand.'
'Of course, sweetheart. How much?' Tony had heard about this dowry payment in a conversation with Bert one night; however, at that moment, he was fearing the worst.
'My sister married man from Wales seven years ago. He gave two hundred thousand baht to my mama and papa.' Tony did a quick calculation in his head. He worked it out to be around four thousand pounds. He felt happy to match that.
'I can give two hundred thousand too.'
'You can?'
'Yes, you're worth every baht.'
'I phone mama.' Pooki pulled her phone out and, within a minute, was having a very excitable conversation. Tony sat back and sipped his beer; he didn't understand a word of what was being said.
Ten minutes later, a smiling Pooki came off the phone.
'They very happy and want to meet you. I tell them we will see them on our way back from here.'
'Wow, so quick.'
'They very nice, darling. They will love you, too. My sister will come with her husband.'
'Sounds great. I hope they don't think I'm too old for you?'
'They not think that. I tell you before, I not worry about it. My sister is thirty-three and my brother-in-law is seventy-two.'
'Seventy-two?' Tony immediately felt better.

The remaining time in Koh Chang went very quickly. Tony couldn't believe his luck. As he looked at his future wife, he couldn't remember the last time he felt so happy.
'You okay, darling?' Pooki noticed Tony staring at her.
'Yes, I'm feeling fantastic. I love you.'
'I love you too.' Once the scooter was loaded on the back of the truck, Tony started the long journey to Pooki's family home.
As they waited to board the ferry back to the mainland, Pooki leaned over and kissed Tony on the cheek.
'Can we come back here one day, darling?'
'Yes, it's beautiful here. Maybe come back for our honeymoon.'

'Ka, I would love that. We stay at my mama's home one night, darling.' As Pooki spoke, her phone started to ring.
'It's my sister.' Pooki answered as Tony followed the car in front onto the ferry. Pooki chatted away with her sister for most of the ferry crossing. Eventually, she closed her phone.
'Everything Okay?'
'Yes, darling. My sister at mama's already. She take mama to temple this afternoon to arrange a good day to get married.'
'I see. Where will we get married?'
'At home. Monks come to our home and they marry us. Will be a big wedding; all village will come. My cousins, auntie and uncles.'
'Wow, how many are we talking here?'
'My sister say, about three hundred.'
'Three hundred?' Croaked Tony.
'Maybe a few more. Don't worry, darling. My papa wants to talk to you. He will want to talk about wedding and money.'
'Does he speak English?'
'No. Don't worry, I will translate.' Tony drove in silence for a while. He was beginning to wonder what he was getting himself into.

'Not much further, darling.' Tony looked at his watch; they had been driving for over six hours since they came off the ferry.
'Good, I need a pee.'
'Me too. Gasoline place not far, we can stop there. Use toilet and get a few bits to take home.'
'Okay, shall I get some drink?'
'Ka, papa likes whiskey, maybe get bottle and some beer.' Tony liked that idea; he was thinking he might need a few beers to get through the next few hours. He couldn't believe he was meeting his future in-laws; he thought he'd left that sort of thing way behind.

As they went down a very bumpy road, Pooki grabbed Tony's arm. 'We here.' Pooki had driven from the gasoline station and drove the truck into the driveway of a very nice house.
'My sister husband build house for family.'
'That was nice of him.' As Tony spoke, he could see people coming towards the truck. There was no mistaking Pooki's sister, slightly

bigger, but with the same beautiful face. An elderly man came towards him, using a walking stick.
'You must be the famous Tony?'
'I am.'
'Pleased to meet you, I'm Peter.'
'Nice to meet you, Peter.' Tony picked up the Welsh accent. Pooki came over holding her sister's hand.
'This is my sister, Jeab.' Pooki's sister did a wai and then hugged Tony.
'Welcome, Tony.'
'Come on then, let's take you to meet mama and papa.' Jeab grabbed Tony's arm and led him towards the house. As he walked around the back of the house, about ten people were sitting around what Tony assumed was an outdoor kitchen. Again, Tony didn't have to guess who was Pooki's and Jeab's mum. An older version of the two girls stood up.
'This is mama, Tony. She not speak English. Tony did a wai.
'Sawadee Khab, mama.'
'Give mama a hug, darling.' Pooki joined them, and the three of them hugged.
'This my papa.' Tony turned and saw a small man who he guessed wasn't much older than him. Again, Tony did a wai and a Thai greeting. Pooki's papa gave him a western handshake and smiled. He spoke to Pooki.
'We go indoors, Tony. Papa want to speak to you.' Thinking this would be interesting, Tony followed Pooki and her papa indoors. Jeab came and joined them in a very nice lounge.
Once they were all seated, Papa spoke to Pooki.
'Papa ask if you love me?'
'Yes, tell him I love you very much.' Pooki spoke, and her papa listened. Then he spoke again.
'Papa want to know that you take care of me?'
'Yes, of course. I will take very good care of you.' Pooki translated. Papa stood up and picked up a pen and a notepad. He scribbled something down and passed it to Pooki. After a conversation between Papa and the two girls, Pooki turned to Tony.
'Papa ask if you can pay this amount. He say the numbers are very lucky.' Passing the piece of paper to Tony, he couldn't help but smile.

The amount written on the paper was 209,999. He was getting squeezed for another 10, 000 baht.
'Lucky numbers?' Tony asked Pooki.
'Yes, Papa say very lucky, bring us a happy life.'
'Yes, of course, I will pay.' Pooki spoke to Papa, and after a few moments, Papa came and hugged Tony.
'Papa very happy, Tony,' announced Jeab.
'I guess we will have to sort out a date for the wedding next.'
'We do already, mama and me went to temple. We get a lucky day for you to marry my sister.'
Tony looked at Pooki, who had a slightly worried look on her face.
'Oh, great. When's our lucky day going to be?'
'1st December, very lucky day to get married.' Jeab smiled at Tony.
'For a minute there, I thought you said 1st of December?'
'Yes, that a very lucky day.'
'But that's only about five weeks away.'
'I know, we have much to do. Come, let's go and tell the family.' Jeab grabbed Tony's arm again, and for the first time in his life, he felt like a lamb to slaughter.

'Congratulations, Tony. Welcome to the family.' Peter came and sat down next to Tony.
'You've struck gold there, mate. Pooki is a lovely girl.'
'Yes, she is.'
'The wedding will come along quickly.'
'Yes, I was thinking more of a wedding next year.'
'Well, if you love her, why wait?'
'Do you know what, Peter, you're right?' Tony looked at his bride-to-be as she hugged and smiled with her family and friends. She was perfect for him, and he knew it.

After a night of eating and drinking, Tony was awoken by a lot of noise coming from the rear of the house. He'd slept in a bedroom that was Pooki's when she came to visit. Pooki had slept with her mama. Checking his watch, it had just gone 5 am. Sticking a pair of shorts and a vest on, Tony made his way towards the noise.
'Good morning, darling.' Pooki was already showered and changed and sitting with her mama, who was busy crushing chilli peppers in a pot.

'We feed monks soon.'
'What, they come here for breakfast?'
'No, we wait front of house.'
'I see, I'd like to see that.'
'Of course, darling. Go take shower, I make you some breakfast. We feed monks and go. Need to get back to Pattaya today. Much to do with wedding. Don't worry, my sister help me.'
'I never asked, where do your sister and Peter live?'
'Pattaya.'
'You never said you had a sister living in Pattaya?'
'Ka, she live there long time.' Tony went off for a shower, knowing there was a lot about Pooki he didn't know. He guessed it was the Thai way, if you didn't ask, you wouldn't get told.

After feeding the monks, and watching Pooki and her mama pray. It was time to head back to Jomtien. After saying goodbye to the family, Tony drove away, waving back at the smiling faces.
'Your family is lovely, Pooki.'
'They you're family too, darling. Mama and Papa will be so proud of me when we get married.'
'It seems a lot to organise in a short time.'
'Don't worry, darling. Mama will do everything, and we will have a good wedding day. My sister will help, next week we choose dress and a suit for you.'
'A normal suit? Or a Thai traditional?'
'Normal suit for our wedding day, darling. You must wear traditional for our wedding photos.'
'How's that work? Do I have to change from one suit to another on our wedding day?'
'No, darling. We have wedding photos taken in Pattaya before we get married. Don't worry, I sort everything, okay?'
'Yes, I'm more than okay.'
'Will you ask friends from the UK?'
'I doubt it, it's only just over a month away. Doesn't give them much time to get here. It's a long way to come.'
'I'm sorry, darling. I should have told my mama and sister to make the wedding next year.'
'Don't worry, I doubt if they'd come anyway.'

'I love you, darling. I will make you happy in your life.'
'That, I do know.'
'Can we stop soon? I'm hungry.' Tony smiled away; his wife-to-be was always hungry.

It had just turned 2 pm when Tony pulled up outside the shop. Boss came over and helped Tony get the scooter down from the back of the truck.
'Right, I'll leave you to it. I will come back later, we can go and get something to eat.'
'Okay, darling. Come here about eight.' Pooki was too shy to cuddle Tony in front of Boss, so she did a wai.' Tony smiled and returned the wai.

After emptying his case back in his hotel room, Tony decided a late afternoon swim in the pool was in order. He knew he had to tell Bob the latest development, but decided that call could wait. Putting on a pair of swim shorts, Tony ventured downstairs and straight to the pool. Lying on a sunbed between two girls was Bert. Seeing Tony walk over, he sat up.
'There you are, I've been a bit worried about you.'
'I've been to Koh Chang for a few days, Bert. I thought I told you I was going?'
'You may have done, I get forgetful in my old age. You going for a swim?'
'Yes, thought I'd have a refreshing dip after all that driving.'
'Good man, that'll save me getting wet. I promised these two lovely's I would teach them how to swim. Come, girls, my friend here will teach you, and no pulling his shorts down.' Bert patted the bum of one of them. Tony smiled and marvelled at Bert's lust for the opposite sex.

After some splashing around in the pool, Bert gave the two girls some money and sent them on their way.
'A night off tonight, young man.' Bert had ordered two beers and passed one to Tony.
'I don't know where you get the energy from, Bert. You always seem to have two at a time?'
'The magic pills. That reminds me, how are you getting on with them?'

'To be honest, I've not tried them since that first night, and that is a night I want to forget.'
'Yes, I remember. You don't fancy trying a ladyboy again?'
'No, I don't. Can I tell you something, Bert?'
'Of course, you haven't caught a dose, have you? I told you, always wear a condom. It's the golden rule over here.'
'No, it's nothing like that. I've met someone.'
'That's grand, lad. What bar does she work at?'
'She doesn't work in a bar. She runs that scooter hire shop, just along from the hotel.'
'I know the girl, a bit of a beauty.'
'Yes, that's her. I took her to Koh Chang with me, and had a fantastic time.'
'That's the trouble here, Tony. You meet a nice girl, fall in love, and then you have to go home. Unfortunately, you're soon forgotten; next week, some other man is filling your shoes.' Tony smiled at the ever-cynical Bert.
'I know that, so that's why I'm not going home, I'm staying. I'm renting a condo in Pattaya for a year.'
'Good for you, Tony, are you staying because of this girl?'
'I won't lie, I did sort of think about it before I met her, but obviously, it helped influence my decision. I'd been to the complex and thought, yes, I could live here. I met a nice guy who rents there, and he lives on a small pension similar to mine. He has a beautiful wife and, as far as I could see, is living the dream. He said the secret was to meet a nice woman to settle down with. If I live here full time, Bert, I won't be able to afford to go to bars every night.'
'No, it's not a cheap hobby. I don't blame you. I have to go home for six months every year. I have my children and grandchildren. If it wasn't for them, I'd be out here all the time. Have you got kids?'
'Yes, I have a daughter.'
'What will she say about you staying out here?'
'Oh, I think she will be happy for me. The hard part is going to be telling her I'm getting married to a girl the same age as her.'
'Getting married?'
'Oh …. Yes, I was coming to that bit.'
'That's all a bit quick if you don't mind me saying, Tony.'

'Yes, it is. But do you know what, Bert? I don't care what other people think. That girl is perfect for me. She has made me smile again; she is funny and smart. Has a lovely family and just wants to be happy with someone who won't let her down. She knows I don't have loads of money, but she is happy to accept me as I am. Look, Bert. I don't have much to return to the UK for. I need to rent a cheaper flat now because I lost my job. My pension is not going to be enough to live on, so I need to find another job. And trust me when I tell you, Ipswich isn't a thriving town when it comes to employment. If I go back now, I'm heading straight into another UK winter. No, I know I'm making the right decision.'

'Well, when you put it like that, it's a bit of a no-brainer. I have my reservations, Tony, but you're a smashing bloke and I hope it all turns out well for you. We'd better have another beer to celebrate. Have you set a date yet?' Tony felt embarrassed to say it, but just blurted it out.

'Yes, the 1st of December.'

'That's just over a month?'

'Well, we thought, what's the point in hanging around.'

'If your minds are made up, why not? It's certainly a whirlwind romance.'

'Yes, you could say that.' Tony sat back and sipped his beer. He smiled to himself; he didn't have any doubts in his mind about his future with Pooki.

8 pm, on the dot, Tony arrived at the shop. He'd spent an hour composing a long email to his daughter. He hadn't mentioned the wedding, only that he was staying out in Thailand for a bit longer. He saw he had many missed calls and messages from Bob. He decided to give some thought to how he was going to break this latest development to his best friend. So sent the briefest of messages back. "Will call you soon. Everything is good here, so don't worry."

Pooki looked lovely in a vest and small denim shorts that showed off her perky behind. Pooki caught him taking a peek.

'Does my bum look big in these shorts?'

'No, it looks very sexy.'

'Thank you, darling. I want to show you something before we go eat. Sit down.' Tony sat down, and Pooki opened an A4-size notepad.

'I have been working out the cost of the wedding, darling. I try to keep costs down, but I want to show you.'
'Can I say something before we do this?'
'Of course, darling.'
'I love you, Pooki, you have come into my life and changed it for the better. I can't remember ever being so happy as I am now. I trust you; I know you will do the best for us. I know the wedding is going to cost a bit, but it's your special day, and I want it to be perfect. I'm not worried about what it will cost.'
'Thank you, darling. I love you too, and you perfect man for me. You have a good heart, and my family love you, that makes me very happy. Let me show you anyway.'
'Yes, of course.'
'My sister knows a wedding photographer shop owner. She will do all our photos, with two different dresses, and two suits for you for 20,00 baht. She will take some photos on a beach and we will have a lovely album to show.' Tony quickly worked that out to be four hundred pounds. It sounded cheap to him.
'That sounds good, Pooki.'
'I can take both dresses home to get married in, you can have the western suit for the wedding day. I know you not want to get married in a traditional suit.'
'Well, I would feel a tad uncomfortable, to be honest. So, we have our photos done before we get married?'
'Ka, darling. My sister will arrange invites, we get three hundred printed. You write your name down. Not want mistake on invite.'
'Of course.' Tony wrote his full name down.
'I will need some money soon, darling. Not much, but I need to pay deposit at photograph shop, the invites will be 1,500 baht.'
'Okay, I need to send some money over from the UK. I could do with a Thai bank account, make life easier.'
'I phone sister.' Pooki picked up her phone and very quickly was chatting away and laughing. Occasionally, Tony would hear his name mentioned.
'You go with my sister tomorrow. She has friend who work in Bangkok Bank. You get bank account.'
'We have to go to Bangkok?'
'No, Bangkok Bank in many town.'

'Oh, I see. Your sister knows many people.'
'Yes, she real estate agent. She gets to meet many customers. Mama phoned, they arrange catering and music. Monks will come at seven minutes past seven to marry us.'
'What, in the morning?'
'Yes, darling. Lucky time to get married.' Tony was beginning to realise he was marrying a very superstitious woman.
'Is that it?'
'Nearly; one more thing, darling.'
'It's tradition to buy me some gold, it will come to about 40,000 baht. It's important to wear when we get married.' Tony held Pooki's hand.
'I've said already that I love you and will pay whatever you need.'
'After wedding, darling. I sell gold back to shop. I want to finish payment on truck. I want to be free of paying 5,000 baht every month. It will be our truck, darling.'
'How much do you have left to pay?'
'About 50,000 baht.' Tony looked across at the truck. Pooki had taken good care of it, and it was immaculate. It would save him from buying a car, so he felt paying roughly one thousand pounds to clear the finances was a good option and would please Pooki immensely.
'Wait till I get some money sent over, and I will pay off the truck for you. It will be handy for me to use sometimes. I want you to keep the gold, Pooki.'
'You such a good man for me, darling. I win lottery day you come to me.'
'I'm a very lucky man. Tell me, are you hungry by any chance?'
'Ka, let's get some food and eat on the beach.' Tony jumped on the scooter, and Pooki climbed on behind and gave him a big hug.

Tony looked at his laptop; he had put off the Skype call to Bob long enough. This was his last night in the hotel. Tomorrow, he was moving into the apartment in Pattaya with Pooki. It was four and a half weeks until the wedding, and he needed to bring his best friend up to date with developments and get important documents sent over. Pooki had told him that the wedding was part of the tradition. They would register the wedding at a later date. To do this, Tony needed to get a freedom to marry affidavit from the British embassy. To do that, he

needed his divorce papers. Opening Skype, he could see Bob was online. As soon as they connected, Bob had a little dig.
'Oh, you're alive then.'
'Sorry, Bob. I've been really busy sorting things out with the new apartment. Oh, and planning a wedding.' Tony threw the remark in not knowing how Bob would react.
'What wedding?'
'Are you on your own, mate?'
'Yes, the sisters glum are out, why?'
'Well, I have some news for you, and I wanted you to be the first to know.'
'Are you getting married, Tone?'
'Yes.'
'When?'
'1st of December.'
'What, this year?'
'Yes, Bob. Now, I know you will think I'm mad, but I've fallen for the sweetest and kindest girl here. I know it's all a bit quick, but she's right for me, mate.'
'Bloody hell, Tone. I don't know what to say. Congratulations, I suppose. It is quick, but you're old and ugly enough to know what you're doing.'
'I need some stuff sent over, Bob. Get a pen and paper and write down my new address.' After giving Bob his new address, he gave him a list of things he needed to be sent.
'The main things I need are my birth certificate and divorce papers. They should be in that briefcase that was in my wardrobe.'
'Yes, I've seen them, Tone. I'll send them to you tomorrow.'
'Make sure you send by registered post, Bob.'
'I will, don't worry. So, you haven't told Emily yet?'
'No. I sent her a long email, bringing her up to date. But did not mention the wedding to her. It's difficult, Bob. Pooki is the same age as Emily, I'm not sure how she'll be about it.'
'You, lucky bastard, that's all I've got to say. So, the girl is called Pooki?'
'Yes. You might see her in a minute, she went off to get an ice coffee. So, how are things there, Bob?'
'Well, your flat is empty. I left it nice and tidy, so you shouldn't have any trouble getting your deposit back.'

'Thanks, Bob. I did email the agent, and he wrote back and said he'll pay back the deposit once he's checked the flat and got the keys. I have a set here. Seems a pain sending them to the UK.'
'Don't worry, Tone. I'll get a spare set cut and I'll drop them off at the agents for you.'
'Thanks, Bob. You're a bloody good friend. What about the car and motorbike?'
'The car has gone. I got two grand for it, which is about the right price considering its age.'
'I'm surprised you got that much, well done mate. Any luck with the motorbike?'
'Well, I rode it here from your flat. It's been years since I had a motorbike, and I really enjoyed riding it. So, I'll buy it from you.'
'No, you won't. You can have it. Let's say it's a thank you for all the running around you've done for me.'
'You sure, Tone? It must be worth a bit.'
'I'm glad to see it go to a good home.'
'Thanks, I'll most probably mothball it until next spring. So, do you want me to mention anything to Janice?'
'Give it a couple of days, Bob. I'll write an email to Emily; I'd better tell her myself before her mother gets the chance to stir things up.'
'I would, Tone. No disrespect, but Susan is a bloody nightmare. I can see her poisoning Janice. Always picking fault with me.'
'Well, she's a bloody expert at that. Listen, Bob, you need to remind her whose home she's staying at. Hang on.' A knock at the door signalled Pooki's arrival. Tony let her in.
'I get green tea, darling, coffee not good this time of night.'
'Thank you. I'm just talking to my best friend Bob in the UK. Come and say hello.' Pooki sat down in front of the laptop.
'Sawadee ka, how are you?'
'Yes, I am well, thank you. Congratulations on your wedding.'
'Khob khun ka. You not worry, I take good care of Tony. You come and see us?'
'Yes, I will. I've wanted to visit Thailand for a long time.'
'You will like it here. Okay, I let Tony talk.' Pooki gave a wai, then got up so Tony could sit down.
'Wow, she's lovely, Tone.'
'She is, mate. Right, I'd better go. Don't forget the documents.'

'I'll do it first thing in the morning. I'll get the keys cut and drop them all off at the agents as well. Don't forget to email Emily.'
'I won't. Okay, Bob, I'll give you a call in a few days once I've moved and settled in the apartment.'
'Okay, Tone. Take care, mate.' Tony waved and cut the call.
'He nice man.'
'He is. He's been a very good friend to me. Well, this time tomorrow, we'll be in our new apartment.'
'Ka, and two days we get wedding photos done.' Tony smiled. He knew Pooki would look beautiful in the photos.
'I hope they can airbrush a few years off me.'
'No need, you, handsome man, for me.' Pooki stood up and rubbed her tummy.
'I'm hungry.'
'Me too. Let me write a quick email to my daughter, and we can go and eat.'

As Bob pulled up on the driveway, he could see Susan and Janice looking through the curtains. He was tired after a long day on the production line. He was completely envious of what Tony was doing and wished he had the balls to do it himself. He looked at the pair of them staring out at him and longed for the day when his sister-in-law announced she was moving out. He'd done all the jobs for Tony on Saturday morning. He hadn't mentioned the wedding and felt quite chuffed that he knew something they didn't, or so he thought. As he walked in through the front door, Susan came into the hallway to greet him.
'Did you know?' She said in a slightly raised voice.
'Good evening to you too, Susan.'
'Answer her, Bob. Did you know?' Janice had followed her sister into the hallway, where Bob was trying to get his coat and shoes off.
'What is this, the Spanish Inquisition?'
'Did you know Tony is getting married to a child bride?' Susan stood with her hands on her hips, demanding an answer.
'You do know how ridiculous you sound, I hope. I'd hardly call thirty, child bride age. I have to ask you, Susan. What are you getting so upset about? I mean, you didn't give a shit about Tone when you started shagging young Frankie, did you?'

'Bob, don't speak to Susan like that.'
'Listen, you two, I've just come through the door after a hard day at work. I'm tired and I'm hungry. I don't need this sort of shit as soon as I get home. In answer to your question, yes, I did know. In fact, I've spoken to Tone's girlfriend and bride-to-be, and she is beautiful and very nice. I can certainly see the attraction of what he's doing.'
'Well, don't let me stop you.' Shouted Janice.
'Don't tempt me,' Bob looked furious. He put his shoes back on. It was rare for Bob to fall out with Janice, but she and her sister had pressed the wrong buttons.
'Right, I'm going to the pub for my dinner tonight. When I get home, I want you gone, Susan. Do I make myself clear?'
'You're not kicking my sister out,' protested Janice.
'This is my house, and I want her out. She is causing problems between us, Janice. You need to take those damned blinkers off.' Bob went back out of the door and slammed it behind him. He had a wry smile as he climbed back into his car.
"That told them," he thought to himself as he drove away.

An hour and a half later, Bob returned to the house. Having tucked into a nice carvery meal and two pints of lager, he was feeling a lot better. His mood had softened, and he started to feel a bit guilty in the way he spoke to Janice and Susan. As he walked into the lounge, Janice was sitting watching television.
'Have you calmed down, now?'
'Yes. You should know better than to have a go at me as soon as I walk through the door from work.'
'Yes, I'm sorry. Susan had no right to speak to you like that. You want a cup of tea?'
'That would be lovely, thank you.' Janice smiled at him and disappeared into the kitchen. As she went in, her sister came out and sat opposite Bob.
'I apologise. I shouldn't question you about, Tony. I know he's your best friend, I guess I was just shocked when Emily phoned me and told me about her dad getting married.'
'It was a shock to me as well, Sue. But he asked me not to say anything until he'd spoken to Emily.'

'Yes, I understand that, now. If it's alright with you, I'll move out tomorrow. I've never been on my own, and it's a frightening thought.'
Bob immediately felt guilty and relented.
'Stay, Sue. I was just angry at the time. Stay as long as you like.' He cursed himself after he realised what he had just said.
Janice returned with a cup of tea and a tin of biscuits.
'All made up?'
'Yes. I can't eat a biscuit, Jan. I've had a carvery at the Rose and Crown.'
'I've not cooked anything yet.'
'Go and have a carvery, my treat.'
'Do you fancy, Sue?'
'Yes, you never know, I might meet a nice man there.'
Bob sat back and waited for the two women to get ready.
'Will you be okay, Bob?'
'Yes, I'm just going to have a shower and watch a bit of TV.'
'Okay, see you later.' The two women went out of the front door. Bob turned the television off and listened to the car driving away. Going upstairs, he switched the laptop on. After a quick shower, he went back to the spare bedroom and sat down in front of the laptop.
Opening his wallet, he pulled out a small piece of paper with a website address and a password. After connecting to the internet, he went to a Thai dating site.
'What's good for the goose,' he mumbled to himself as he logged in to the website.

## Chapter 4

Tony was sitting on the balcony of the new apartment, enjoying a cup of tea, and he was admiring the view while he waited for Pooki to get ready. She had insisted that he wear a matching T-shirt and shorts as part of the wedding photos. Pooki knew what she wanted, and Tony was more than happy to go along with her plan. The apartment looked over the swimming pool, and as Tony looked down, he could see the familiar figure of the tubby tattooed Barry, logged out on a sunbed. Tony checked his watch; it was only 08.30. He thought it strange he was there so early and alone. Having only moved in the day before hadn't seen either Barry or Alan on his travels. Moving in was easy, he'd collected the keys from Tom and introduced Pooki to him and his wife, Suk. The two girls seemed to hit it off straight away. He also mentioned the forthcoming wedding to which Tom and Suk congratulated them both, without passing comment.
'I'm ready, darling.' Pooki stood by the fridge, drinking a glass of water.
'I not put make-up on, the girl in shop will do.'
'You don't need make-up, you're a natural beauty.'
'Thank you for say that, shall we go?'
'Yes. I see a guy I flew over with lying by the pool, let's go that way to the truck and say hello.'
'You can ask him to the wedding.'
'I could, but I think he flies back in a couple of weeks.'
Taking the elevator down, Tony held Pooki's hand as they strolled to the pool.
'Bloody hell, Barry. Have you shit the bed?' Barry, who was half asleep, struggled to sit up.
'Hello, Tony. I heard from Tom that you moved in, everything okay?'
'Yes, we moved in yesterday, everything's great. I looked out for you and Alan, but I did not see either of you about.'
'I was in bed most of yesterday, dodgy guts. You'd think I'd have learnt my lesson when it comes to eating spicy food. Alan's still in bed; he went out last night, so he won't surface until this afternoon. I had a night in. I can't remember ever doing that before in Pattaya. It's not often I see the mornings.' Barry started laughing and then took note of Pooki.
'Sawadee Khab.' Barry gave the Thai greeting.

Pooki said hello and gave Barry a wai.
'So, I heard a rumour, young Tony. A little birdie tells me you're getting married.'
'Yes, I've met and fallen in love with this beautiful woman. This is Pooki.'
'Have you set a date yet?'
'1st of December.'
'Bloody hell, Tony. You don't let the grass grow under your feet, all a bit quick, isn't it?'
'Well, it is quick. But why wait? I love her and the 1st of December is a lucky day to get married.'
'Lucky for who?' Asked a sceptical Barry.
'For both of us.' Replied Tony.
'Well, I wish you both good luck and happiness.' Barry stood up and shook Tony's hand, and gave an awkward kiss on Pooki's cheek.
'I can't wait to tell Alan it's true.'
'Well, we have a busy day ahead, don't go getting yourself burnt, Barry. Your body isn't used to the morning sun.'
'No, I'm having another thirty minutes then strolling up the road for a pint and a cooked breakfast.'
'Beer with your breakfast?'
'Yes, I have a craving for a Guinness.' Barry smiled as Tony and Pooki headed for the truck.

Pooki drove, and after a hectic drive in traffic, she managed to park the truck right outside the big wedding photographer shop. Once inside, Tony couldn't believe how big the shop was and that there were three floors.
Pooki explained the day's itinerary to Tony.
'We get make-up and some photos in these clothes, darling. Then, you get changed into traditional suit and we have photos taken in studio. We eat, then this afternoon you get a western suit and we go to beach for more photos.'
'Sounds great.' Tony felt relieved that he didn't have to venture outside in the Thai traditional outfit that he'd have to wear at some point during the day's proceedings.
After a long wait for Pooki to have her make-up done, Tony was summoned to the chair. He'd never had makeup applied before, and

he wasn't at all comfortable with it. However, he didn't complain as this was Pooki's day, so he just grinned and bared it.

After being led out to the rear of the shop, there was a small garden and a very stylish bench, which the photographer had them sit in various poses. There was a square of grass and big boards that were placed behind them, of various designs. After quite a few photos, Pooki told the photographer that she wanted some taken of them standing by the truck. Tony suddenly realised why Pooki insisted on getting the truck cleaned on the day they were moving into the apartment. After the photographer had taken around thirty photos, they were led back inside the cool shop.

'You follow this lady upstairs, darling, her name is, Jin. She will help you choose traditional suit.' Tony looked at the "Lady" who he thought had bigger shoulders than him.

'After you, Jin.' Tony gave Pooki a half smile and followed the ladyboy upstairs.

Jin asked Tony to sit down and picked up a large, thick folder. As she opened the album, there were A4-size photos of the Thai traditional suits. Tony didn't have a clue, so he asked Jin what she thought would look good on him.

'You want something cream and burgundy; it will go well with your hair colour.'

'You speak very good English, Jin.'

'Thank you, ka. My mama's husband is Australian, so I learn from him.'

Tony looked at Jin. If it wasn't for the solid build and the slightly deeper voice than you would expect, Jin was very much an attractive woman. She had a beautiful face and complexion and was very fair-skinned for a Thai.

'I see, well, Jin, you seem to know what you're talking about, so I will let you pick something for me. I honestly haven't a clue.' Jin smiled at Tony.

'Okay, ka. I need to measure you. Stand up, please, ka.' Tony loved the way women said, ka.' Pooki had told him it was polite to say that. Jin picked up a tape measure and started to measure Tony's chest.

'You big man.' She wrote down the size and then measured his waist.

'Oh, you a little pom pooie.' Tony guessed that meant fat.

'Err ... Yes, I have been eating and drinking too much lately.' He admitted.

'I joke, you look good.' Jin bent down and measured Tony's inside leg. He was sure she brushed his manhood on purpose as she stood back up.
'Neck.' Jin stood very close to Tony as she measured.
'You smell lovely, Jin.'
'Thank you, ka. You think I'm a beautiful lady?' Tony could feel the heat rising in his head.
'Yes, of course.' Jin smiled when he said that.
'I go and find clothes now. You can make coffee or water in fridge.' Jin pointed to a little side room where there was a kettle and a mixture of coffee and tea.
'Okay, thank you.' Jin walked off, and Tony went in search of water.

About twenty minutes later, Jin returned carrying a lot of clothes all wrapped in cellophane. She opened a curtain to reveal a small changing room.
'I find very nice outfit for you, Khun Tony. You take shirt and jeans off, then I help you get dressed.' This statement sent a cold shiver down his back. Jin could see the fear in Tony's eyes.
'No worry, I help many men.'
"I bet you have," Tony thought to himself as he walked into the changing room. Reluctantly, he took off his shirt and turned his back to Jin as he dropped his jeans.
'You, shy man?'
'Me? No, I used to play rugby. I share a big bath with fourteen other men.'
'Really, ka.' Jin looked at Tony, who was still trying to get his jeans off.
'I help you, ka.' Jin bent down and was at eye level with Tony's crutch.
'I can manage, thank you.' Jin wasn't listening; she was looking at Tony's manhood outlined through his pants as she helped him pull his jeans down. As Tony struggled, he lost his footing and tumbled over Jin and onto the floor. As he fell, the curtains opened, and Tony looked up to see Pooki and another assistant standing looking down at him.
'You, okay, darling?'
'Err, yes. Just had a spot of bother getting my jeans off.' Jin stood up and spoke to Pooki. After a brief conversation, they both started laughing. Pooki turned and spoke to Tony.

'You no need to be shy, darling. Jin, only here to help you. She want you to relax.'
'Of course, I am relaxed. I'm just a bit nervous, that's all.'
'Okay, well, I go put dress on now and when you ready we can get photos done.' Pooki looked at the clothes Jin had chosen.
'You will look very handsome in photos, darling.' Pooki disappeared with her assistant, leaving a slightly embarrassed Tony to deal with Jin.
'Right then, let's get back to getting these jeans off.'

Twenty minutes later, and after a few minor changes, Tony was dressed head to toe in a Thai traditional outfit. He looked in the mirror and thought, "I look a right plonker." Looking like he was auditioning for a part in Aladdin, he vowed never to let any of his friends see a photo of him dressed as he was. He sucked it up and did his best to hide his feelings from Jin.
'What do you think, Jin?'
'Your girlfriend right, you look very handsome. If she change mind, you come and marry me, okay.' Jin stood there smiling, leaving Tony to wonder if she/he was joking or not.
'We go to studio now.'
'Where is the studio, Jin?' Tony prayed and hoped he wouldn't have to leave the building dressed as he was.
'Upstairs, follow me.' Tony followed Jin up a narrow stairway; he was sure Jin slowed down so his face was close to her behind.
As they reached the studio, Tony got his first glimpse of Pooki, dressed in a traditional outfit. She looked stunning.
'You okay, darling?'
'Yes, you look beautiful.'
'Thank you, ka. You look handsome, too. We get photos taken now. Then we can eat, I'm feeling hungry.'
'Now, there's a surprise.'

An hour later, Jin was helping Tony off with his outfit.
'My goodness, thank God I didn't have to walk far in those shoes. I bet Aladdin will be glad to get them back.' That little joke from Tony sailed straight over Jin's head.
'I get some western suits for you to try after eat. We go to a quiet beach and take more photos.'

'Okay, I'll leave it in your capable hands.'
'Where you go eat?'
'I think Pooki said there is a nice restaurant nearby.'
'Yes, I come too.' Tony didn't know what to say, so he just smiled.
Once he was back in his jeans and t-shirt, they went downstairs. Pooki was sitting waiting for them. She still had all the makeup on. Before Tony could speak, Jin said something to her, Tony didn't have a clue what was said. Pooki turned and smiled at him.
'You such a nice man, telling Jin she can eat with us as a thank you for helping you.' Tony looked at the smiling Jin.
'Well, it's the least I can do; she's been a great help.'
'I better ask, Nid, to come. She been good help for me too.'
'Yes, of course, you must.' Tony realised his lunch bill had just doubled.

The afternoon was far more enjoyable for Tony. The lunch bill only came to around twelve pounds. Jin had picked him a very nice dark suit, and it fitted like it was made for him. Pooki was in a lovely white wedding dress and again looked stunning. Jin accompanied them as they were driven by the photographer.
After a thirty-minute drive, they were standing on a very quiet beach.
'Wow, how come there is no one around?'
'Not many tourists know about this beach, darling.' Tony looked around and was very impressed.
'It's a beautiful beach, we must come and have a picnic here someday.'
'Ka, we can.'
'So, is this the dress you take home to get married in?'
'Ka, this one, and another shorter one.'
'Two dresses?'
'Ka, one for day, and one for evening. Wedding last all day and night, darling.' Tony gave a half smile. It was beginning to dawn on him that the wedding was going to be one hell of a long day.

While Tony was embroiled in all the wedding arrangements, his best friend had arrived home from work to hear some surprising news from Janice.
'You'll never guess what?' She asked him as he walked into the kitchen.
'Your sister is moving out?' He asked, forever hopeful.

'No ... And stop saying that. You did say to her she could stay as long as she likes, you shouldn't have said it if you didn't mean it.'

'Alright, calm down. So, what won't I guess?' Bob bitterly regretted that moment of weakness when he told Susan she could stay, but lived in hope she would get the hint.

'Susan has had a letter from her solicitor, Frank has offered to buy her share of the house. He's offered her one hundred thousand pounds.'

'Shit, where's he got that sort of money from?'

'I don't know, but that's about how much she was expecting to get from the sale of the house.'

'She could buy a flat, now.'

'Yes, so be nice to her, you may get your wish after all.'

'What a terrible thing to say, Jan. I love having your sister here.' He replied sarcastically.

'By the way, where is she?'

'She's upstairs on the laptop, looking at flats.'

'Oh, I'll pop up and see her.' Bob tried to keep calm. He was worried his sister-in-law might unearth some of his recent activity online. Susan worked for a company that dealt with computer fraud. She knew the ins and outs of all types of computers and software; this was a big worry for Bob. A guy at work had told him that even by deleting your website history, a computer expert could find it.

'Well, dinner will be about another twenty minutes, so get yourself showered.'

'Okay, I'll tell Susan.' Bob quickly went upstairs. Opening the door, Susan was sitting scrolling through pages of properties.

'Hi, Sue. Well, that sounds like a fair offer from Frank, don't you think?' Susan swivelled the chair around to face Bob. She had an angry look on her face. Bob was expecting the worst.

'Fair offer? The bastard only lived there for just over a year.'

Bob breathed a sigh of relief.

'No, what I meant was, it will save you the hassle of trying to sell the house, at least this way you haven't got to pay out for estate agent fees and all that.'

'Yes, I know. But it doesn't seem fair after all the years I've owned that house.' Bob nearly mentioned how she took Tony's half of the house in the divorce settlement, but thought better of it.

'Look, I've found an interesting website, have you seen it?' Again, Bob's heart missed a beat.
'What website?'
'It's a property auction site. There is an auction in two weeks, looks like two or three properties might be worth bidding on. Look at this one, a converted house, down by the river. A downstairs flat that comes with a garden, one bedroom, kitchen, bathroom and a nice-sized lounge. It will start at sixty thousand pounds.'
'That's cheap.'
'I doubt it will sell for that, but I might get lucky.'
'Can you view the properties before the auction?'
'Yes, it says if I want to view, I have to contact this auction house.'
'Well, if you want to take a look, I'll come with you. I can check if the property is sound or not.'
'Thanks, Bob. I'll see if I can get appointments to see a few this weekend. Do you want to get on the laptop?'
'No, I'm just going to get showered before dinner. Jan said it won't be long.'
'Okay, I'll just contact the auction house, and I'll close down. You want your back scrubbed?'
'What?' Bob was shocked.
'I'm joking with you, Bob Bates.'

It hadn't taken Tony long to fall into a nice routine. He'd go out for an early morning ride on his recently acquired mountain bike. Sometimes he'd meet up with his neighbour, Tom. They would ride out for about an hour, trying out all the different routes. When he got back to the complex, he'd spend an hour in the small gym and finish off with a swim. He would make sure he was back at his apartment by 9 am so he could have breakfast with Pooki before she went to the shop. At lunchtime, he'd ride down on his newly purchased scooter and take food to Pooki. He always made sure they had lunch together. In the afternoon, he would often leave Pooki at the shop and spend a couple of hours on the beach. Pooki was a typical Thai girl; she wasn't keen to have too much sun. Old Bert had explained to him about girls wanting to be white; they saw it as a higher social standard. Tony loved Pooki's olive skin; however, he understood her reluctance to sit on the beach.

This particular morning, however, the routine had changed. They were heading off to Pooki's home for the wedding. Pooki said they wouldn't be leaving until 10 am, as they would be following her sister and brother-in-law in their car. This gave Tony time for a workout, a swim and breakfast before they hit the road. Getting out of the pool, he decided to have ten minutes on a sunbed before going up to the apartment. Lying down, he couldn't get over how quiet the complex was. Alan and Barry had headed back to the UK. They'd exchanged phone numbers and both were now in contact on Skype. He liked the pair of them and missed their banter. He certainly wasn't missing anything from the UK. He'd spoken to Bob the previous evening, and he had told him it was wet, cold and horrible. Bob had filled him in on the latest news about Susan and how they were going to a property auction the weekend.

Bob was praying that Susan would be successful in bidding on a property. Tony could tell his friend was getting stressed by having Susan living there.

As he stretched out, he smiled. He couldn't believe it was nearly December, and there he was, laying out in just a pair of swim shorts.

'Darling.' Tony looked up and could see Pooki waving at him. She was holding a mug, signalling that she'd made him a cup of tea. He waved back, grabbed his towel and headed up.

'Something smells good.' The waft of a fry-up hit him as he opened the door.

'I make you American breakfast, darling.' This was a skill Pooki had learnt from a brief time she worked in a hotel.

Tony walked out to the balcony and sat down as Pooki brought out a plate containing eggs, sausages, bacon and toast.

'This looks lovely, thank you, sweetheart.' Tony wasn't over-keen on the rubbery processed sausages, but he never said anything.

'Don't forget to bring money, darling.'

'I won't. It's all in the safe. Three more days and you'll be Mrs Fellows.'

'I know. When we get back, we need to do paperwork for marriage. Maybe wait until after honeymoon, do it January.'

'Well, we have three weeks after the wedding before we go to Koh Chang, but whatever you decide. I have the documents ready to take to the embassy.'

'Ka, I go shower.' Pooki bent over and kissed Tony's cheek.
'I love you.'

Back in the UK, Bob was trying to hide his disappointment. He'd gone with Susan and Jan to the property auction. Unfortunately, all three of the properties Susan had been interested in had gone above her limit.
'I can't believe how much those flats went for.' Susan couldn't hide her disappointment.
'Don't worry, there'll be others, won't there, Bob?' Jan tried to stay positive.
'Yes, bound to be. Don't forget, this is our first time at an auction. We'll be better prepared next time.'
'The prices won't change though, will they?'
'Well, perhaps you need to look a bit further out of town or consider taking out a small mortgage. I mean, you have a good job.'
'But I'm fifty-two, I'll have trouble getting a mortgage at my age.'
'I know a guy at work who has just taken out a ten-year mortgage, Sue. Not ideal, I know, but it's an option, it will raise your limit and give you more of a chance when we go to another auction.'
'Maybe, I'll look into it. Thanks, Bob.'

Back home, the sisters decided the best way to get over the disappointment was to go and indulge in a bit of retail therapy. Something that didn't interest Bob in the slightest.
'You sure you don't want to come?' Asked Jan, knowing full well the answer.
'No, you go. I'm going to have a tinker with the motorbike and do a few odd jobs.'
'Okay, do yourself some lunch and I'll cook tonight.' Bob carried on reading the paper until the sisters had driven away. He decided to have an hour on the laptop first. Taking a cup of tea with him, he switched on and checked his Skype account. Nothing from Tony, so he went onto the internet and logged onto his favourite website, "friendlythaiwomen.com"
He smiled when he saw he had six unread messages. He opened each message and marvelled at the beautiful women writing to him. He knew that if he wanted to write back to these women, he would have to sign up to the site. This was something he'd been reluctant to do.

He knew that if Janice found out, there would be hell to pay. He scrolled through the new members' section; he couldn't take his eyes off the photos and profiles. He eventually sat back in the swivel chair. He desperately wanted to join this site, but he needed to find a way to join without giving his bank details. He suddenly broke into a smile. He would ask someone at work, he'd give them the cash, and they could put their credit card details in. He knew he might have to add a small financial incentive, but he knew it would be worth it, save the chance of Janice finding out. It was the first time in a long while that he couldn't wait to go to work.

In Thailand, the wedding preparations for Tony and Pooki's wedding were taking shape. Tony was glad to have his future brother-in-law, Peter, there to help explain all that was going to happen. An open-backed truck pulled up, and an elderly Thai man started to set up some very large speakers. Within ten minutes, he was playing some very loud Thai music.
'Christ, what's all that about?' Asked Tony.
'Oh, he'll be blaring that out all day and most of the night.' Replied Peter.
'It's a way of letting the village know there is a wedding taking place. Don't worry, you'll see most of them turn up tomorrow, have the food, drink the whiskey, and then clear off.
That's why they cater for so many at a wedding. There'll only be about one hundred invited guests; the rest will be the locals. That's why the money will be displayed tomorrow, it's about showing how well their daughter has done.'
'I see.' Tony watched all the activity going on around him. People were putting out tables and chairs, and some guys were finishing off by putting up a huge marquee roof. Women were putting up displays and flowers. A huge board was at the entrance to the house, decorated with flowers and announcing the wedding of Pooki and Tony. Pooki's sister Jeab was busy organising everything. At the back of the house, about twenty women were busy preparing food. In the middle sat Pooki, she was laughing and joking with the women while she shredded coconuts with what Tony thought was an oversized cheese grater. Looking up, she saw her husband-to-be.
'You okay, darling?'

'Yes, I was wondering if you needed me to do anything?'
'No, darling, you just relax. Why don't you and Peter go for a drink?'
'Okay, you sure you don't mind?'
'No, many people here, so go.' Pooki smiled, and Tony didn't have to be told twice to go and have a drink. Peter was sitting in the shade watching the activity.
'Hey, Pete. Pooki suggested you and I ship out for a beer. What do you think?
'Let me get my car keys.' Peter was up and heading indoors at a pace Tony hadn't seen before.

Peter managed to manoeuvre the car out through all the obstacles.
'Might have been easier to walk.' Suggested, Tony.
'Hardly, the nearest so-called bar is about ten clicks away, Tony.'
'Really, nothing closer?'
'No. There are places you can buy drinks, but an actual bar is about a fifteen-minute drive away.'
'Christ, this place really is out in the sticks.'
'Yes, it is. I did have designs about retiring out here, that's why I got the house built and sorted out a nice big bedroom with an en-suite and a small lounge office area for myself. However, after being here a few days I start to get twitchy, no one speaks English, and there is only so much I can do on the computer or watch on TV. Plus, you must have noticed it's a lot warmer here than in Pattaya.'
'Yes, it seems a lot warmer here.'
'It's okay to come here for a short break every so often, but you want to forget any thoughts of retiring out in the country. There is a guy who lives a few houses down; we might see him tomorrow. He married a Thai girl and ended up building a house, as I did for her parents. She insisted they live here now. Poor bloke, it's turned him into an alcoholic. Nothing to do, so he does what a lot of the local men do here: drinks himself into a stupor every day. The last time we were here, I found him sitting by a tree. He was so pissed he couldn't walk home. What a state to get yourself in.'
'Yes, that's something to avoid. What I've seen so far is that it can be very easy to fall into the drinking culture.'
'Keep yourself busy, Tony, that's the key.'

'Well, I've got myself a mountain bike, so I get out on that most mornings, I use the gym and swim every day.  My friend Tom said he would take me fishing on the beach when we got back from the wedding.  He goes late afternoons after the heat has gone out of the sun.'
'Sounds good, Tony.  Those sorts of things don't cost a lot of money to do.  Here we are.'  Peter pulled into a small car park.
'Been here a few times, has a nice shaded area at the back.'  Peter led the way, and soon they were sitting nursing a cold bottle of beer each.
'Cheers.'
'Cheers, Peter.  I'm guessing I need an early night tonight?'
'I reckon.  You'll be up at about 3 am.  The girls are having their make-up and hair done at 4 am.  There'll be a rush for the bathroom.  I'll be up, give me a knock, and you can use our bathroom to get ready.'
'Thanks, Peter, I can imagine there'll be quite a queue forming in the morning.  Bloody early time to get married?'
'It is, they have some strange ways over here.  It's going to be a long day, followed by a long evening.  All the uncles and the local Herberts will get pissed before the evening session.  There are thirty tables, two bottles of whiskey on each.  Trust me when I tell you, they'll all be gone by the evening.'
'Oh well, it's Pooki's day, so as long as she can look back and think that was a great wedding day, that's all that matters.'
'Well said, Tony.  I wish you both a happy and long marriage.'

As predicted by Peter.  Pooki's alarm on her phone started playing music at 3 am.
'You sleep a bit longer, darling, I get sister and we start get ready, I call you later.'
'Tony wasn't going to argue, however, once the bedroom light came on, getting back to sleep wasn't going to be easy.  Eventually, the light went off, and he started to drift off.  This moment of semi-consciousness didn't last long.  The man with the music at the front of the house decided that 3.30 am was a good time to announce the start of festivities.
Tony sat upright; he couldn't believe how noisy the music was.  Realising that was the end of any more sleep, he climbed out of bed.  Sticking some shorts on, he wandered out to the back of the house,

where the outside kitchen was. About ten women were there organising the cooking and preparing more food. Pooki was sitting with her mama and sister, drinking coffee.
'You not want to sleep, darling?'
'Err ... No, I thought I'd get up and help.'
'No need. Sit here I make you a coffee. You want American breakfast?'
'No, I'll sort something out later. Don't worry about me, you concentrate on getting ready.'
'I make you coffee first. Make-up lady here.' Tony looked to where Pooki was pointing. The make-up lady was, in fact, a ladyboy.
'She'll do you later, darling.'
'Will she now?' Murmured Tony, causing Pooki to giggle.

An hour later, the wedding preparations were in full swing. Pooki, her mama and her sister were locked away in her mama's bedroom getting their hair and make-up done. The lounge area had been emptied, and a row of cushions and all sorts of Buddhist gala were being laid out. There were by now about thirty people milling around. Peter surfaced from the bedroom, minus his jacket, but already in his suit.
'This is where you'll get married, Tony. The cushions are where the monks will sit.'
'I see.' Peter could see that Tony was a bit overwhelmed by the occasion.
'Come and have a coffee, mate. You can get showered and changed in here.' Tony followed Peter into his bedroom.
'You've made it very nice in here, Pete.'
'Well, I wanted to make it comfortable for when we stay here. Now, you fancy a little stiffener with your coffee?'
'That would be great, thanks, Pete.' Opening a cupboard, Peter pulled out a nice bottle of brandy.
'Drop of the good stuff.' Peter made the coffee and poured two big measures of brandy into glasses.
'Too good to waste in the coffee. Cheers.'
'Cheers, Pete.' The two men clinked glasses.
'Well, I'd better have this, then think about getting ready.'
'Yes, only an hour to go. Don't worry, Tony, I'll be with you. Think yourself lucky, when I got married, I had no one to talk to. It's a long day, so pace yourself with the drink.'

'Yes, says a man who is giving me brandy at 6 am.' Tony started laughing.
'There's mouthwash in the bathroom, so don't sweat. You want another?'
'No thanks, as you said, I'm in for a long day.'

The time Tony was showered and changed, it was getting near 7 am.
'How'd I look, Pete?'
'Very smart. The monks are here, so we'd better get out there.' Peter opened the bedroom door, and Tony walked out and straight away spotted Pooki. She looked stunning. Pooki came over.
'You okay, darling?'
'I'm sorry, do I know you? Who is this beautiful woman?' Pooki smiled and grabbed his arm.
'I can look like this every day if I have three hour to get ready.'
'No need. You always look beautiful to me.'
Pooki smiled at her husband-to-be.
'Not long now, darling. You wait with Peter while the monks get ready.'
Tony walked over and stood next to Peter.
'Have you taken a peek outside, Tony?'
'No, what's out there?'
'About a hundred locals.'
'You think we'll have enough whiskey?'
'Don't know. We'll have to do a stock take after the morning session. Hey up, looks like we're about to get underway.' Tony looked across and could see Pooki waving at him to come over. The monks started their prayers, and Tony wished he'd taken that offer of a second brandy.

As Tony was beginning the start of a long Thai wedding endurance test, his best friend back in the UK was busy doing a spot of late-night internet surfing. It had cost him a ten-pound bribe to get a workmate to let him use his credit card details. As he didn't want to keep using someone to do this task, he signed up to the Thai dating website for twelve months. All in all, it had cost him fifty pounds to become a member. However, he was already reaping the benefits. He had twelve women in his favourite box and was chatting with most of them. He couldn't remember the last time he had so much fun. Janice and

Susan were fast asleep, courtesy of a bottle of white wine. Bob loved this fantasy world he had created. He looked at the calendar on the desk. He looked for a cross, something he put on a date he had sex with Janice. He flicked back the months; it wasn't until he got to March that he came across the little cross marker.

"Nine months," he mumbled to himself.

"Bloody ridiculous." As he sat there scrolling through hundreds of beautiful women, he thought about his friend in Thailand. He knew he'd done the right thing. What on earth would he want to be living in the UK for? He couldn't help but feel extremely envious of Tony. If only he had the chance to do the same. He was beginning to hate the way his life was now. He had no sex life, and he had his sister-in-law living with them. This was beginning to look increasingly like a permanent arrangement. He was fed up at work; he was a qualified fitter by trade. But, because of a downturn in production, he was demoted to a line worker five years ago. He was forty-nine at the time. He was offered a redundancy package, or he could take a pay cut and work on the production line. Because of his company pension and the lack of jobs in the Ipswich area, he decided to take the pay cut and become a production worker. Unlike Tony, he wasn't old enough to get the pension at the time. If it were offered now, he'd take it in the blink of an eye.

The chat box sprang to life, bringing Bob back to reality.

"Hi, my name is Mooka, how are you?" Bob brought up Mooka's profile. He liked what he saw. The photos of Mooka showed a very beautiful woman. Reading her profile, he could see she was thirty-two and a hotel receptionist. Bob got typing.

"Hello Mooka, my name is Bob. I'm very well, thank you." After about a minute, he got a reply.

"You ever come to Thailand?" Bob thought about how to reply to that question.

"No, I have never visited Thailand, but it's on my wish list." Bob waited for the reply.

"You have lady?" Bob decided not to mention Janice.

"No, I am a single man." Bob wrote that without feeling any guilt.

"You handsome man, you should have lady." That compliment had Bob grinning like a Cheshire cat.

"Well, that's why I joined this site, I want to meet a beautiful Thai lady." After a brief pause, came the reply.
"Okay, you come to Thailand, you can meet me."
"I'd like that. Maybe I will." As Bob waited for a reply, the bedroom door opened. Luckily, he'd arranged the laptop so the screen was hidden. As the door opened, he hit and held the power button that shut the laptop down. Susan stuck her head in.
'Oh, I was going to use the laptop myself, I thought you'd be asleep?'
'I'm just checking my eBay bids,' he lied.
'Will you be long?'
'No, about five more minutes.'
'Okay, I'll go and make a coffee while you finish off.'
'Right you are, I'll leave the laptop on.'
'Thanks, Bob.' Susan disappeared out the door, leaving a frantic Bob switching the laptop back on. He needed to clear the history, especially with Susan about to use the computer.
He just about cleared everything off when Susan returned, carrying a mug of coffee and a packet of biscuits.
'All done.' Bob stood up and silently cursed his sister-in-law as he went to bed.

For the first time that morning, Tony felt relaxed. After the wedding blessing, feeding the monks, the traditional walk along the road, followed by about fifty relatives and locals carrying all sorts of gifts, and planting two banana trees in the backyard, it was time to sit down and eat. Pooki was in her element, walking around the tables and chatting to friends and relatives. Peter hobbled over and sat down next to Tony with a plate of food.
'It wasn't too bad, was it?'
'No, to be honest, apart from having to be on my knees for about thirty minutes, it went okay.'
'You'll have to go with Pooki and Pa in a minute, collect the envelopes.' Informed, Peter.
'Really? What's that about?'
'The guests will put money in the envelopes, it will help with the cost of the wedding.'
'I see.' That bit of news brought a smile to Tony's face; he was thinking he would be tapped up for a contribution.

'I suppose we'd better crack open the whiskey.' Peter opened the bottle and poured out two glasses.
'It's a bit rough, Tony, but after a couple, it gets better. Cheers.'

By midday, the majority of guests and locals had gone. The uncles and aunts were helping Mama clear the tables and wash up. A couple of the uncles had set up a karaoke machine and were belting out some Thai songs.
'Christ, it's enough to make your ears bleed,' commented Peter.
'What happens now, Pete?'
'Well, not much until this evening. Then it will be another feed, some music and dancing. A lot more relaxed than this morning.'
'Thank God for that.' Tony watched as Pooki and her sister came over smiling.
'You okay, darling?' Asked the new Mrs Fellows.
'Yes, I'm fine. How are you?'
'I'm so happy. Mama and Pa are so proud of me. We just counted the money from the envelopes, nearly fifty thousand baht, we get more tonight.'
'Will that be enough to cover the cost of the wedding?'
'I think so, darling.' Tony knew Pooki's parents didn't have a lot of money.
'Let me know if it doesn't, I will help them if there isn't enough.' Pooki hugged her husband.
'You good man for me, darling. You should go and have a sleep, we not do much now.'
'What about you?'
'I help Mama and aunties cook food for tonight.' Pooki headed off to the back of the house.
'Thank you, Tony. You make my sister very happy.'
'She makes me happy, Jeab. I'm one lucky man. I feel like I've won the lottery.'
'I might have a kip myself,' announced Peter.
'You not have time. You drive Mama and me to the market, we have food to buy.'
'Right, well, I'll leave you to it.' Tony slipped off, not making any eye contact with Peter.

After a good power nap, a shower and a change into shorts and a vest, Tony ventured outside, where there was still plenty of activity in the kitchen area. Pooki was changed into casual gear and was busily flitting about.

'Hello, darling. Why don't you go and sit with my uncles and have a sing?' This was something Tony wanted to avoid.

'Oh, right, you sure you don't need any help in here?'

'No, you go and enjoy yourself. Peter's over there.'

Tony wandered around the side of the house where the most awful singing was bellowing out. Six Thai men were laughing and shouting out; in the middle of them sat Peter. Sitting in just a pair of shorts, he looked glassy-eyed and drunk.

'Pacing yourself then, Pete.'

'About time you woke up, bloody lightweight, here have a drink.' One of Pooki's uncles passed Tony a glass, and Peter did the honours, filling Tony's glass up with the equivalent of about four measures of whiskey.

'Easy, we have a long night ahead.'

'No problem, it's just a party, Tony. I don't know about you, but I fancy a beer.'

'Yes, better than all this whiskey.'

'We're running low on beer, Tony. I've been waiting for you to get up. We need to take a drive to the shops. I'm beyond driving, so you can drive my car.'

'Well, let's go now, then, before I drink this whiskey.'

'Good idea, mate. Let me get a shirt on.' Peter rose to his feet in an unsteady fashion, much to the amusement of the uncles.

'Won't be a minute,' he shouted back as he limped indoors.

Twenty minutes later, Tony loaded the last of the cases of beer into the back of Peter's car.

'Christ, seems a lot, Peter.'

'Better to have more than not enough, mate.' Tony walked over and paid for the beer.

'How much?' Asked Peter as Tony climbed back into the car.

'7000 baht.'

'That's not bad for twelve cases. The uncles will organise the ice man to come and they'll put the beer in dustbins of ice.'

'You're looking a tad worse for wear, Pete.'

'I'm alright, the time we get back and unloaded, it will be time for a quick freshen up and change, then part two.'
'Yes, I need to have another shower and stick the suit back on. How many will turn up tonight, Pete?'
'Oh, quite a few, I would imagine, especially all the locals. They won't pass up on some more free food and drink.'
'What do the local men do here?'
'Farming mainly, working in the fields. Bloody hard graft for a pittance. I think I told you, the majority of them are alcoholics. That's why I can't stay here for long periods; I'll end up like them. I mean, look at the state of me today.'
That little observation from Peter had both men laughing.

By the time Tony drove back and helped unload the beer into dustbins filled with ice, it was less than an hour before the evening party was due to begin. As Tony entered the bedroom, Pooki was putting on her second wedding dress.
'Wow, who's this beautiful woman?'
'It's your wife, ka.' Pooki smiled and kissed Tony.
'You smell of drink, darling. You need to shower and get ready.'
'Yes, I'm just waiting for Peter to get showered, and I'll use his bathroom. There are about ten people queued up waiting to use the other bathroom.'
'You like?' Pooki did a twirl.
'Yes, very much, the dress is nice too.'
'Thank you. I'll never forget this day, darling. You make my dream come true. Okay, I go and help Mama get ready.' Pooki kissed Tony's cheek and headed out of the bedroom. Tony sat on the bed; he felt like the luckiest man alive.

Not for the first time since Tony arrived in Thailand, he awoke with a massive hangover and wondered where the hell he was. One thing he was certain of, it wasn't Pooki lying close to him making a horrendous snoring sound. Sitting up, he realised he was on Peter and Jeab's bed. Peter was comatose in just a pair of baggy Y-fronts. The familiar banging sound coming from the back of the house meant someone was preparing food. Tony had slept in the suit trousers that were looking decidedly worse for wear. After using the ensuite, he staggered out

and checked Pooki's empty bedroom. Wandering outside, he was greeted by about twenty people who were sitting around eating.
'Good morning, darling, I make you American breakfast.'
'Err ... Maybe just a coffee for now.'
'Peter still asleep?' Asked Jeab.
'Yes, I didn't want to disturb him. Sorry, I'm not sure how I ended up on your bed.'
'You drink and sing karaoke with uncles, you still singing at 3 am.'
'Really? What's the time now?'
'It's 1 pm, darling,' announced Pooki.
'Christ, not the wedding night I was hoping for, sorry.'
'It okay, ka. We have our whole life in front of us. I happy you enjoy yourself.' Tony looked around.
'Where's your papa?'
'He still asleep, he so drunk he sleep in front garden.' Pooki turned and translated what she said into Thai, causing an uproar of laughter.
'Oh, he had a good time then.'
'Ka, he very happy. You need to eat, darling, make you feel better.'
'I don't know about that, maybe a bit of toast.'
'Ka, with egg and sausage.'

As Bob arrived home from work, he noticed Janice's car was missing. He guessed she was either out with Susan or working late. When he went in the front door, he could hear the TV, so he knew Susan was home alone.
'Hi, Sue, Jan not home from work yet?'
'No, she phoned, some order came in late, so she won't be home until around nine.'
'They take the piss out of her, that firm. She doesn't get paid any more money for working late.'
'So, she said, I've got some fish out of the freezer, I'll make a start now your home.'
'Great, I'll have a quick shower then give you a hand.'
'Okay. I'm glad we are alone. I need to talk to you. Have your shower first.' Bob wondered what she wanted to talk about. Hopefully, it was about her moving out; he wanted his house back to how it used to be.
'There's some wine in the fridge, I won't be long.'

After showering, Bob slipped on some jogging bottoms and a sweatshirt and headed down to the kitchen. Susan was busy preparing some vegetables.

'You want some wine, Sue?' Bob opened the fridge door.

'Yes, please.' Bob pulled out a bottle of wine, opened it and poured out two glasses. He handed one to Susan.

'Cheers.'

'Cheers, Bob.'

'So, what do you want to talk to me about?' Bob sat down at the kitchen table. Susan stopped what she was doing and came and sat opposite.

'Are you planning to do a "Tony?"' Bob immediately felt his heart starting to race. He did his best not to show any concern.

'What do you mean by that? Do a "Tony." I haven't a clue what you're on about?'

'Oh, I think you do, Bob.'

'Have you been snooping on my laptop?'

'Your laptop? I thought it was yours and Jan's laptop.'

'You know what I mean. Well, have you been snooping?'

'Why, have you something to hide?'

'No, of course not.'

'You're a bloody liar, Bob Bates, something you're not very good at. You seem to forget I deal with computer fraud every day. Do you think I can't see your browsing history? For your information, I wasn't even looking. I was checking out properties last night, and a chat pop-up came up on the screen. By the way, Mooka sends her love and wants to know when you're going out to see her?'

'I don't know who that is. It must be spam.'

'Hark at you, you don't even know what spam means. I checked, Bob. You've joined a Thai dating site, what the hell is the matter with you?'

'What's the matter with me? I'll tell you, you, nosy bitch. I have the same trouble as young Frank did. No sex, no affection. Tony told me you were frigid; no wonder young Frankie didn't stick around. What's the saying? The apple doesn't fall far from the tree. Janice has the same problem; we've not had sex since last March. Bloody nine months, isn't it any wonder I look elsewhere?'

'It's all about sex with you men. That's all you bloody think about.'

'That's utter bullshit, and if you think nine months is okay to go without sex, then you don't have a clue.'

'You know Jan is going through the change, you should understand what that means. Her hormones are all over the place.'

'Not that old chestnut, this has been going on for over ten years.'

'If that's what's making you go on those sites, you have a problem, Bob.'

'What? A problem because I crave some love and affection?'

'Don't say that, Jan loves you. She always puts you first, you're too blind to see it. For goodness' sake, Bob. You don't think this living the dream lifestyle of Tony's is going to last, do you? I give it a year max, he'll be back soon enough with his tail between his legs. He'll come back, have nowhere to live, and spent all his money on the young Thai girl. That's not something you want to do, surely. Okay, I can see the attraction: a beautiful young girl, a trophy on your arm. But what would you have in common with her? Hardly speaking any English, trust me, Bob, the novelty will soon wear off.'

'Maybe so.' Bob didn't have an argument to put up against Susan's thoughts on Tony's Thailand adventure.

'Listen, Bob. I'm not going to mention any of this, too, Jan. I can understand you're frustrated, but just watch some porn, get rid of it that way.'

'Oh ... Well, I don't normally look at those types of sites.'

'Bob, do I have to remind you what I do for a living? It's a wonder that the laptop is still functional with the amount of porn hidden in the archives.'

'Err ... Well, I might have stumbled across a few sites.'

'Yes, you certainly did. Now, I want you to stop using the Thai dating site. Will you?'

'Yes, I was just fantasising, Sue.'

'Right, well, there is no more to be said on the subject. Drop more wine?'

'Go on then.' Bob played along. There was no way he was giving up the dream. He knew he'd have to stop looking at the Thai dating site for now. He'd have to work out how to stop Susan from snooping on the laptop. He needed to find a computer expert. A visit to a computer shop was in order.

Bob broke into a smile as he poured the wine out. "Susan had won the battle, but not the war," he thought to himself.

Like every other wedding, the day after was all a bit flat. Tony was nursing a giant hangover, and Pooki was busy helping her mama and sister clear everything up. The marquee had been taken down, and a big lorry and trailer had arrived to take away all the tables and chairs. That evening, just the close family sat at the back of the house, eating and chatting away. Tony sat and listened to all the laughter and chatter, not understanding a word, but happy to be with his beautiful wife. Now and again, she would squeeze his arm or leg, making him feel special.
'We go home tomorrow, darling. I need to get back to shop.'
'Okay, you sure you don't want to stay a few more days?'
'No, need to get back, we have honeymoon soon.'
'Oh yes, Koh Chang, I love that island.'
'Yes, very nice. Thank you for take me there.' Tony smiled at his wife.
'I love you.' He whispered in her ear.
'I love you too.'

Bob pulled his car up outside a small computer repair shop down a very small side street on the outskirts of Ipswich. This shop had been recommended to him by a couple of different work colleagues. The sign read that it not only sold computers but also serviced and repaired them.
As he opened the door, a buzzing sound could be heard. This brought out a young man of about twenty-five. Thick-rimmed glasses, long hair tied back into a ponytail and reeking of tobacco. He looked like a computer nerd without even asking.
'Hi, man, how can I help you?' Bob quite liked the laid-back approach of this young man.
'Well, I'm after a bit of advice, really.'
'Okay, my advice is free; anything else you have to pay for.' The boy smiled at Bob, then pulled a tobacco pouch out and started making a hand-rolled cigarette.
'Is there a way to hide my browsing history on my laptop?'
'That's easy, man.'

'Hang on, let me finish. I know how to delete my browsing history, but for some reason, my sister-in-law seems to retrieve it, even though I've deleted it.'
'How's she doing that?' Asked the boy as he lit the cigarette in his mouth.
'Well, I was hoping you could tell me. I should mention that she is very knowledgeable with computers and works with them all day.'
'Does she now? Interesting? There is a way, bloody difficult, but it can be done. She most probably has a software program she uses to get to the deleted folders. Has she found something naughty?'
'No, nothing like that, just stuff I don't want her to see. What's the best way to stop her?'
'There isn't, you're stuffed, man. The only way to stop her from getting on the laptop is to put a code lock on it. I can set up a password for you.'
'No, I can't do that, she'll know straight away that I'm up to something.'
'What are you trying to hide from her, man? I mean, it's nothing illegal, is it? You know what happened to that pop star.'
'Of course, it's nothing illegal, if you must know, I'm chatting to a few Thai women behind my girlfriend's back. Her bloody sister started snooping and found the site I'd been using.'
'Thai women?'
'Yes, my mate has just moved out there, and married a Thai bird, and he looks very happy.'
'I bet he does, where would you rather be? Sunny Thailand or a wet and cold December afternoon in Ipswich?'
'I know, it's a no-brainer. So, there is nothing you can do?'
'Not with your sister-in-law's snooping, and your reluctance to put a password lock on.'
'Looks like I'm stuffed then.'
'There is an alternative, man. Why don't you buy a second laptop?'
'How will I explain that, plus they're not cheap.'
'I have just the thing for you, man.' The boy disappeared into the back and returned holding a small notebook computer.
'Christ, that's a small laptop.' Observed Bob.
'This here is a notebook. For your purpose, it's ideal. Easy to hide, has a ten-inch screen and Windows. Bonus: a built-in webcam, for when

you want to video call. It has easy access to the internet and is ideal for chatting to beautiful Thai women.' Bob picked it up.

'It doesn't weigh much. I could hide it in the rucksack I use for work; my girlfriend never touches it. Does it have the same functions as a laptop?'

'It will do everything your laptop will do, apart from it doesn't have a CD or DVD function.'

'That's not going to be a problem. How much?'

'To you, man, sixty quid, and for that, I'll chuck in an internet dongle as well.'

'What's that?'

'Pay as you go internet, same as a mobile phone. It's handy if you want to use the internet outside your home.'

'What, I can plug it in, say in my car and use the internet?'

'That's the kiddie, just top it up the same way as a pay-as-you-go phone.' Bob looked at the notebook and didn't need any more convincing.

'Okay, I'll take it.'

'Nice one, I'll just go and get the box and the rest of the bits,'

'I don't need the box, just the charger, I'll slip it into my rucksack now.'

'Right, well, I'll sort out the charger and the dongle. Card or cash?'

'Cash,' the last thing Bob needed was this purchase showing up on his credit card statement.

Christmas day couldn't have been any more different for the two friends. For Tony, it meant enjoying the afternoon on a beautiful beach in Koh Chang. Having enjoyed a nice steak for lunch, he was content to chill out. Pooki was happy lying in a shaded area, with the occasional jog into the sea.

'I not want to get any darker, daring,' she explained to Tony, who by now had a lovely tan. There was nothing special about Christmas in Thailand. He'd noticed a few bars advertising Christmas Day lunches, but on the whole, it was all a bit low-key. He couldn't believe it when, a few days before they drove to Koh Chang, he popped into a big Tesco and only a very small part of an aisle was dedicated to Christmas goodies.

Of course, for Bob, it was the same old. Well, apart from the added bonus of having his sister-in-law staying with them. The supermarkets were packed with Christmas decorations, sweets and all sorts. The adverts for Christmas had begun way before Guy Fawkes' time. Where Tony was wearing vests, t-shirts and flip-flops, Bob was walking around in his full winter garb. At 11 am UK time, 6 pm in Thailand, Bob called his best friend. Tony and Pooki were sitting on the balcony of their hotel, waiting for Bob's prearranged Skype call.

'Here we go,' Tony called out as the familiar ringtone started. Walking into the room, Tony clicked the answer tab.

'Merry Christmas, Bob.'

'Hello, Tone, Merry Christmas, mate. Christ, you look very dark, Tone.'

'It's the sun, Bob, it does that to you.'

'Well, I'll let you know in another six months' time when we may start to get a bit of a summer.'

'Pooki wants to say Merry Christmas.' Tony swung the laptop around, and Pooki came into view.

'Merry Christmas, Khun Bob. How are you?'

'Merry Christmas, Pooki. Yes, I am okay, thank you. I loved the wedding photos Tony emailed over, you looked beautiful in your dress.'

'Khob Khun ka.' Pooki gave a wai.

'You come and see us?'

'Yes, I will. It's on my wish list.'

'Okay, take care.' Pooki waved and spoke to Tony.

'I go and make bath.' She smiled and disappeared into the bathroom.

'I had to laugh, Bob. Pooki is thirty and this is the first time she's had a bath. It's unusual to get baths in hotels, so she's loving it.'

'I bet she is. How are you, Tone? No regrets?'

'What do you think? This place is beautiful, Bob. Everyone smiles, the sun always shines, and I have a beautiful, kind wife. What more do I need?'

'No, it sounds great, Tone. You're certainly living the dream.'

'You sound a bit fed up, Bob.'

'Oh, you know, the usual shit. I hate that bloody job, I come home knackered every night. That production line work is a young man's game. It's cold and miserable, and I still have my wonderful sister-in-law staying here. She's started spying on my laptop, I tell you, Tone, I don't know how much more of this I can take.' Tony felt sorry for his friend.

'Is she making any effort to move out?'

'She says she's looking at properties every day, but she's got her feet well and truly under the table now. Jan loves having her here, so I'm buggered, Tone.'
'She'll find somewhere eventually, just hang in there, mate.'
'Well, I can't do anything else, can I? Anyway, enjoy the rest of your Christmas day, Tone. I'll give you a call in the new year.'
'Okay, Bob. You take care and keep your chin up.' Tony gave a wave as Bob closed the call without saying goodbye. It was unusual behaviour from Bob, plus it was always Tony who finished a call. He'd never seen his friend like this before. Bob was always cheery and smiling. Tony felt a tad concerned for his friend.

Bob entered the lounge as the sisters were busy chatting over a coffee.
'Tony alright?' Asked Janice.
'Yes, he's fine. He said Merry Christmas to you both,' he lied.
'Bloody wind-up merchant,' commented Susan.
'Dinner will be about 2 pm. Mum said she'll be here about 1 pm. You want a coffee, Bob?' Asked Janice.
'No thanks, it's Christmas day, I think I'll have a brandy.' Bob headed to the kitchen.
'Bit early for that?' Remarked Susan.
'So, you don't want one then?'
'Well, as it's Christmas day, why not?'
'Jan, you want one?'
'A glass of wine will be nice. Hurry up, we can have a game of Trivial Pursuit before Mum gets here.'
Bob walked into the kitchen, grabbed the bottle of brandy and poured himself a large one.
"Merry Bloody Christmas," he mumbled to himself.

## Chapter 5

## *"Six months later."*

The idyllic lifestyle continued for Tony. He often forgot what day of the week it was. Pooki was still working at the scooter hire shop; she was a lot happier now that Tony had paid the remaining finance owed on the truck. It didn't take him long to realise, after making new friends in and around his complex, that a lot of their wives and girlfriends were high maintenance, drinkers and always after money. He knew that he had struck gold with Pooki. She didn't drink or smoke, enjoyed cooking and took good care of him. She didn't waste money and wasn't at all demanding. He recently had a real battle to persuade her to buy a new phone. Her old one kept switching itself off, and when Tony offered to get her a new one, she told him her old one was okay. In the end, he went out and bought her the latest model and surprised her at the shop.
'You such a good man to me, darling.'
'It's because I love you and want to take care of you,' he replied.
After his usual routine of riding along the beach on his bike with his neighbour, Tom. Followed by a workout and swim, for the first time since they had moved into the apartment, Pooki hadn't cooked him breakfast. He normally caught a waft of bacon as he opened the apartment door. As he walked in, there was no sign of Pooki. He could hear her coughing in the bathroom.
'You okay, sweetheart?' he shouted to her through the door.
'Ka, sorry darling, I can't cook this morning, it's making me feel sick.'
'Don't worry, I can sort myself out.' As Tony listened, he could hear Pooki retching.
'Do you want some water, sweetheart?'
'Ka.' Tony went to the fridge and poured some water into a glass. He went back to the bathroom door and called out.
'Here you are.' Tony waited, and eventually, Pooki opened the door. She looked very pale.
'I told you it's not good to eat raw crab.' Tony couldn't believe it when he watched Pooki eat a very spicy Thai salad, which contained fresh, uncooked river crab. Pooki drank the water.

'Thank you, darling. It's not the food, I going to have baby.' Tony was speechless for a moment.
'Are you sure?'
'Ka,' Pooki held up a pregnancy test kit.
'You going to be a daddy again, darling.' Tony's face turned as pale as Pooki's.

Back at the forklift truck manufacturing plant in Ipswich, Bob was getting worried. He'd been summoned to the Human Resources office. Sitting outside waiting to be called, he was glad to see his union rep, Trevor White, turn up. Bob had a lot of time for Trevor. He was a long-standing shop steward whom Tony had often spoken highly of.
'Alright, Bob. How's it going?'
'You tell me. Am I in trouble?'
'No, of course not. You're going to be offered a redundancy package, something you can't refuse.
'Really? What if I don't want that something?'
'Then you'll wake up tomorrow morning with a horse's head lying next to you.'
'I do most mornings anyway, it's called the girlfriend.' Trevor started laughing.
'Nice one, Bob. No, things are not good here, mate, they're looking to reduce the headcount again.'
'They're going to offer me a redundancy package?'
'Aye, you're in the right age group, Bob. They will want you to stay until shutdown, but that's less than four weeks away. Let's see what they offer up. I'll tell them you need the weekend to think it over.'
'Cheers, Trev. To be honest, I've been wanting to get out of here for ages. But now it's going to be offered, I don't know so much.'
'Big step, Bob. But I don't think it's negotiable if you get what I mean.'
'Yes, I know. Walk or be pushed.'
'Look on the bright side, you can go and see our old mate Tony now. How's he getting on? Do you still hear from him?'
'Yes, we Skype about once a month. He's still living the dream.'
'Lucky bugger. Just goes to show, Bob. There's a whole new life outside of this factory.' Before Bob could respond, the office door opened and Trevor led the way in. The personnel officer was a young dowdy-looking woman called Helen Gotter.

'Take a seat, Mr Bates. Now, I take it that Trevor has explained the company's position. Schedules are down for the last quarter; early signs are showing a considerable downturn for at least the next eighteen months. Because of your age and service, Mr Bates, we'd like to offer you a redundancy package, along with the chance to take your pension.'

'Yes, a pension that will be reduced by 49% because of my age.'

'Unfortunately, Mr Bates, that's something that is outside of our control.' Trevor intervened.

'Well, Helen, don't get me started on the company's lack of respect for our retirees; otherwise, we'll be in here all day. You know damn well the company could have put more money into the pension scheme. Had they done so, then we wouldn't be taking big chunks out of people like Bob here, monthly figures. However, that being said, I think it's only fair to give Mr Bates his figures and let him digest this offer over the weekend.' Bob could see why Tony liked him so much. Trevor didn't need much of an excuse to have a dig at the company. Bob did smile when he noticed Helen and Trevor were on first-name terms, and he was referred to as Mr Bates.

'As I've already mentioned, many times, Trevor, the pension scheme problems are outside our control. As for Mr Bates, yes, of course. Take the paperwork with you and come and see me on Monday, let me know your decision.'

'And if I say no?'

'Well, that's something the company will have to discuss with you if you decide upon that route. Have a nice weekend, Mr Bates.'

'Don't start with that heavy-handed shit, Helen.' Trevor stood up, and that was the signal to depart the office. Outside, Bob spoke to his union rep.

'It's pretty obvious I'm on the way out, one way or another.'

'Sorry, Bob. As much as I like to have a dig at her, there's not much I can do for you. As you know, it's all changed here. There used to be a time when company service meant something. You know, the old last-in-first-out system. Unfortunately, that is not an option anymore. The bloody equality brigade has deemed that as unfair. Apparently, if we use that rule, we're discriminating against a new starter. I tell you, Bob. The country is going mad.'

'I understand, Trevor. It's not your fault. You're right, though, all these new laws, the bloody health and safety have gone well overboard, I'm glad my working life is coming to an end, not the beginning.'
'Yes, I make you right, Bob. You come and find me on Monday, and I'll come with you to see old iron britches. Did you see what she had on? Looked like she was auditioning for the Prime of Miss Jean Brodie.'
'Yes, she looks like a woman you don't want to mess with.'
'Take no notice of her, Bob. Trumped up nobody. They changed the name from Personnel to Human Resources shit just to give themselves a pay rise and make them sound more important than what they are. Just because she has a university degree, she thinks she knows it all. Trust me, she has no life skills and knows jack shit.'
'I take it you don't like her?'
'Whatever gave you that idea?' Trevor smiled as they headed back to the production line.

A few days after the initial shock of Pooki's pregnancy, Tony was warming to the idea. The only worry he had was the financial side and the small apartment they were living in. He spoke to Pooki about his worries.
'Don't worry, darling. We can always go and live at Mama and Papa's house. Plenty room, mama be very happy if we live there. We not have to pay rent like we do here.'
'Yes, well that's good to know.' Tony thought back to all the warnings his new brother-in-law, Peter had given him about living in a village environment. He pictured himself sitting against a tree, drunk.
'We stay here until contract finish, then we decide what to do. I call Mama and tell her we may come in December. Our baby go to my old school.' Pooki's lovely smile and happiness helped soften the blow.

That evening, he called Bob on Skype to tell him the news. The past few months, Tony had noticed a decline in Bob's mood. There was only so much he could say to try and cheer his mate up, and he wondered what mood he was in today.
'Hello, Bob, how are you, mate?'
'Alright, Tone. Yes, I'm okay, I have some news for you.'
'Good, I have some news for you too, you go first.'
'Well, I'm taking early retirement.' Tony was shocked.

'Really? How's that come about?'
'Oh, you know, the usual shit, downturn in schedules and all that jazz.'
'What did Jan say?'
'I've not told her yet. You know the score here, Tone. We hardly talk, not since the bust-up a couple of months ago.' Bob was referring to the day Jan confronted him with his hidden notebook, conveniently found by his snooping sister-in-law. The fallout from that episode was still ongoing.
'You should have kicked her out months ago, Bob.'
'Easier said than done, however, I'm making moves to sort things out. I'm seeing a solicitor on Tuesday to see where I am legally with the house. If she won't kick her sister out, I'll sell the bloody thing.'
'That sounds a bit extreme, mate. What will you do if you sell the house?'
'Rent, as you did for a while. Give myself a bit of time to see where I'm going. I'm not happy, Tone. Something has to change; my life is passing me by. A bit like you, being made redundant may well be the making of me.'
'Well, see what the solicitor says, mate, you're not married, so that's one blessing, and you don't have kids to worry about. I have a feeling Jan will have some rights regarding the house, she's been with you a long time.'
'Getting on for thirty years. I'm sure she's entitled to something; I just need to hear it from an expert. Anyway, I'll keep you posted, Tone.'
'You still checking out the Thai dating sites?'
'No, not since Jan smashed my notebook, I daren't look on this laptop, you know what Susan is like, she'll be straight to Jan telling tales.'
'Yes, well, don't do anything rash, mate. Get the legal advice and weigh up the options.'
'I'm going to, Tone, don't worry. Anyway, enough about my woes, what news have you got for me?'
'Well, Pooki's pregnant.'
'Jesus H Christ, Tone. Are you fu***** mad?'
'It wasn't planned, Bob. It just happened.'
'When's it due?'
'Middle of February.'
'You'll be fifty-six?'

'I know, don't remind me. But I guess that's the price you pay for marrying a younger woman.'
'Have you told Emily?'
'No, not yet. I only found out a couple of days ago. I will email her today, so keep it under your hat for now.'
'I will, Tone. Christ, can you afford a baby? I mean, you'll have to rent a bigger place, won't you?'
'Maybe, we can always go and live with Pooki's parents, they have a big house.'
'You told me a while back it was bloody boring there, that you got stir crazy after a few days, now you're thinking of moving there?'
'Well, it's just one of the options, Bob. I'm hoping to persuade Pooki to stay here and go back to work. I can help take care of the baby.'
'You want to be taking care of a baby at your age? Can't you get a job?'
'Not easy out here, Bob. Lots of restrictions. Christ, it's hard enough in the UK, \ out here, I do not speak the language, it's going to be nigh impossible.'
'Oh well, Tone, I'm sure you'll work it out.'
'For sure, as I said, worst-case scenario, we'll move into Pooki's family home. It's plenty big enough, and no, it's not ideal, but a good fallback position if needed. So, you have a date for leaving work?'
'Three weeks, they want me to work up to the summer shutdown. I've got this weekend to make my mind up, but without actually saying the words, they're only giving me one choice.'
'I know that feeling, mate. You'll be alright, look at me, turned out to be the best thing that ever happened to me.'
'Yes, I know, Tone. It's time for a change, mate. I'll give you a call next weekend, I'll have a clearer picture of things by then.'
'Okay, Bob. Hey, you have no excuse not to come out to see me now.'
'I know, Tone. And I will, I just need to get everything sorted here first before I think about that.'
'Of course, mate, I understand. I'll speak to you soon.'
'Send me a text when you've told, Emily. I want to get some enjoyment telling the sisters grim.'
'I bet you do, leave it until tomorrow, I'll send her an email now. Take care, Bob.'
'You too, Dad.' Bob was smiling as he closed the connection. This was the first time Tony had seen a smile from his best friend for quite a

while. Knowing Bob wouldn't hang around telling Janice and his ex-wife, Susan. He started an email to his daughter Emily.

The developments of the past twenty-four hours had prompted Bob into gear. He needed to start making plans. He had a solicitor's appointment for Tuesday late afternoon; this appointment was made on his way home from work after being told of his imminent departure from his current employment. He was determined not to waste his Saturday, so after breakfast, which he ate alone in the kitchen, he put on his motorbike jacket and left the house without a word being said to Janice. Riding into town, he parked up and went to the same letting agent Tony had used previously.
A man of about thirty was in the agency on his own.
'Good morning, another fine day. A motorbike enthusiast like myself, I see.'
'Yes, certainly the weather to being out on two wheels.' The man shot his hand out.
'Hi, my name is Robert Barker. I'm the manager here.'
'Nice to meet you, Robert. I'm Bob Bates.' The men shook hands.
'Take a seat, Bob. Now, I take it you're looking for a place to rent?'
Bob sat down and explained his situation.
'To be honest, Robert, I'm not sure exactly.' Bob told Robert all the details that had led him to the agency that morning, everything apart from the Thailand connection and the secret notebook.
'Well, Bob, whatever you decide to do, you can count on the agency's discretion. I can show you some flats we currently have on our books in your sort of price range. I won't add you to our mailing list until you let me know. You're welcome to come here anytime to pick up the paperwork on the latest properties we have.'
'Thanks, Robert. I'm seeing a solicitor on Tuesday to see where I stand legally.'
'I would imagine after all that time, Bob, she'd be entitled to half the house.'
'Yes, that's what I'm expecting, but I obviously need to be sure.'
'Well, it won't hurt to appoint a solicitor, let him do all your dirty work.'
'What do you mean?' Bob wasn't sure what else a solicitor could do for him.'

'Well, you could get him to write to your girlfriend, let him explain the situation to her. They write some great letters, he'll tell her to get legal representation herself, and not to discuss anything about the house with you. It will be money well spent, Bob, in my opinion.'
'I never thought of that, thanks, Robert.'
'You're welcome. As I said, you can pop in anytime, I'm sure we will be able to sort you out a nice flat when the time comes.'
'I hope so. Thanks again, Robert.' The men shook hands, and Bob rode home feeling a lot happier with life.

As he turned the motorbike off on the driveway, the twitching of the curtains and the appearance of Susan at the front door alerted Bob that the cat might be out of the bag concerning Tony's forthcoming second fatherhood status.
'Have you heard?' Susan walked up to Bob.
'Have I heard what? Are you leaving?'
'No, you're stuck with me.'
'Not for much longer.'
'What's that supposed to mean?'
'Wait and see.' Bob headed indoors.
'Have you heard about your so-called best friend?'
'He is my best friend, stop with the shit-stirring, you nasty bitch.'
'Don't you dare talk to me like that?'
'I'll talk to you however I want. If you don't like it, just piss off.' Bob left Susan standing there in shock as he went into the kitchen. Janice was busy emptying the washing machine. Bob opened the fridge and pulled out a can of beer.
'A bit early for that, isn't it? Or are you toasting the baby's head?'
'Oh, very droll, Jan. I take it that's why your sister was waiting in lay to tell me.'
'He must be mad.'
'For once, Janice, I agree with you. I told him that myself. But he's a grown man, he can do whatever he likes.'
'You need to wake up and smell the roses, Bob. You think the grass is greener in Thailand. Just look at Tony now, having a kid at his age. What on earth do you think Emily thinks of all this? He's making a fool of himself and his family. Poor Susan, he's not considered her feelings once through all this.' Bob took a big swig out of the can.

'You talk some real shit, Janice. You seem to forget that it was your sister who started all this. Tone was very happy with his lot before your slag of a sister decided she wanted a toy boy on her arm.'
'Don't speak about Susan like that.'
'What, the truth hurts, does it? Do you know what, I wish I had the balls to do what Tone has done. Oh, I know he has the baby business now, but I'd swap places with him in an instant if I had a chance.'
'Well, don't let me stop you, go and join him. You'll soon be back, tail between your legs.' Bob downed the last of the beer.
'I tell you something, Jan. We were fine until your sister moved in, now look at us. She has to go today.'
'Don't go blaming, Susan. It wasn't Susan who was hiding a sordid secret notebook and being a member of a Thai dating website, you bloody pervert.'
'You know what, I've had enough, I'm leaving you.' Bob headed for the kitchen door.
'Good, take your things and say hello to your mum for me.' Bob slammed the door as he went upstairs. He quickly packed a case, took the laptop from the spare bedroom and headed out of the front door without looking back. Twenty minutes later, he pulled up outside a familiar house. An elderly lady was tending her garden. Bob climbed out of his car and wandered over.
'Hello mum, put the kettle on.'

Monday morning Bob was sat outside the H/R department like a naughty schoolboy. He was glad when his union rep, Trevor White, strolled in.
'Morning, Bob. How was your weekend?'
'I've had better.' Bob didn't want to discuss the weekend's events with anybody.
'Here, is that right, old Tony has put a Thai bird up the duff?'
'Where on earth did you hear that?' Bob was shocked that Tony's news had spread so fast.
'I heard it in the union office this morning. Steve was telling us.'
'Who? Is that bloody Steve Sherwood gobbing off again? Funny how he's become brave now that Tone is out of the country. How did he find out?'
'I don't know, Bob. So, it's true then?'

'Yes, it is true. Not sure why all the gossip, I mean, they got married last year, so it's no big deal.' Bob tried to make it sound like a normal occurrence.
'I think it's the fact that he's an old git, Bob.'
'He's not that old, besides, he's over the moon about it.'
'Oh well, good luck to him. Send him my regards next time you speak to him. We go back a long way; he was a good steward.'
'I will, he'll appreciate hearing that.'
'So, have you made your mind up?' Any second thoughts Bob had in his head had disappeared over the weekend.'
'None, Trev. Where do I sign?'

Bob was on a roll; he'd signed the paperwork to leave the company and receive his pension starting on the 1$^{st}$ of August. He had just under three weeks left at work; however, he was owed six days' holiday, so he decided to work a three-day week for the remaining time. The letting agent had quite a few properties ready for him to view. This was becoming a priority as living with his mother was becoming very stressful, not helped by Janice phoning his mother and telling her all that he'd been up to. He wanted to put the house up for sale but held back until he'd spoken to the solicitor. In a way, he begrudged paying for legal advice, but after talking to Robert in the letting agents, he thought it would be a wise thing to do. So, Tuesday afternoon, he found himself sitting opposite a very young-looking man who could very easily pass as a student.
'That's about all of it, Mr Jeffery's. I'm keen to sell the house, but want to make sure I don't cause any problems.' Mr Jeffery looked at the notes he'd been taking.
'So, the obvious question I need to ask you is there any possibility of a reconciliation between Miss Ashkettle and you?'
'Highly unlikely, we both want different things. Having her sister move in last year sort of tipped the relationship over the edge, so to speak. Look, Mr Jefferys, I want to do the right thing with her. Getting on for thirty-odd years, I know she has entitlements. I'm okay with that. What I want you to do is to represent me through the process of selling the house and informing Janice, I mean Miss Ashkettle, that she can't stop the sale.'

'I can do that for you. I will write to Miss Ashkettle, inform her of your intentions and advise her to get some legal advice of her own. My advice to you, Mr Bates, is to wait a few days before contacting an Estate agent. Give Miss Ashkettle a chance to absorb the situation.'
'How long before she hears from you?'
'My secretary will draft the letter this evening and post it out first thing tomorrow. She should receive the letter by Thursday.'
'That's great, I'll wait to hear from you.' The two men stood up and shook hands.
'Just stop by my secretary on the way out, you'll need to pay a deposit.'
'Yes, of course.' Bob, for once, thought this was money well spent.

Two days later, Bob pulled up on his Suzuki Bandit next to a very nice Yamaha. Standing next to the bike was Robert Barker.
'Hiya, Bob, you found it okay then.'
'Yes, been around this way a few times, it's certainly the posh side of Ipswich.'
'It's nice here, I only live around the corner myself. Now, let me say this flat won't be on the market for long. We have an advantage, though. The owner is keen to rent it too … How can I put it? A more mature client, someone who will take care of the place and won't be a nuisance. Now, being it's a ground-floor flat, you don't get the back garden, but you get the front garden, garage and driveway. So, you can park your motorbike in the garage out of sight and be able to park your car off the road.'
'Sounds promising, Robert. To be honest, I'm no gardener, so the back garden isn't a problem. I think I could manage to take care of the front.' Bob smiled as he talked; the whole front garden had been block-paved.
'Can we take a look inside?'
'Yes, I think this place has your name on it.' Robert led the way around the back.
'This door is for the downstairs flat. The front door is for upstairs. You'll be pleased to hear that an elderly retired gentleman lives there. Robert unlocked the door to a small but nicely furnished one-bedroom flat.
'It's not very big?'

'Compact, Bob. You have to remember you're coming from a three-bedroom house. This flat has everything you need, comes fully furnished, has two TVs, a well-stocked kitchen, nice bathroom with a power shower. What with the garage and off-road parking, I tell you, for the money you're looking at, you won't find a better property.'

'Do you think the owner would budge on the price?' Bob was always hopeful for a deal.

'I think I could get it down to three-fifty a month if you sign for a year.' Bob walked around for a second time and wandered around to the front of the property. It seemed a nice, quiet area, and he could see himself living in the flat.

'I like it, Robert. If you can get it for three-fifty for a year's lease, we have a deal.'

'Let me make a phone call.' Bob let Robert have some privacy and went back inside the flat. All he had to bring was his clothes, as Robert had mentioned, the flat had everything he could need, even a small dishwasher in the kitchen. Bob was trying out an armchair when Robert came in.

'Congratulations, Bob, and welcome to your new home. The owner has accepted your offer.'

'Thanks for your help, Robert.' The two men shook hands.

'Okay, I'll sort out the paperwork. Can you pop into my office tomorrow and sign?'

'Yes, of course. I take it I'll need to leave a deposit?'

'Yes, one month's rent. You'll also need to pay a month in advance before you move in. What date are you looking at, Bob?'

'As soon as possible, next week would be good, how about next Monday?' Bob needed to get out of his mother's as soon as possible.

'No problem, I'll get the date put on the contract. Ring me if you have any questions.'

'Will do. I'll come tomorrow straight from work. Take it easy on the bike.' Robert smiled, waved and roared off.

Bob sat on his bike looking at his soon-to-be new residence. He felt confident he'd be happy there while all the upheaval that was soon to come his way was sorted. Once the house was sold, he could decide what to do next without any time constraints.

The happy mood he was in didn't last long. As he pulled into his mother's turning, he could see Janice's distinctive Mini parked up. Pulling up outside, he debated whether to keep his safety helmet on. Walking in through the front door, he took off his leather jacket and boots, not sure what was waiting for him on the other side of the lounge door, Bob took his time. Eventually, he entered the lounge to see his mother consoling Janice.

'Bob, what's got into you? Janice has shown me this nasty letter from a solicitor.'

'My solicitor, mum. He's representing me and my well-being.'

'Wellbeing? You're going to give up your home and thirty years of happiness for what? I thought you just had a row, I was expecting you to be back home by now.' Janice turned to him, brandishing the letter in her hand.

'We could sort this out, Bob. We've always talked things through in the past. It's like I don't know who you are anymore. Oh, I know you've been influenced by Tony Fellows, I can see you have a green eye. Is that what you want? A young Thai girl on your arm, a baby in your mid-fifties. Do you want to give everything up to follow your mate to the other side of the world? You going to give up your job, your family?' Bob still hadn't revealed he was leaving work.

'Janice thinks you're having a midlife crisis, son. I tend to agree, this is not like you. Riding around on that bloody motorbike, you'll end up killing yourself. I think you should pack your things and go home. It's not healthy for you to be living here. Go home and cancel this solicitor, selling the house? Whatever next.' Bob had half expected his mother to side with Janice, so it came as no surprise.

'I think it does say in that letter, Janice, that we're not to discuss the sale of the house. Any questions you have about what's going on, I suggest you get legal representation yourself. You can feed my mother a load of shit if you want, but we both know what's behind this. I've asked you many times to tell your sister to leave our home. She's a nosey, manipulating sponger. All this crap about not wanting to be on her own it's just an excuse to live at ours for free. Now, I'm not going to get into a slagging match with you. I will put the house on the market, and once sold, I will give you fifty per cent of the profits. The furniture you can have, I don't want anything except a few personal things, I will pick up at some point. I won't be coming back to the house after I've done that. Don't panic, mum, I've got myself a flat and I'm moving into it next week. Luckily, we have our own bank accounts, so it's just the credit card bill we need to split. You can stay in the house until it's sold, but you are responsible for the utility bills. Maybe get your sister to contribute for a change. As I said, you should get yourself a solicitor, as I'm not prepared to discuss this with you any longer. Right, mum. I'm going for a shower. I'll treat you to dinner tonight. Oh, Jan, please don't come around here again until after I've moved out.' Bob headed off upstairs without a second glance.

'I don't know what's got into you, boy?' Bob was treating his mum to dinner, but was still getting an ear bashing. Bob ignored the question. 'I can recommend the carvery, mum. Listen, I didn't say anything in front of Janice, and I don't want you telling her, but I'm being pensioned off from work.'
'Oh my God, son. What are you going to do? How on earth are you going to get another job at fifty-five?'
'That's why I get a company pension, mum. So, I don't have to get another job, unless I want to.'
'You're not going to move to Thailand, are you? I mean, you're not going to leave me on my own?'
'You won't be on your own, mum, you have Deride and Joan to keep an eye.' Bob had two younger sisters who lived locally.
'Once everything is done here, I may go out to Thailand and visit Tone, and have a well-deserved holiday. That won't be for some time yet, as I want to get the house sold and everything sorted.
'Jan's, right, son. You have changed. I always thought you two were happy. Is it because of Tony?'
'No, mum. For goodness' sake, it has nothing to do with him. If you must know, this has been brewing for a long time, we're not, how can I put it?'
'Sex?'
'Whoa, mum, keep your voice down. Yes, that's part of the problem. But it's all come to a head since her bloody sister moved in.'
'Don't let your cock rule your head, son.'
'Mum, keep your voice down, for goodness sake.' Bob was mortified when it came to discussing anything sexually related with his mother.

'I'm just saying, you can't blame Susan for everything. Okay, I know she found your little computer. You should have known better. She's a bloody computer expert, Son. She was bound to find all your sordid stuff. I couldn't believe it when Janice phoned me and said they'd found all this porn and Thai dating stuff.'
'I'm not discussing it anymore, mum. Come on, let's fill our plates up.'

Tony was sitting, sifting through his emails, when he spoke out aloud.
'Holy shit.'
'You okay, darling?' Pooki came over and put a hand on Tony's shoulder.
'It's my daughter, Emily. She's coming out to see me. I mean us.'
'That's good, darling. When is she coming?'
'Next week, she's coming with her husband. They are going to visit his family in Australia, but have altered their plans and are having three days in Thailand to break up the journey. She's asked if I can pick them up at the airport.'
'Of course, we can, darling. I'll get Boss to look after shop.'
'She wants me to sort out a hotel for three nights, somewhere close to us.'
'You can do that tomorrow, darling. I come with you, get discount.'
Tony smiled at his wife, always after a discount.
'I happy to see your daughter, darling.'
'She will be happy to see you too.' Tony hid his feelings; he was worried Emily wouldn't approve of his new lifestyle and having a baby on the way. On the plus side, he was feeling excited to see his daughter. Although they didn't see each other much after she got married, she would ring him at least three times a week to check he was okay. Although she never said anything, he knew she was upset with her mother after she divorced him and set up home with Frankie. He wrote an email back, saying he was looking forward to seeing her and her husband, John. He asked for her flight details and the exact time they would be in Thailand. He told her he would look for a nice hotel close to the complex where they were living.

Bob pulled up outside the house. There were three estate agents' for sale signs plotted in various positions in the front garden. He knew Janice and Susan would be at work. He'd picked up the keys to the flat, so he felt this was a good time to collect all his personal belongings. He also decided to take some bedding and towels, which he didn't have at the flat. In the kitchen, he took the toaster and sandwich maker. He filled the inside of his car with everything he needed. He took every piece of clothing, shoes and boots. The flat didn't have a Hoover, so he took that as well. In the garage, he selected as many tools as he could fit in the boot of his car. He didn't want to come back, so he took his time checking for the essential items he thought he might need.

By the time he'd finished loading the car, there was just about enough room for him to fit behind the steering wheel. He sat looking at the house for a minute. He would miss the place, but not the atmosphere he'd endured the past few months.

"No time for sentiment, Bob." He said to himself as he started the car and drove off.

By mid-afternoon, Bob was moved into his new flat. He'd found room for most of his clothes, some he put in a dustbin sack and would drop off at one of the charity shops. He had stocked the kitchen and was now sitting with a coffee, playing with his laptop. Eventually working out how to connect to his wi-fi, he gave Tony a Skype call. A lot had happened since they'd last spoken. Tony's bronzed face came into view.

'Hello, Tone, how are you?'

'Good, mate. Where are you? I don't recognise that place.'

'I'm in my new flat, Tone. I moved in today.'

'Jesus H Christ, you didn't let the grass grow under your feet. What happened?'

'What happened, Tone, is I saw the light. To be honest, everything is a bit of a blur. After we last spoke, I ended up having yet another row with the pair of them. This time I had enough. It was obvious Janice wouldn't chuck her sister out, so I moved in with my mother. That was a total disaster, so I went to the letting agent you used. Guy called, Robert. Nice guy. Anyway, this flat came up, it is great, Tone. I'm about two minutes from that new Tesco.'

'I know that area, a bit of a trek to work though.'

'Well, considering I have only four working days left, that's not a problem.'

'True, I forgot about that.'

I went and got advice from a solicitor. I'm giving Janice half the house, which I guessed would be the case. The house is on the market with multiple agents. I just want the thing sold.'

'What about Janice? I can't see her just taking it on the chin, plus she'll have Susan winding her up.'

'True, she did turn up at my mum's while I was there, but I told her she wasn't to discuss things relating to the house with me. I think the solicitor's letter got the wind up her.'

'Bloody hell, Bob. I hope you're not rushing into things.'

'No, I don't feel like I am. It's not like the problems have just started, Tone. Like you, I want a bit more out of life. Now I have this place, I can chill a bit and decide what to do next.'

'That's great, mate. So, when are you coming out to see us?'

'I will, Tone, I promise. I just want to get everything sorted here first. Once the house has sold and everything has been put to bed, I'll come out for sure.'

'I look forward to that, mate. Now, I have a bit of news.'

'You're expecting twins?'

'What? No, don't say that for Christ's sake. No, my Emily is coming out to see me.'

'When?'

'This Friday. She and her husband, John, are stopping off for three nights on their way to Australia.'

'Wow, that's great, Tone. I'm happy for you.' Tony couldn't tell Bob his fears as Pooki was sitting in the lounge with him, watching TV.

'Yes, it should be great.'

'It will be, Tone. Blimey, it must be a while since you saw her?'

'Yes, I was trying to think. It must have been my birthday last year before I came out here.'

'I bet that will put Susan's nose out of joint.'

'I hope so.' The two men laughed.

'Okay, Tone. I'll give you a call next week, you can tell me how the visit went.'

'Okay, Bob. Glad to see you smiling again. You take care, mate.'

'Will do, say hi to Pooki.' Bob waved and cut the call.

After making himself a coffee, he opened the internet, and he bought up his favourite Thai dating website. After logging in, he went to the chat room and smiled.

"There you are." Bob started typing.
"Hi Mooka, been a long time, how are you?"

At Suvarnabhumi Airport, Bangkok, a rather nervous Tony was waiting in the arrival hall.
'How'd I look?' Tony faced a smiling Pooki.
'Handsome. You lucky, you not getting fat like me.'
'Hardly, you still look slim and beautiful.'
'You think daughter will like me?'
'She will love you, sweetheart.' Tony checked the people heading his way, and he spotted his tall son-in-law.
'Here they come.' Tony walked forward and spotted Emily waving at him. Rushing over, he gave his daughter a big hug.
'Hiya, how was your flight?'
'Long, it's good to see you, Dad.' Emily hugged her dad again.
'It's good to see you too.' Seeing his son-in-law, Tony freed a hand up and they shook.
'Thailand life suits you, Tony. You look great.'
'Thanks,' Tony suddenly remembered Pooki, who was standing watching the reunion.
'Emily, this is my wife, Pooki.' Pooki did a wai and hugged Emily.
'Wow, you're more beautiful than your photos. It's lovely to meet you, Pooki. This is my husband, John.' Pooki gave a wai to John and they did a bit of an awkward hug.
'I pleased Tony daughter come to see him. He always a happy man, but today, he smile a lot.'
'I'm happy my dad has you, Pooki. I've been worried about him. But I can see he is happy and safe with you.'
'I love your dad, he very good man for me. We take care of each other.' Emily hugged Pooki again. Tony and John waited for the embrace to finish.
'Right then, let's head to the truck.' Tony was keen to hit the road.
'How far is Pattaya, Dad?'
'A couple of hours, it's motorway all the way. Should just about get there in time to see the sunset.'

Bob was in the kitchen cooking one of his favourite meals, Spaghetti bolognese. He'd been in the flat a couple of weeks and was already

settled into a nice routine. He was surprised he hadn't felt lonely; he was thoroughly enjoying the freedom of doing what he wanted and having to answer to no one. As per normal, when it came to spaghetti, he'd cooked way too much. As he dished up the meat, the sound of his doorbell ringing made him jump. He hadn't had a visitor since he moved in, and that was the first time he'd heard the loud doorbell. Opening the door, he was surprised to see Janice standing there, holding a bottle of red wine.
'Hi Bob, I have some post for you, and well, I just thought I'd see how you're getting on?' Bob was a bit unsure but decided on the nice approach.
'Oh, hi Jan, that's kind of you. How did you know where I lived?'
'It wasn't difficult, your mum told me you had moved onto this estate, and your car is on the driveway. Plus, I could smell the spaghetti, about the only thing you can cook.'
'Hang on, I do a mean beans on toast.'
'Can I come in?' Bob looked behind Janice.
'I'm alone if that's what you're worried about?'
'Err ... No, of course not. Come in, I'm just dishing up. I made plenty if you want some?'
'That would be nice, thank you. You have a bottle opener?'
'Yes, somewhere, try looking in the drawer.' Jan opened the drawer and then spotted the toaster sitting on the worktop.
'Susan was well put out that you took the toaster.'
'Good, I take it she's still living with you?'
'Yes, for now. Although it looks like we have someone interested in the house.'
'So, I heard. The estate agent rang me this morning. They have to sell their property, though, so let's keep it on the market and see what happens.'
'Yes, of course.' After pouring out two glasses of wine, Janice took a walk around, checking the bedroom and bathroom. In the lounge, she stopped by the TV and checked for dust.
'This is a nice little flat, Bob. Can I be nosey and ask how much you're paying?' Bob walked into the lounge holding his wine.
'Three fifty, I was lucky to get it at that price. Right place, right time.'
'That's good, I've been looking myself, although I'll hang on until the house gets sold.' For the first time since he'd walked out, he felt a tad

sorry for Janice. He'd left her and didn't think of the consequences for his long-time partner.

'Maybe you can rent somewhere with Susan?'

'Yes, it's a possibility.'

'Come on, let's eat.' Bob led the way back to the kitchen, where there was a small table and two chairs.

'Hope it tastes as nice as it smells.'

'It's the old Bates recipe, passed down through the generations.' Bob smiled; he was glad of the company. Janice poured some more wine.

'I'll only have a small glass, I'm driving.'

'Yes, you want to be careful.' Bob didn't mention she was already on her second glass.

'I'm sorry, just to turn up like this, I just wanted to check you're okay.'

'Well, as you can see, I am. It's my last day at work tomorrow, I don't have to be in until nine. Quick presentation, photo and cheerio.'

'I didn't know you were leaving work. Have you taken early retirement?'

'Not through choice, they are cutting down on the staff, and unfortunately, I'm a casualty.'

'What will you do, Bob?'

'Well, I suppose I'll take a stroll down to the job centre on Monday. I won't hold my breath, but I wouldn't mind something part-time.'

'Blimey, that's a shock. I hope you find something.'

'Well, the good news is, I can take my time, I'm sure something will turn up eventually. Look, Jan, I'm glad you came. There is no reason for us not to stay friends. I don't know what's happened between us, I guess I've changed.'

'You have, Bob. It's no good for me to blame, Tony. He never lost your job. He's your best friend, and I know you miss him. What with him moving to Thailand and Susan moving in didn't help the situation, I know that. But what could I do? She is my sister, and I have to stand by her. She's mortified that we've split up, blames herself.'

'So, she should. Anyway, let's not go down that road again. You're right, it's not Tone's doing. He's made a new life for himself, and good luck to him.'

'Will you go out and see him for a holiday?'

'I said I would, but not until the house is sold and everything is sorted. There's no rush. The good news is, we're talking, and who knows what the future holds for any of us.'

'True. Did you know, Susan and I are off to Menorca next week?'

'No, I didn't know. That will be nice for you.'

'Yes, I'm looking forward to it. I need a holiday after the past few months.' Bob decided to change the subject in case Janice brought up the Thai dating site.

'That was a surprise, Emily going to see Tony.'

'Emily's going to see Tony? When?' Asked a shocked Janice.

'When I said going, I mean gone. She must be there by now. They are stopping off for a few days in Thailand on their way to Australia to see John's parents.'

'Christ, she didn't tell Susan about that. She thinks she's going directly to Australia.'

'Well, Tony is her dad after all. Of course, she'll want to see him.'

'Yes, I know. I wonder why she didn't mention it to her mum? Susan knew she was going to Australia for a month, but never mentioned anything about Thailand.'

'I don't know, most probably didn't want to upset her.'

'Well, I'm not surprised. Between us, Bob, I don't think Emily is very happy with her mum. She was embarrassed when she left her dad for that greasy, Frankie. The way she treated Tony, well, I think Emily felt desperately sorry for him. I'm guessing she's happy he has met someone and found happiness. Mind you, I wonder what she'll think of having a half-brother or sister?'

'I'm sure she'll be happy for him. She's closer to her dad than you think. Tony used to tell me that Emily would phone him regularly, especially in the early days of the divorce, checking he was okay.'

'Well, I won't say anything to Susan; I will let her find out for herself. Hopefully, she won't hear about it until we get back from our holiday. This is delicious, Bob, thank you.'

'You're welcome. Listen, Jan, don't be a stranger, we had some great times together. There's no need not to see each other because we don't live together anymore.'

'Yes, it will take time, Bob. You've hurt me more than you can imagine. But I can't see why we can't remain friends.'

'I'm sorry for how things have turned out. Hopefully, we can build a bridge between us. More wine?' Bob topped Jan's glass up.

Emily and John's whirlwind visit to see Tony and Pooki was coming to an end. Having shown them all the sights in and around Pattaya. They spent hours on the beach and ate out every night. Pooki took Emily to some of the local markets where they would spend hours browsing the stalls. Emily liked Pooki; she felt she was more like a sister than a stepmother. Tony enjoyed supping a few beers with his son-in-law, where they would discuss many things and also the joys of retirement in Thailand.

It was a slightly sombre mood when they had to travel to the airport to say their goodbyes. As they stood by the check-in desk, Emily hugged Pooki and didn't want to let her go. Tony shook John's hand.

'Well, thanks for a great time, Tony. I'm so glad we stopped here. I know Emily has been very worried about you, but hey, look at her now.' The two men looked at the two girls still hugging, both tearful. Emily walked over and hugged her dad.

'You take care, Dad. Don't forget to Skype me anytime, okay? I'm so happy you have made a good life for yourself here. Pooki is lovely, I am going to miss her.'

'Miss me as well, I hope?'

'What do you think? I miss you every day.' That comment from his daughter made Tony's eyes well up.

'Right, we'd better get checked in.' John, seeing the emotional state of father and daughter, put his arm around Emily and steered her to the check-in counter.

'Thank you for come to see us.' Pooki did a wai and grabbed Tony's hand. After watching Emily and John book in, they waited until the reluctant couple started to walk away. Tony waved a couple of times until they were out of sight.

'Well, that's that.' Muttered Tony. Pooki turned to her husband as he wiped his eyes. It didn't take long for her to make him smile when she came out with a comment he'd heard a hundred times.

'I feel hungry, darling.'

'There's a surprise, I don't think they sell chicken feet in here?'

The alarm buzzing awoke Bob from a deep sleep. He knew this was his last day at work and cursed that he'd forgotten to set the alarm for a later time. Hitting the off button on the alarm clock, Bob stretched out while trying to bring himself into the land of the living. It took a few seconds and the noise of the toilet flushing to make him aware he wasn't alone. Janice came walking into the bedroom. Her hair was wet, she had a towel wrapped around her head and another around her waist.

'That's great, your power shower, Bob. Really wakes you up.'
Jan sat on the edge of the bed, her ample breasts swinging freely.
'Thanks for last night, I needed that.' Bob sat there bemused, the events of the previous evening slowly coming back to him. Red wine always made Janice horny. Bob was convinced years ago that it was the reason she'd changed to white wine.
'Yes, me too.' Bob smiled as Janice leaned over so he could feel her breasts.
'You want more?' Asked Janice in a seductive voice.
'Yes, please.'
'I bet you do. Unfortunately, you lost that right when you left me. Taking advantage of me like that, have you no shame?'
'Now, hang on a minute.'
'No, Bob. You hang on. You've ruined everything. We could be looking forward to a nice retirement together. But no, you want to get some Thai girl on your arm and look like a complete arsehole like Tony. Middle-aged men chasing young girls, it's perverted.' Janice ranted at Bob as she hurriedly dressed.
This attack caught Bob off guard and took him a minute to have a go back.
'Well, it didn't take long for you to get back to normal. I'm perverted, am I? Well, at least I don't need a bottle of red wine to get me in the mood. I've said it before; you and your sister are a couple of frigid mannequins. You'll grow old and be like some old spinster sitting knitting in an old people's home. Bloody right, I will find myself a nice Thai girl, and I'll shag her noon and night, now, f*** off from my home and don't come back.' Janice pointed at Bob.
'Susan told me all about what she found on the laptop. Japanese schoolgirls, I have a good mind to go to the police.'
'They were dressed as school girls, you stupid bitch.'

'Oh, that makes it okay then, does it? Listen to yourself?'
'Just get out, Janice.'
'You know something. I feel sorry for you. No one will love you as I do. You want to remember that.' Janice picked up her handbag and headed for the door. She stopped and turned back, she couldn't resist one last dig.
'You're a pathetic, perverted human being Bob Bates. I can't wait to see you make a complete fool of yourself.' With that, Janice went out of the flat and slammed the door.
Bob lay back down; he'd never seen her so mad. Thank God she'd gone, he was thinking just before the sound of smashing glass had him jumping out of bed. Going through to the lounge, he could see a rock sitting on his rug, surrounded by broken glass. Opening the curtains, he could see a large hole in one of the fanlights. Janice was standing by her car, looking furious.
'Wanker.' She shouted out as she climbed in and sped away, smoke coming from the tyres.
As Bob watched her disappear, the neighbour from upstairs came out to see what all the commotion was about and to inspect the damage. Bob had spoken to him a couple of times. He had told Bob he was a retired policeman and was glad his new neighbour downstairs wasn't some young man who would be noisy and disrespectful, but an older person who respected the peace and quiet of the neighbourhood.
'Everything alright, Bob?' He called out as he lit his pipe. Bob opened the window so he could speak more clearly.
'Yes, sorry about that, Ted. It was my ex, she's not taken the break-up too well.'
'A woman scorned, eh?'
'Yes, something like that. Don't worry, she won't be coming back.'
'Good job. You watch your back, Bob. I remember a case I was on as a young constable. I'd only been on the beat a few weeks when I got called out to the most horrendous crime. I was the first to arrive; a crime of passion was the headline in the papers. The jilted wife crept into her ex-husband's house in the middle of the night. She took a carving knife out from the kitchen, went to the bedroom and stabbed him and his young girlfriend to death. He was stabbed over a hundred times. Frenzied attack. I'd never seen so much blood; it was everywhere, up the walls and curtains. She just stood there smiling

when I arrived, still holding the knife. I can still smell the waft of death when I cook liver.'
'Really? Well, Ted, I'll bear that in mind when I go to bed tonight. Liver, you say?'
'Yes, I don't know why, but the smell always reminds me of that night. Anyway, fear not, she died in prison. If I see anything suspicious or a woman hanging around, I'll let you know.'
'Yes, thanks for that. Right, I'd better clear this mess up. I'll have to board the window up for now. I'll get it sorted this afternoon.'
'Right, you are, Bob. Pop up if you ever fancy a cuppa and a chat.'
'Will do.' Bob went into the kitchen where he had a dustpan and brush. Looking at one of the worktops, he had a block containing various-sized knives. Picking it up, he hid it in one of the cupboards. He made a mental note to himself to get locks for all the windows. "What a start to the day," he mumbled to himself as he started to pick up the pieces of glass.

## Chapter 6

After what seemed a long and sometimes stressful period, Bob, at last, was crossing the finishing line. Five months had passed since his house was put on the market, and that morning, the letter had finally arrived informing him that the contracts had now been signed and the house was sold. The solicitor had enclosed a cheque, which Bob held in his hand and was admiring. A certain type of knock on the door alerted Bob that his cynical neighbour from upstairs, Ted, was waiting to come in. He always did the same knock and most mornings if Bob was in, he'd pop down for a chat and a coffee and empty the biscuit tin. As much as he came across as a doom and gloom merchant, Bob had grown to like the retired policeman and his way of steering any conversation to another tale from his life in the constabulary. Bob opened the door.
'Morning, Ted. You must have heard the kettle go on.'
'Well, I saw the postman arrive and stick a letter through your door, any news?' Bob had mentioned last week that he was waiting for a cheque from his solicitor.
'No wonder you're chairman of the neighbourhood watch, nothing gets past you, does it, Ted? But, for your information, yes, I'm pleased to say that at long last the cheque has arrived and I believe everything is just about sorted.'
'Well done. I bet you thought this day would never come.'
'You're not wrong. A couple of false starts to begin with, but I got there in the end. Anyway, let me make the coffee. Can I ask, why are you wearing a coat to come downstairs?' Ted was wearing a green duffel coat.
'When you get to my age, you have to be careful, these late November mornings can be bitter you know.'
'Yes, they can, but I've got the central heating on, so you don't need to wear it in here.'
'Right, you are.' Ted took his coat off and hung it by the door, he then sat down at the kitchen table.
'So, can I ask, what are your plans, Bob?'
'Well, it's high time I went to see my friend in Thailand. As it's only a month to Christmas, I will most probably spend the festivities in the place they call the land of smiles. I'll sort out a flight and hotel later on

my laptop.' Bob had never mentioned his online chatting with Thai women. He knew Ted would frown at that, plus, of course, it would give him another opportunity to tell him some gruesome tale or other.
'Nice time to get away, Bob. Mind you, you need to be careful about what you eat in those sorts of countries. One of my colleagues went to the Philippines one Christmas. Nice fella, I played rugby with him. Fit as a fiddle, but do you know what? The food killed him, you see, our bodies are not used to the spicy Asian food, Bob.'
'What on earth did he eat?'
'A blowfish.'
'Well, no wonder, even I know not to eat one of them.' Bob shook his head in disbelief. But Ted wasn't finished.
'You want to watch out for extreme sunburn too'
'Really? Well, Ted, I'm just going to have to risk it. I'll take a high-factor sun cream, also, I thought about going into town and having a few sunbed sessions, you know, get a bit of a head start.'
'Christ, that takes me back.'
'What, you had a few sunbed sessions in your younger days, have you?' Bob joked with the old man.
'No, a gruesome discovery.' Bob tried not to laugh; he knew another story was coming his way. Carrying the coffees over, he sat down opposite the story master.
'Have a biscuit before you tell me.'
'Thanks, don't mind if I do.' Ted opened the biscuit tin and pulled out a handful of chocolate bourbons. After dipping a biscuit, he started to tell Bob another one of his never-ending supply of policeman tales.
'Must have been the mid-eighties. Me and my partner, George, were on an early-shift patrol. It's ironic when I think back. We'd just been to see a woman who had reported her husband missing. He hadn't arrived home from work the previous evening. I was just telling her that in my experience he was bound to turn up sooner or later when we received a call to go to an incident at a health club. Well, it was advertised as a health club, but behind closed doors, it was a lot more than that if you know what I mean.'
'I think I'm getting the drift, Ted.'
'Basically, it was a knocking shop. You could have a sauna or steam, a sunbed if you were vain enough, or, if you were that way inclined, a topless massage.' Bob let the vain comment pass over his head.

'What did you plump for, Ted, a topless massage, I bet?'

'No, nothing, I was on duty, plus the fact it wasn't open for business that time in the morning.'

'So, what was this gruesome discovery?'

'Easy tiger, I'm getting to that. We pulled up outside the premises, where a distraught woman was waiting to show us inside. It turned out she was the cleaner and the person who had called the police. She'd arrived that morning to clean the place and found a dead body under one of the sunbeds. I went in, and that's when the smell hit me.'

'Not the liver smell again?'

'What, no. There was no blood, Bob. No, this time it was the smell of burning flesh. He was cooked, Bob. God knows how long he'd been under the canopy; the sunbed was still on. The timer had got jammed, they seemed to think he was under the sunbed canopy for about ten hours. No one had checked the room before they closed up for the night.'

'So, he was a bit overdone, I take it?'

'Overdone, he was crispy, Bob. You know, I could never eat a bag of pork scratchings after that morning. Similar smell, you see. Burnt pork. Never seen someone so red before, the poor man was literally cooked to death. Turned out to be the missing husband. In some respects, he had a lucky escape.'

'Lucky escape? Not sure how you work that one out, Ted?'

'You never saw his wife, beast of a woman.' That comment had Bob chuckling.

'You've seen some sights over the years.'

'I have, Bob. Well, thanks for the coffee and biscuits. I'll leave you to book your holiday. Let me know how you get on, I have a fascinating story for you about the last time I flew … It was …'

'Save it, Ted. Tell me next time.' Bob ushered Ted to the door. The last thing he needed was to hear a story about an aeroplane disaster before he was just about to book a flight.

'Okay, Bob, be seeing you.'

Ten minutes later, Bob was on the Thai dating site and typing away to the Thai girl called Mooka. He'd grown fond of her ever since he dabbled in the world of Thai dating.

"Hi Mooka, good news, everything here is sorted at last and I'm about to book my flight to Thailand. I hope we can meet up at some point." After a brief pause, Bob got a reply.
"Ka, Bob. That so good, so, when you come?"
"I booked a flight and hotel today. I will let you know, I am looking to stay over the Christmas and New Year period."
"Okay, I can pick you up at airport."
"I'm not sure, I have a friend I want to see while I'm there who lives in Pattaya. So, I will book a hotel there.'
Bob waited for a response.
"Ka, no problem, darling. I can still pick you up at airport, I take you to Pattaya after I show you my home."
"You sure you don't mind?"
"Of course not, darling. I want you to see where I live, meet my family. I want them to meet my handsome boyfriend." Unfortunately for Bob, like many men, he was easily sucked into the compliments.
"Well, as long as you don't mind."
"I not mind, I wait long time for you to come and see me."
"Yes, you have. I thank you for waiting for me. I will bring you a nice present when you come."
"Thank you, you bring gift for my sister too."
"Yes, of course. I didn't know you had a sister; you didn't mention her before?"
"ka, she speak good English and drives."
"Okay, I'll get her a nice present too, don't worry. I'll talk again after I book the flight. You okay to stay with me in Pattaya?"
"Ka, no problem, I can't wait to see the man I fall in love with. I stay with you. No need to book hotel in Pattaya, I do that for you, get discount."
"If you are sure?"
'Ka, I sure. Let me know day you come to Thailand. I get sister to bring me to airport."
"That will be great, I can't wait for the day I finally have you in my arms."
"Ka, I want that day to come soon."
"It will be soon, I promise. Okay, I'll go now, talk later."
"Ka, love you, sexy man."

"Love you too." Bob came out of the site. Before he went searching for flights, he looked at the photos, Mooka had sent him over the past few months. He couldn't get over how beautiful she looked in all the photos.

"Not long now, sexy woman."

In Thailand, Tony was driving Pooki to the local government hospital for an overdue six-month check-up. He'd managed to persuade her to stay in the apartment for another six months. He knew he was borrowed time regarding living in Pattaya. He reluctantly agreed to give it a try and move to the family home once the six months were up. Pooki promised him that if he couldn't settle, they would move back to Pattaya.

Although it was less than a twenty-minute drive to the hospital, Pooki felt uncomfortable.

'Truck not good for baby, darling.'

'Sorry sweetheart, these trucks are a hard ride, you can feel every bump.'

'Ka, I know.' Tony looked across at his wife. The past few weeks, she'd started to blossom.

'You look beautiful.'

'I fat, darling. I not fit in any of my clothes.' Pooki lifted her top to reveal the top of her jeans were open wide.

'Well skinny jeans when you're nearly seven months pregnant are not ideal. Once we finish at the hospital, we can go to the market and get you some more comfortable clothes.'

'Ka. We should have come on the scooter, darling.'

'Safer in the truck, sweetheart. Anyway, we're here now. Look, I'll drop you off, you go to the antenatal and I'll come and find you once I've found a parking space.'

'You know where to go?'

'I'll ask someone if I can't find it, don't worry.' Tony pulled up close to the entrance and Pooki waddled off. For the next ten minutes, Tony drove around the car park waiting to find a space. Eventually, he spotted someone pulling out and managed to squeeze the truck into the vacant spot.

Like many hospitals, the place was heaving with people. This was a bit of a culture shock for Tony. It was the first time he'd come to the hospital with Pooki.

Looking up at the signs, Tony didn't have a clue where the antenatal was. The reception area was massive and there were desks and counters everywhere, with long queues of people waiting. Seeing a nurse sitting behind a desk on her own, Tony marched over.

'Good afternoon, I'm looking for the antenatal department?'

The woman, whom Tony estimated to be in her fifties, sat there blank-faced. Tony tried again.

'The antenatal department, you know where it is?' The woman again didn't answer; instead, she stood up and called over to a woman in a white tunic and trousers, and what looked like about twenty military ribbons on her chest. The woman walked over. Tony wondered what all the ribbons meant. Was he about to speak to a high-ranking hospital officer?'

'Can I help you, sir?' The woman seemed to speak good English.'

'Yes, I'm looking for the antenatal department.' The woman repeated the look her colleague had just given.

'I not understand?' Tony tried again.

'Antenatal?'

The two women looked at each other.

'My wife,' Tony pointed to his wedding ring.

'She is pregnant, she is expecting a baby.' Tony used his hand and showed the woman an exaggerated fat stomach. He then held his arms together as if he were cradling a child.

'You need antenatal, second floor.' The woman walked off, leaving Tony dumbfounded.

As he reached the escalator, he found himself behind a young couple. The girl was heavily pregnant, so Tony held back and hoped they were heading towards the same destination. Luckily for him, they were.

'I been getting worried, darling.' Pooki was relieved to see her husband finally arrive.

'Don't ask, bloody parking is a nightmare.' Tony didn't mention his recent encounter downstairs with the two nurses.

'I know, that's why I said bring scooter.'

'No worries, we're here now. Once we move to your mum's I'm going to do an extensive Thai course.'
'Ka, darling. Your Thai is very good.'
'Antenatal.'
'Yes, darling, this is the antenatal department.' Tony let out a silent whistle.
Another highly decorated nurse called Pooki's name out, and Tony followed his wife through some doors into a small room where the nurse invited Pooki to lie on the bed. After pulling the curtains around, she disappeared and then returned with a trolley carrying what Tony assumed was some type of ultrasound equipment. After plugging the machine in, the nurse lifted Pooki's t-shirt and exposed her fat tummy. The nurse shared a joke with Pooki that Tony didn't have to guess what it was about, as he saw Pooki trying to do the zip-up on her jeans. A male doctor came in and spoke to Pooki. He then turned and smiled at Tony, but didn't speak to him. The doctor rubbed some gel on Pooki's stomach and started to rub the sensor slowly around. Talking away in Thai, Tony didn't understand a word. But he could see the baby on the screen and hear a fast heartbeat.
'That's our daughter, darling,' smiled Pooki. Tony walked over and held her hand. Up to that point, he didn't know the sex of the baby; deep down, he wanted a son, but he wasn't disappointed.
'She's going to be beautiful, like her mother.' Tony could feel his eyes welling up. The doctor spoke to Pooki. After he finished, she translated to Tony.
'Doctor say I need to get booked in five January.'
'What's that for, another check-up?'
'No Ka, five January I have baby.'
'I thought the baby was due in February?' Tony was confused.
'Scan say I thirty-five week. Five to go.'
'No wonder those jeans are so tight. Well, we better start stocking up on nappies.'

After a long Skype call to his daughter Emily, in which Pooki sat and chatted as well, Tony gave Bob a call.
'Hello Bob, how the devil are you?'
'Hiya Tone, yes, life is good mate.'

'Hello, that makes a change. Don't tell me the contracts have been signed.'
'They have, and I've paid a very healthy cheque into the bank.'
'Well done, Bob. Well, you have no more excuses now. When are you coming out?'
'End of next week, I fly Thursday night and get to Bangkok around 4 pm on Friday.' Tony looked at his calendar.
What's that, Friday the 11$^{th}$?'
'That's it, I'm coming out for four weeks. Fly back on the 8$^{th}$ of January.'
'That's great news, Bob. Been too bloody long. Well, you'll be here when the baby is born.'
'Really? I thought the baby was due in February.'
'So, did I mate? Seems like they got their dates wrong. Pooki's booked in for the fifth of January. Doesn't matter, so you'll have to give me your flight numbers and I'll pick you up at the airport. What hotel did you book?'
'Err ... Slight change of plan, Tone. I'm meeting a girl at the airport.'
'Meeting a girl? How did this come about? You never said anything about a girl. Who is she?'
'Don't panic, Tone, her name is Mooka, and I met her through a Thai dating site.'
'Bloody hell, Bob. Why didn't you tell me? It's okay, I can pick you both up.'
'Her sister is picking me up, they are taking me to meet the family, and then we'll come to Pattaya. Mooka said she would sort out the hotel. She said if she books the hotel, she can get me a discount.'
'Maybe that is true, however, why you have got to meet the family straight away? Where does she come from?'
'Not sure, she did tell me once, but I forgot. Don't worry, I'll go and meet the family, it's what Mooka wants. Most probably spend a few days there, then we'll come to Pattaya.'
Tony wasn't happy with this new development.
'Listen, Bob, and don't take this the wrong way, but these dating sites can be very dangerous. Now, I'm sure this Mooka is fine, but let's be honest, you know nothing about her. I think you should come here for a few days first, get to know her, then if everything is okay, travel up and meet the family.'

'You're most probably right, Tone. Let me talk to her and I'll get back to you.'
'I don't want to scare you, Bob, but I've heard some real horror stories out here. I'd feel more comfortable knowing you were coming here first. Just book a hotel in Pattaya, get a move on as a lot of them will be full for Christmas and New Year.'
'I'll get looking as soon as I've finished talking to you. Tell me, how much money do you think I need for a month? I was thinking around three grand.'
'That should be plenty, Bob. Depends on how much you want to spend on this Mooka?'
'I won't go mad, Tone. Maybe I'll bring a bit extra just in case.'
'They have plenty of ATMs here, Bob. Just notify your bank you're coming here, and you can always get money out if you run short.'
'Good idea. What about clothes? I bought a couple of pairs of nice jeans, and a couple of nice sweaters for the evenings.'
'Sweaters? Bloody hell, you will be sweating if you wear them. Look, let me show you something.' Tony unplugged the laptop and carried it into the bedroom. He slid the door back on the cupboard.
'This is my entire wardrobe, Bob. Vests, four lightweight polo shirts, two pairs of tailored shorts, and about six pairs of sports shorts and pants. I have a pair of trainers and one pair of flip-flops.'
'Is that it?' Bob was shocked.
'That's it, mate. You won't need jeans or sweaters out here. Too hot, even at night. My advice, travel light. There are loads of markets to buy clothes here. The shirts in the UK are too thick. You need lightweight stuff; otherwise, you'll be sweating like a good un.'
'Bloody hell, those jeans and sweaters cost me over a hundred pounds.'
'Can't you take them back?'
'I cut the labels off, mind you, they should still be in the dustbin. I'll go outside and see if the dustmen have been yet.'
'Okay, well I'll call you tomorrow, you can let me know what you're doing.'
'Right you are, Tone, I'll be seeing you soon.' Bob cut the call, donned his coat and went outside to check the dustbin.

'Thrown something out you shouldn't have, Bob?' Straightening up, Bob turned around expecting to see his neighbour Ted, standing there.

'I'm up here.' Bob looked upstairs and could see Ted standing, holding a pair of binoculars.
'You look like you're going for an audition for Dad's army.' Joked Bob.
'Just checking the birds. What have you lost?'
'Some labels I cut off some clothes. I've found them now. Pop down, I'll stick the kettle on.'

Five minutes later, Bob was waiting for Ted to steer the conversation to another policeman's tale.
'So, you fly next Thursday?'
'I do, Ted. Nine in the evening. Direct flight, arrive in Bangkok 4 pm Friday.'
'That's a long flight, nineteen hours.'
'Get a grip, twelve, Ted. They're seven hours in front of us don't forget.'
'Of course, they are, what am I on about? Mind you, even twelve hours is a long time.'
'You're not wrong. Mind you it will be worth it, get away from this wet and cold, and all the Christmas palaver. Right, I need to get these labels back on these clothes.' Bob held up one of the sweaters.
'You taking them back to the shop, Bob?'
'I am, I bought this and another sweater, and two pairs of jeans to take to Thailand, but my mate Tone said I won't need them.'
'So that's what you were retrieving from the dustbin.'
'Yes, not a pleasant task. Did you put fish in the dustbin by any chance?'
'Guilty as charged,' laughed Ted.
'I always get a cold shiver down my spine when I open a dustbin lid.'
"Here we go," thought Bob as Ted prepared for another tale.
'Cold shiver, Ted, why's that?'
'Gruesome discovery. The smell stayed for me for years, Bob.'
'Smell of liver or burnt pork?' Asked Bob jokingly.
'What? No, it was the smell of death. Rotting flesh, it hit me like a bullet. I couldn't eat rare steak again after that day.'
'Well, I'm with you on that, Ted. I've always liked my steaks well done. So, what was in the dustbin?'
'A dead body had been chopped up and placed in a dustbin. They seem to think the body had been in there for weeks.'

'Had the dustmen not been, Ted?'
'No, the dustbin was hidden in a garage. My sergeant had asked me to have a look around. A woman had come to the police station worried about her missing sister. She said her sister's husband was a nasty piece of work and suspected he had something to do with her disappearance. We went to see the husband; his eyes were too close together, Bob. There was something sinister about him, but I couldn't quite put my finger on it. As I said, my sergeant spoke to the man and he asked me to check around outside. I opened the garage door; it was then that the smell began to hit me. I just knew something was in the dustbin.'
'Christ, Ted. It must have taken some nerve to lift that lid?'
'It did, Bob. But it had to be done. I held my breath and took the lid off and there it was, the bottom half, still with the tail attached.'
'Tail?'
'Yes, the bastard had killed and chopped up the family dog.'
'Jesus Christ, Bob, I thought you were going to tell me it was his wife.'
'Wife? No, turned out she'd run off with the postman.'
'Bloody hell, Ted, you were wasted in the police force, you should have been on the stage.'
'Thirty years a policeman, there's not much I didn't come across.'
'Well it's a wonder you can eat anything, I mean, you can't eat liver, pork scratching, rare steak. Pity you can't eat bourbon biscuits; you'd save me a fortune.'
'Aye, I'm okay with them. It's going to be a quiet Christmas without you around.'
'What's your plans for Christmas, Ted?'
'Nothing special. My nephew normally pops in for a while on Christmas morning. Then I'll most probably cook a small chicken and put my feet up in front of the television.'
'I see.' Bob felt sorry for the old man. It made him feel even more determined that he wouldn't end up living in a cold climate and on his own.
'You're not getting a small turkey then?'
'Can't eat turkey, ever since I was on the case tracking down some turkey rustlers, fascinating case ….'
'Well, you'll have to save that one, Ted. I must crack on. I need to take these clothes back.' One story was enough for Bob per visit.

'Right, you are. Be seeing you then.' Ted put his coat on and left Bob to it.

It was two days before Bob was due to fly to Thailand, and he had a major concern. He'd not heard a word from Mooka for nearly a week. He'd left message after message, but he hadn't had a word back. This was out of character, as she always left him a message if he wasn't online. Not sure if she would be at the airport to meet him, he decided to give Tony a Skype call. After a few rings, his tanned friend came into view.

'Hiya Tone.'
'Alright, Bob, I bet you're getting all excited?'
'I am Tone. Listen, I might need you to pick me up at the airport after all.'
'That's not a problem mate. I was coming to see you at the airport anyway.'
'You were?'
'Yes. I'm a tad concerned mate. You don't know this girl, yet you're prepared to travel to god knows what part of Thailand to meet the family? I'd rather you bought her here, get to know her a bit, then if you're happy, go and see her family.'
'Yes, you're most probably right, Tone. I've not heard from her for over a week?'
'Really? I thought she was keen on you; I wonder what's happened to her?'
'Most probably with husband,' called out Pooki from the sofa.
Tony turned around and asked Pooki what she meant.
'Hear many time, darling. Tell your friend internet dangerous. Many girl have three or four men. Your friend send her any money?'
'What did Pooki say?' Asked Bob.
'She said you need to be careful. There are a lot of liars on these Thai dating sites. Have you sent her any money?'
'Yes, not much. I sent her five hundred pounds a week ago, so she can afford to take time off work when I come.'
'That's a lot of money for a Thai, Bob. She most probably only earns around nine- thousand baht a month. You've just sent her nearly twenty-five thousand. What does she do, anyway?'
'She works as a hotel receptionist.'

'What hotel?' Pooki again called out.
'I don't know, tell Pooki not to worry. Mooka has sent me hundreds of photos, many of them from her family home. I trust her, well, I did until she disappeared. But there could be an innocent explanation.'
'Yes, there could.' Tony didn't want to upset his friend, so he didn't pursue the subject.
'I'll be at the airport in case she doesn't show up. It won't be a problem; you can rent an apartment in our complex. I spoke to my friend here, and he has the keys to a few. He can sort out an apartment for you for a month.'
'Thanks, Tone. You have my flight details?'
'Yes. You should land around four. Don't worry, I'll be there waiting for you.'
'Thanks, mate. It will be good to see you.'
'It will be good to see you too. Funny, when you left me at Heathrow, I'd never have guessed what would happen next.'
'Yes, who'd have thought it. Proves the point, though, we never know what's around the corner. Listen, do you want me to bring anything over for you?'
'If you have room in your case, I'd love a pack of PG tips, I miss a decent cup of tea.'
'No problem, anything else?'
'Yes, bring a couple of papers with you, I've not sat and read a newspaper for over a year.'
'You can't get newspapers over there?'
'You can, but they're always old editions and very expensive.'
'Leave that with me, I'll pick some up at the airport.'
'Cheers Bob. Changing the subject, have you heard anything from Janice?'
'Surprisingly, yes, I got a Christmas card through the door a few days ago. She'd put a note inside letting me know her new address and hoped I was happy. Here, get this. She said if I was on my own for Christmas, I was welcome to have dinner with her.'
'That was nice of her. Emily told me her mum and Janice are renting a house together. Christmas dinner? I guess she didn't know you were coming out here?'
'Obviously not.'
'Did you send her a Christmas card back?'

'I did, Tone. No need to continue all these hostilities.'
'Well, you didn't help the situation by sleeping with her that time.'
'No, I didn't. Right then, Tone. I'd better crack on.' Bob didn't want to dwell on his moment of weakness when he woke up at the flat and found Janice coming out of his bathroom.
'Okay, I'll see you at Suvarnabhumi airport on Friday afternoon.'
'God willing. See you soon, Tone. Is Pooki coming with you to the airport?'
'No, the truck is very uncomfortable for her. Best she waits here.'
'Okay, well, say bye to Pooki.'
'Hang on.' Tony turned the laptop so Bob could see her sitting on the sofa.
'See you Friday, Pooki.'
'Ka, I look forward to meet you.' Pooki did a wai.
'Safe flight, mate.' Bob waved and then cut the call.

Thursday morning, Bob felt reasonably happy and excited. He'd still not heard from Mooka, and he couldn't help but feel disappointed. In his suitcase, he'd packed perfume for her and her sister, just on the off chance she was waiting for him at the airport. The taxi was booked for 3 pm. Checking his watch, he had three hours to kill.
Switching on his laptop, he went to make a coffee while he waited for it to start up. As if by magic, Ted knocked at the door.
'Come in, it's not locked,' he called out to his elderly neighbour.
'Bloody hell, Ted. You must hear the kettle going on.'
'Well, I know you have a taxi coming at three, so I thought it best to pop down now. Here, this is for you, Merry Christmas.' Ted handed over a wrapped present.'
'Thanks, Ted. Sorry, I haven't got you anything. I'll bring you something nice back from Thailand.'
'Anything in her late twenties will do.'
'Me too,' joked Bob, causing both men to laugh. Bob unwrapped the present and knew by the feel of it that it was a book.
'A Thai phrase book. Thanks, Ted, that's very thoughtful of you. Sit down and I'll make the coffee.' Ted sat down in front of the laptop.
'I've often thought about getting a computer, but I feel I'm a bit too long in the tooth to learn how to use one.'

'Well, if I can learn, I'm sure you can, Ted. Wait until I get back, and I'll show you the basics. It will give you another interest. You could write a book about your time in the police force.'

'That's an idea. I'll take you up on your offer, thanks, Bob.' As Bob was making the coffee, a familiar sound came from the laptop. A notification bleep that was linked to him receiving a message from the Thai dating site.

Bob walked over and could see he'd received a message from Mooka. Not wanting Ted to see, Bob picked the laptop up and placed it in the lounge.

'Don't want to spill coffee on it,' he announced as he came back into the kitchen. Bob was now in a dilemma; he was dying to read the message from Mooka, but he didn't want to be rude to Ted. So, he sat there impatiently while Ted rambled out another policeman's tale. Something Ted picked up on.

'You okay, Bob. You look a bit nervous?'

'Preflight jitters, Ted. I'm not the best of flyers as it is, what with having to fly for twelve hours.'

'You'll be fine. Night flight, have a couple of whiskeys and you'll sleep most of it.'

'Good idea, Ted. Don't let your coffee go cold. You might as well finish these bourbons up; they'll only go soft while I'm away.' Bob thought dunking the biscuits would soak the coffee up quicker.

Eventually, Ted stood up and slipped his coat on.

'Well, Bob, I wish you a safe flight and a great holiday. Come back safe and sound, my dear friend.'

'Thanks, Ted. I'll be fine, don't worry. You have a nice Christmas and I wish you a Happy New Year.'

'Thank you. I'll keep an eye on the place, don't worry.'

'Oh, I know you will. Thanks again for the phrasebook.'

'It might come in handy.' The two men shook hands, and Ted went out the door. Bob nearly broke into a run to get to the laptop.

He opened the message from Mooka.

"Hi my darling Bob. Sorry I not be in touch. Many problem here with electric and internet. My mama get knocked off her motorbike and I go home to help. She okay now and electric and internet back on.

'I come with my sister to airport to meet you. My family very happy my handsome boyfriend come to say hello. We will be waiting for you at arrival Friday afternoon.
You come see me make me very happy lady. I love you."

Bob read the message twice. He didn't know what to think. Tony's and Pooki's warnings were playing in the back of his mind. He decided he'd wait until he was at the airport, meet Mooka, and then decide. He trusted Tony's judgement, so he would be guided by him. He opened the file containing all of Mooka's photos. And for about the hundredth time, he browsed through all the images of this beautiful woman.

As the taxi approached Heathrow, Bob thought back to his last visit to the airport when he dropped Tony off. He couldn't believe it was over a year ago that he took his best friend to the departure lounge. It was cold, wet and dark as he stepped out of the taxi. After paying the driver, he plonked his case on a trolley and went inside to find his check-in desk.
After a lengthy wait at the check-in, Bob was pleased to wave goodbye to his case. Things didn't move any quicker as he queued to get through the security and immigration. Eventually, he made it through to the departure lounge. It was two hours until take-off time. He did what his friend Tony did before him: he went and had a pint.

Unlike Tony's flight, where he was wedged into a seat in the middle of the plane, Bob found himself sitting in a very nice seat next to an emergency door. Plenty of room to stretch his legs out, and he was very happy. Things got even better when a beautiful, young-looking Thai lady came and sat next to him.
'Good evening.'
'Sawadee Ka,' replied the woman as she placed a small bag in the overhead locker. Sitting down, she smiled at Bob. Being out of chat-up practice, Bob tried to think of something to say.
'Are you going to Thailand?'
'Ka, I hope so, otherwise, I'm on the wrong plane.' The woman started to laugh. Bob sat there wishing the ground would swallow him up. After a short while, he tried to engage in another attempt at conversation with this beautiful woman.

'This is my first visit to Thailand.'
'Really? Thailand is a beautiful country. Many fine temples and the countryside. A lot of history that would be of interest to you. Obviously, the one that stands out is Kanchanaburi, you must have heard of the bridge over the River Kwai and the death railway to Burma. You should visit many museums and war cemeteries. You won't be far from Erawan National Park. It has seven levels of waterfalls.'
'Sounds interesting, I'd love to visit the bridge of the River Kwai. It's a famous film.'
'So, I hear. You should spend some time in Bangkok, it very busy, but has great markets, the best street food. The Grand Palace is certainly worth a visit, and the Temple of the Emerald Buddha, the most sacred Buddhist temple in Thailand.'
'Sounds fascinating. I'm Bob, by the way.'
'Hi Bob, my name is Porn.'
'Porn? That's an unusual name.' Bob did his utmost not to laugh.
'Quite common in Thailand.'
'Is it? You speak very good English, Porn.'
'My father is English, I just come for a visit. I live in a place called Chiang Mai; you must have heard of it?'
'Yes, of course,' lied Bob.
'I live in a place called Ipswich.'
'I not know this place. My father live in Dorset.'
'I know Dorset, nice part of the UK.'
'So, where you stay in Thailand, Bob?'
'I'm going to visit my best friend, he lives in a place called Pattaya, have you heard of it?'
'Yes, unfortunately, I have.' Bob noticed a slightly disdainful look on Porn's face and a complete change in attitude towards him. On that note, she faced forward, opened a magazine and started to read, bringing a stop to any more conversation.

'I'm just going to see, Tom.'
'Okay, darling. You happy your friend coming?'
'I am sweetheart. He has been a very good friend to me for many years.'
'I hope he like Thailand.'

'I'm sure he will. Don't forget it's winter in the UK now, he is coming to a beautiful climate. I'm just a bit concerned about this girl he's been talking to online.'
'Ka, he need to be careful. I speak with girl when he come here. I find out if she good lady or not.'
'Thanks, sweetheart, I won't be long.'

Tony knocked on his neighbour's door, and Tom's wife Suk, opened up.
'Hi, Suk. Is Tom in?'
'Ka, come in, Tony.' As Suk opened the door, Tony could see Tom sitting at the table, earphones on and watching something on his laptop. Seeing Tony, he removed the headphones.
'Hello, Tony. Everything alright?'
'Yes, fine.'
'What Pooki doing?' Asked Suk.
'Oh, she is just watching TV.'
'I go and see her.'
'Yes, she'd like that.' Pooki and Suk had become good friends since they moved into the complex. After she left, Tom pulled a couple of beers out of the fridge.
'Here you are, mate, what can I do for you?'
'I have my friend, Bob, coming over tomorrow afternoon. I'm not sure what he's going to do yet, but I wanted to double-check if those apartments are still available, just in case.'
'The one on the second floor definitely is. Mind you, he'll want twenty-five thousand for a month's rent.'
'That's okay, still a lot cheaper than a hotel.'
'He'll be lucky to get a hotel room; most will be fully booked over the Christmas period.'
'That's what I was thinking. He sort of sprung it on me the other day that he's been talking to some Thai girl online, so I'm not sure what his plans are. I'm going to the airport tomorrow afternoon to meet him. I'm not sure if he will be coming with me, coming here with this girl, or going off somewhere else with the girl?'
'Online dating? I tell you something Tony, at the bar I do the quiz, there's a lovely girl that works there. But she has four different men sponsoring her. She gets money from all of them, and now and again she disappears for a few weeks when one of them comes for a visit,

then she's back at the bar working. She's making a small fortune. She told me she meets them on a dating site. You know the worst of it, she has a Thai husband and a kid. She sends money home every month, so the husband is very happy.'

'Christ, do you think the husband knows what she does?'

'Most probably, but the money's coming in, so he's not bothered. How old is your mate?

'Same age as me, coming up for fifty-six.'

'Well, he's old enough to know better.'

'He is, but as we know, once you step off that plane in Bangkok, all sensible reasoning goes out of the window.'

'Very true. You've been extremely lucky, Tony. Meeting Pooki as you did. Unfortunately, I had my fingers burnt a couple of times before I met Suk.'

'Yes, I have been lucky. Mind you, my luck will run out at the end of April when I move to the village.'

'Yes, that's something I would struggle with. You need to make yourself comfortable up there, Tony.'

'I intend to. I'll sort out some air conditioning, internet and cable TV. I'll take the mountain bike and scooter. I will most probably get some dumbbells so I can do a bit of a workout. At the end of the day, I will do my best to make it work, for Pooki's sake. She's in her element when she's home. She becomes that country girl, and if she's happy, well then I'm happy.'

'Good on you, Tony. You'll need to spread the day out, get yourself into a bit of routine.'

'I will. I shall study the language, which will help me communicate a bit better. If I can't settle, then we'll have to come back. But like I said, I want it to work, so I will give it my best shot.'

'Bet it seems strange becoming a dad again.'

'It certainly does, and that will keep me occupied as well. I want our daughter to speak English as well as Thai.'

'Absolutely, my friend Dave has a three-year-old son who doesn't speak a word of English. The kid stays with his grandmother in the village. How sad is that, he can't communicate with his own son.'

'Well, that's something I won't allow to happen.'

'Good on you, mate.'

At Heathrow, the giant plane bound for Thailand was about to take off. Bob was surprised at the number of empty seats. There was no one sitting next to Porn, and he couldn't help but smile to himself as he watched Porn, who had her eyes closed and gripping the armrests tightly as they hurtled along the runway. He felt a sense of relief as the plane soared into the air. Looking out of the window, he watched the lights slowly getting smaller. A few minutes later, the seatbelt light went out and Bob loosened his so it wasn't so tight. As a stewardess walked past, Porn asked her something in Thai. The stewardess replied, and Porn undid her seatbelt and moved across to the empty seat. Bob watched as she blew a neck support up and placed it behind her head. Then she pulled out an eye mask from her bag, placed it over her eyes and reclined her seat slightly. Bob guessed that was the end of any further conversation with her on this flight.

Undeterred, Bob wasn't going to let a stuck-up Thai woman spoil his trip. When the stewardess came around with drinks, Bob had red wine and a lager. After the food, he tried to settle down and grab some sleep. Unfortunately, this proved to be difficult as he was feeling excited and nervous. Checking his watch, he worked out they had just past the halfway mark.

"Christ, another six hours," he mumbled to himself. Plugging in his earphones, he started to watch an episode of the American comedy "Friends." Luckily, he only managed the first ten minutes before he drifted off to sleep.

Pooki had walked down to the truck with Tony.
'You know where to go, darling?'
'Yes, sweetheart. It's motorway all the way.'
'I worry you, should have left earlier.'
'You don't need to worry, I'll be fine. I'm not leaving late; I have plenty of time.'
'Maybe I come.'
'There's no need. The last thing you need is to be bounced up and down for two hours, and two hours back. You put your feet up and relax.'
'What time your friend come?'
'His flight lands around 4 pm.' Tony checked his watch.

'It's 2 pm now, so I should get there just as he lands. It will take him another hour to get through immigration and collect his suitcase. I'll have time to grab a coffee while I wait.'
'I think you leave late, take your time, no racing.'
'I won't race, honestly, I have plenty of time. Right, I'd better get going. I'll ring you once I get to the airport.'
'Ka, make sure you do.' Tony kissed Pooki on the cheek and hugged her. He then climbed into the truck and started the engine. Giving Pooki a wave, he slowly drove off. As he looked in the rear-view mirror, he could see Pooki waddling back to the complex. Ten minutes later, as he drove along the Sukhumvit Road towards the motorway, the traffic suddenly ground to a halt. Tony let out a sigh; he was used to this type of hold-up, but could have done without it today.

As Tony sat in traffic, Bob was woken by a stewardess who was serving breakfast. It took a minute for him to pull himself together. His seating companion, Porn, was tucking into her food and smiled at him.
'You sleep a long time?'
'No, not really. It took me a long time to get to sleep.' Bob checked his watch.
'Blimey, it's 7 am.'
'It's 2 pm actually. We should land in a couple of hours.'
'I'd better adjust my watch.' Bob fiddled with his watch as he played with the rubbery breakfast.
'Seems funny eating breakfast at two in the afternoon.'
'Ka, you need to try and stay awake tonight, try and fall in with Thai time. Otherwise, you will feel jet-lagged for days. Listen, I've been thinking about you. Make sure you venture out from Pattaya. There are many nice places to see. Try the street food, you will enjoy. Buses are cheap, so you have no excuse not to see some of the country while you're here.'
'I will, Porn. Thanks for the advice.' Bob didn't understand the need to lie to the girl; he had no intention of jumping on buses and touring around. He guessed that after her reaction to Pattaya, he didn't want her thinking he was a sex tourist.
'Your friend picking you up at the airport?'
'Yes, hopefully, he'll be there.' Bob thought it best not to mention Mooka.

'What about you, are you getting picked up?'
'No, I get bus to Don Muang airport, then get flight to Chiang Mai.'
'I didn't realise Thailand was so big.'
'Ka, take one hour to fly to Chiang Mai.'
'Well, don't go squeezing those armrests too tight.'

Tony was beginning to get a bit concerned, he'd been held up for over an hour on the outskirts of Pattaya, and it was coming up to 3 pm, and he was a good hour and a half from the airport. He just prayed there wouldn't be any more delays on the route. His mobile sprang to life, and he knew who was calling him without looking.
'Hello, sweetheart.'
'You at airport?'
'Not quite, had a little delay getting out of Pattaya.'
'You not be late for your friend, darling.'
'I won't be late; it will take him an hour to get through immigration and find his suitcase.'
'No racing, darling.'
'I'm not racing, don't worry. I'll speak to you later.'
Tony cut the call and put his foot down.

Bob's ears started to feel pain as the plane descended. Porn, seeing his discomfort, opened a small tin of boiled sweets and offered one to Bob. 'Suck on one of these; it will help.' Bob popped a sweet in and said thank you. Looking out of the window, he caught his first glimpse of Bangkok. He looked across at Porn, who was already gripping the armrests and had her eyes screwed tightly closed. Looking back out of the window, he watched with amazement as this huge plane slowly came into land. A couple of thuds and the noise of the reverse thrusters signalled a safe landing. After what seemed only a few seconds, the plane slowed to the taxing runway speed.
Bob looked across to Porn, who was still gripping the armrests. Tapping her arm, she turned and looked at him.
'Thanks for the sweets.' Bob passed the tin back.
'You're welcome.'
'I take it you don't like flying?'
'No, but I force myself; otherwise, I wouldn't go anywhere.'
'Well, we're here safe and sound, so you can relax now.'

'Thank you, and welcome to Thailand.'
'I can't believe that I've left a cold, wet England and I'm now looking out at a clear blue sky and the sun is shining.'
'Ka, I'm always happy to be back home. I hope you have bought some summer clothes with you. You won't be needing that.' Porn pointed to the sweater Bob was wearing. He thought he would travel in the jeans and sweater he'd recently purchased after the store refused to give him a refund.
'No problem, I have a t-shirt on underneath.'
'That's a very nice sweater.'
'Thank you.'
'It reminds me of something my dad would wear.'
'Really!!' Bob wasn't amused by the put-down.

Tony was still making slow progress towards the airport. Now and again, the traffic would come to a complete standstill. Checking his watch, he knew he was going to be cutting it fine to be there on time. He was hoping his best friend was still on the aeroplane.

As Tony checked his watch for the hundredth time, Bob was standing in a long queue waiting to get through immigration. He could see Porn in another queue that was for Thais only. He gave her a small wave as she looked over. She didn't respond as she approached the desk. His queue hadn't moved as he watched her disappear towards the baggage reclaim without a glance back. Looking around, he noticed the majority of Thais in uniform carried a gun. This was quite unnerving for Bob. At a snail's pace, he slowly made his way to the passport control desk. Eventually, he was next to be seen. A Thai man in uniform pointed at Bob's feet. There was a red line which you were meant to stand behind, and Bob was six inches over it. The man didn't smile, and Bob quickly shuffled back.
'Bloody jobsworth,' came a comment from behind Bob.
'Yes, but he has a gun,' joked Bob without looking behind at the person who made the comment.
The person in front went through, and Bob walked up to the desk and handed his passport over to a woman who didn't smile. She scanned his passport and then stared at Bob. Eventually, she stamped a page

and handed the passport back. Bob let out a sigh of relief as he headed to retrieve his suitcase.

Checking on the large screens, he found what number conveyor he needed. After what seemed like a sponsored walk, Bob found the right conveyor. He knew it was the right one without checking the number, he could see Porn standing with a trolley waiting for her case.

'We meet again.' Bob stood next to his former seating companion.

'Ka, bags taking long time to come through.'

'Oh well, I might go and freshen up while I'm waiting.' Porn didn't answer, so Bob left her and followed the sign for the toilets. He'd treated himself to a nice aftershave and body spray at Heathrow airport, so he decided to wash his face and dab the nice smelly on in case Mooka was waiting for him. Feeling his stomach gurgling, he thought it best to relieve himself while he was at it. He hadn't been to the toilet since he'd left the flat. So, finding an empty cubicle, Bob locked himself in.

Ten minutes later, smelling nice and chewing a mouth-freshening mint, Bob headed back to the conveyor. He was surprised when the crowd of people who were there when he had left had now gone. Only half a dozen or so were now waiting for their luggage. As Bob approached, his distinctive red suitcase came into view. Quickly grabbing a trolley, he hurried over to the conveyor but was a few seconds late as his case disappeared out of view.

'It come round again,' said a man in a blue uniform. Bob walked towards the other side of the conveyor, and sure enough, his case came back into view.

Pulling out his comb, he had a quick flick-through before heading towards the exit.

As Bob was on the escalator heading towards the arrivals lounge, Tony was taking the exit off the motorway towards the airport. He saw the sign telling him he had 3 kilometres to go and again put his foot down. He half-smiled with a sense of relief when he followed the signs for short-term parking. He checked his watch again, it was 5.15 pm. After collecting a ticket, he drove into the multi-story car park.

'Bollocks,' he called out to himself as he hunted for a parking space. After driving up three floors, he eventually saw a car about to drive out. Putting his hazard lights on, he waited for the car to pull out.

'Come on, go.' Tony called out. The car slowly edged out, and Tony pulled past the space and reversed in. This turned out to be a bit of an issue, as the space was just about big enough to squeeze the truck in. Once he had backed in, he had the problem of trying to get out of the truck.

"Jesus Christ," he mumbled as he tried to squeeze himself out of the vehicle without the door hitting the car next to him. Looking at the passenger door, he realised he had a bit more room on that side to manoeuvre himself out. So, he climbed over the seat and managed with some difficulty to get out of the truck.

Breaking into a jog, Tony hurried to the arrivals lounge. It was a fair distance from where he'd parked the truck, so by the time he entered the building, he was breaking into a sweat.

Searching in his wallet, he pulled out Bob's flight number. Looking up at one of the arrivals boards, he could see Bob's flight had landed at 3.55 pm. Checking his watch, he could see it was 5.30 pm. He guessed he must have come through by now. The airport was heaving with people, and he hoped he wasn't too late to meet his friend. He decided to check the bars and restaurants. He kept telling himself he wasn't that late, and he prayed Bob wouldn't go off without saying hello. Just as he started to look, his phone rang. For a half second, he thought it might have been Bob, but when he looked at the number, he knew it was Pooki.

'Hello sweetheart, I'm at the airport.'

'You meet your friend, Bob?'

'Err ... Not yet, the airport is very busy. He may have come through, so I'm just about to check the bars and restaurants.'

'Okay, darling, listen to your wife next time. You get to airport late.'

'Okay, but it's not my fault I'm late; there were many hold-ups. I'll call you in a while. I'd better get looking for him.' Hanging up, he started to search the restaurant and bar outlets; there weren't that many, so if he was in one of them, he would surely find him.

As he walked towards an open bar, a familiar voice called out behind him.

'Better late than never.'

Tony turned around and saw his best friend standing there.
'Bloody hell, aren't you a bit hot in that sweater?'
'Not really, I think it feels quite cool in here.'
'That's the aircon, mate. Wait until you step outside. It's good to see you, Bob.'
The two men shook hands and hugged. Bob pulled the sweater off and wrapped it around his waist. Tony couldn't help but notice a large gold chain around his neck.
'Bloody hell, it's the medallion man.'
'You like it, I thought I'd treat myself.'
'Not the sort of thing to wear out here, Bob. Temptation to muggers.'
'Okay, I'll keep it covered up.'
'I would, and if you go out anywhere, leave it hidden up.' Tony looked at his friend and could see he'd changed in appearance.
'Have you lost weight?'
'I joined a gym, Tone. By the look of you, you've put some on?'
'It's the beer, Bob. But I can see the gym is doing you good, you're looking fit, mate. Just need to get some sun on that milky body of yours.'
'Cheers, Tone, that's what I intend to do. A month of sun, sea and sex.'
'In that order, I hope?'
'Not necessarily, Tone.'
'How was the flight?'
'Not too bad, considering the amount of time it takes. I had a nice Thai lady sitting next to me, all was going well until she asked me who I was meeting at the airport. As soon as I mentioned you and that you lived in Pattaya, she frowned at me and moved seats.' The two men started to laugh.
'Well, I won't take it personally, and you're right, it's certainly a long flight.'
'So, where's your bag, Bob?'
'Over there in that restaurant, Mooka and her sister Nan are looking after it.'
'Oh, she showed up then?'
'Yes, they were waiting for me as I came down the escalator. She's had a few problems at home, which is why she couldn't contact me. But we spoke just before I came here, and all is good. She said she would be here waiting for me, and sure enough, she was. I tell you, Tone, she's

more beautiful in the flesh. Come on, come and say hello.' Tony followed his friend to the restaurant where the two women were eating some Thai food.

'Mooka, this is my friend, Tone.' Mooka stood up and gave Tony a wai.

'Sawadee ka.'

'Sawadee khab, Mooka, nice to meet you.' Tony immediately agreed with Bob's assessment; she was beautiful. Mooka sat back down and continued to eat.

'Err, Mooka doesn't speak much English, Tone.'

'I see, won't that be a bit of a problem?'

'No, Nan speaks very good English, don't you, Nan?'

'Ka, I speak English.' Nan stood up and also did a wai to Tony.

'Nice to meet you, Tone.' Tony stared at Nan; she was as tall as him. He felt he'd been in Thailand long enough to spot what he suspected was a ladyboy. He looked at this tall, beautiful woman and wasn't completely sure of his suspicions.

'Nice to meet you too, Nan.' Tony held his hand out, and Nan did a limp type of handshake.

'So, have you had to drive far?'

'Ka, we live near Chiang Mai.'

'Wow, you have driven a long way,' interrupted Bob.

'I sat next to a girl on the plane who was from Chiang Mai; she was getting a flight there from another airport in Bangkok.'

'Really? That sounds like a long drive.'

Tony was oblivious to where Chiang Mai was situated in Thailand. He'd heard of it but didn't know where it was.

'Ka, it is a long drive, I just go toilet,' Nan stood up, and Tony tried to discreetly look for the tell-tale signs that Nan was born a boy. Unfortunately, the shoulders looked quite small and feminine, which normally gave the game away. Although he noticed her hands seemed quite big. Nan smiled at Tony as she tried to get past him. Standing up, Tony purposely left his hand down by his side as Nan squeezed past. It was at that moment, as she brushed past, that he felt a small bulge in Nan's groin area. Nan smiled and gave a seductive look to Tony that made him feel uneasy. This development had left him in a bit of a dilemma, as to how he was going to break the news to his best friend about Mooka's so-called sister.

Bob sat there oblivious, grinning like a cat that got the cream.

## Chapter 7

After ordering some more drinks, Bob tried to explain the situation to Tony.
'Look, Tone, I've promised Mooka that I'll go and visit her family first, then Nan will kindly drive us to Pattaya in a few days. Bob was holding Mooka's hand, and Tony could tell he was already smitten with her.
Tony wasn't the sort of person to skirt around an issue.
'I understand that, but I think you should spend a few days getting to know her before you head off to the great unknown. Not being funny, but you are not thinking this through. You're in a foreign country, you won't have a clue where you are. What's the big rush to meet her family? You're here for a month after all?'
'I hear what you're saying, Tone, but I've already promised Mooka I'd go to see her family first. I can't go back on that, can I? It won't look good in her eyes, will it?'
Tony looked at Bob and tried to suppress his feeling of wanting to slap his friend around the head. Instead, he turned his attention to Mooka's alleged sister.
'You been to Pattaya before, Nan?'
'Ka, many time. I work in bar on Walking Street.'
"I bet you did," Tony thought to himself.
'You must have been a very popular *lady* at the bar. You are very beautiful.'
'Easy tiger, you're a married man.' Joked Bob.
'Ka, thank you.' Nan gave Tony a wai. There was something about Nan he didn't like.
'Well, I've sorted out a nice apartment at my complex when you do eventually come, so you won't have to worry about booking a hotel. Pooki wants to meet you, and obviously Mooka too. I'm sure we can find a place for you to stay as well, Nan.'
'No need, I have many friend I can stay with in Pattaya.'
'Okay, well that's sorted then.' Tony was not only disappointed, but he was also furious with himself for getting to the airport late. He knew he would have had a better chance of getting Bob to Pattaya straight away if he'd got to him first.
Bob continued to sit there like a lovesick teenager.

'Isn't she a beauty, Tone?' Mooka just kept smiling but sat in silence; she didn't make any effort to speak, and this also worried Tony. Something about the whole situation didn't sit right with him. Bob could see his friend wasn't overly happy.

'I'll ring you, Tone. I don't want you worrying about me.'

'Okay, but you need to get a Thai SIM card for your phone.'

'Do I? What do I need one of them for?'

'Because your network will probably not work out here, and if it does, it will cost you a fortune to make calls.'

'Okay, that makes sense. Where will I get one of these Thai SIM cards from?'

'You'll probably get one in here somewhere, give Nan some money and she'll try and get one for you, won't you, Nan?'

'Ka, no problem, Khun Tony.' Nan spoke to Mooka in Thai, and the two of them stood up. Bob opened his travel bag and pulled out an envelope which was stuffed with cash. Pulling out a 1000 baht note, he handed it to Nan.

'Is that enough?'

'Ka, I get you SIM with credit.' The two so-called sisters walked off, allowing Tony to speak candidly to his friend.

'Look, Bob, I won't lie to you, I'm worried about you going off with these two so-called women.'

'Don't call them that, honestly, I'll be alright, Tone. Mooka's lovely, you have to remember I've been in contact with her for months, and Nan, well, as you can see, she's a nice girl. After a few days meeting her family, I'll be with you and Pooki in Pattaya, so don't worry.'

'You think Nan's a nice girl? I'm afraid you're in for a shock with that one, mate.'

'I'm not worried about Nan, she comes across as a very nice girl, and as you can see, Mooka is beautiful, and what's not to like about her? She's the one I've come out to see and I care about her.' Tony could tell he was on a loser with Bob regarding Mooka, so he changed tack. 'Okay, well, you shouldn't be carrying that sort of cash around with you either. How much have you got in there?'

'I ordered five thousand pounds worth of Thai money at the bank last week.'

'For Christ's sake, Bob. That's way too much to be carrying around, I told you that you can use the ATMs here.'

'I know, but when I inquired, they said each withdrawal is very expensive. So, I thought, I'm here for a month and I want to enjoy myself. What I don't spend, I'll keep for my next visit.'

'Okay, I can understand the logic, but you're taking a chance carrying all that cash around with you. And fancy flashing the envelope in front of those two.'

'She's my girlfriend, Tone. She won't let anything happen to me.'

'You don't know that, be honest, you don't know either of them really, do you? The one you thought you were chatting to for months doesn't speak a bloody word of English for Christ's sake. It's been the other one, Nan, that you've been talking to all this time, I bet you.'

'Yes, I know that, but she's only been translating what Mooka tells her. What I don't understand is why you don't like her sister?'

'Not being funny, Bob, I doubt very much that they are sisters, in fact ……' Before Tony could break the news about Nan's sexuality, they returned holding a small packet containing a Thai SIM card.

'I do for you, Khun Bob, pass phone.' Bob pulled his phone out and passed it to Nan.

'What's with the Khun bit, Tone?'

'It's the polite way of saying your name.' The two men watched Nan quickly swap the cards, a bit too quickly for Tony's liking.

'Here,' Nan passed the phone back to Bob and held the UK SIM card in her hand. Tony relieved her of it.

'You need to keep this UK SIM card safe, Bob. Put it back in your phone when you go home.'

'Right, I'll tuck it in the zip-up part of my wallet.' Bob struggled to pull his wallet out of his jeans pocket. Tony was horrified to see a thick wad of pound notes bulging out from inside it. Bob tucked his UK SIM card inside and put his wallet away. Tony noticed the quick glance Mooka and Nan gave each other on seeing the thickness of the wallet.

'What's your new number, Bob?'

'Err … I'm not sure. I think that's it written on the side of the packet.' Bob struggled to read the number without his reading glasses; he was too vain to get them out in front of Mooka yet, so he passed it over to Tony. Pulling his phone out, Tony keyed in the number that was written down, then tried ringing it. A few seconds later, Bob's phone sprang to life and the theme from the Benny Hill show sang out.'

'Benny Hill? Really?'

'I know, I need to change it. I would if I knew how.' Tony looked at his friend and remembered he wasn't good with computers or mobile phones.

'I'll sort it out when you come to Pattaya. Right, save my number, Bob, just in case you need to contact me in an emergency. Plus, you can let me know when you're heading to Pattaya.'

'Emergency? Don't worry, Tone. I've packed a big box of protection.' Bob laughed to himself. Tony, feeling slightly embarrassed by Bob's admission, kept a straight face.

'Here, I'll save your number under Tony Thai.'

'Yes, very witty. I've saved you under Bob Gullible.'

Nan spoke to Mooka and then announced they wanted to leave.

'We should get going, Khun Bob. Long drive to Mama's home.'

'Yes, of course.' Nan called over to the waitress for the bill.

'How about a photo before you leave?' Tony felt reluctant to let his friend go.

'Good idea, Tone. Can you take one of Mooka and me?' Bob passed his phone to Tony.

Putting his arm around her, Bob had a beaming smile. Tony took a couple of photos and passed the phone back. Pulling his phone out, he went to take another photo.

'You get in the photo too, Nan. I want to show my wife a photo of you two beautiful sisters.'

'I not look good, Khun Tony.' Nan was reluctant to have her photo taken, but Tony was insistent.

'You look beautiful, Nan. Now, don't be shy.' Nan, not smiling, squeezed next to Bob but looked away from the phone. This reluctance for the photo only furthered Tony's suspicions.

'All done.' As Nan faced forward, Tony discreetly took another photo and quickly put his phone away.

The waitress walked over and gave the bill to Bob.

'How much is that, Tone?' Tony checked the bill.

'Nine hundred and fifty baht. About twenty pounds.'

'I thought it was cheap here?' Joked Bob.

'Airport prices. Give her a thousand note, that will cover the tip as well.' Once again, Bob pulled the envelope out from his travel bag and handed over a one-thousand-baht note.

"You're a mugging waiting to happen," thought Tony as Bob stuffed the envelope back into his travel bag.
'Well, Tone, thanks ever so much for coming to the airport to see me, all being well, I'll see you in a few days. I'll ring you when I'm on my way to Pattaya.'
'Ring me tomorrow, I want to make sure you get to Chiang Mai safe and sound.'
'Okay, and stop worrying, I'm in good hands.' Mooka held onto Bob's hand and Nan started to push the trolley with Bob's suitcase on it. Sticking his hand out to say goodbye, Bob was surprised when Tony's hand stayed by his side.
'I'm not staying here, Bob. I'll come to the car with you, I've got to get the truck anyway.'
'Of course, you have. What am I like? I forgot about that?' Nan said something to Mooka in Thai, Tony would have bet money it wasn't anything complimentary.

After a long walk, Nan stopped the trolley by a white Toyota.
'This my car.'
'Very nice,' Bob was impressed with the large salon.
'Christ, how hot is it?' This was Bob's first experience of the Thailand heat.
'I did tell you that you wouldn't need that sweater and jeans.' Bob had thought about changing into shorts, but he was reluctant to expose his lily-white legs yet.
'Car has aircon, Khun Bob.'
'Thank God for that.'
Nan opened the boot and lifted Bob's suitcase in with ease. This was another tell-tale sign to Tony. Nan was too strong for a slender woman. Mooka gave Tony a wai and said goodbye in Thai.
Bob managed to shake Tony's hand this time.
'Stop worrying, mate, I'm going on an adventure, I'll ring you tomorrow.' Bob hugged his friend, then climbed into the back of the car with Mooka.
'Make sure you ring me.' Called out Tony, unfortunately, it fell on deaf ears as Bob was more interested in his travelling companion. Nan closed the boot lid and stood in front of Tony.
'Sawadee Khab, Nan, it's been nice to meet you,' he lied.

'Sawadee ka, Khun, Tone.' Nan did a wai and then climbed into the driver's seat.
'Safe journey, guys.' Tony stood back and waved as Nan slowly pulled away. Nearly an afterthought, Tony quickly pulled his phone out and managed to take a photo of the Toyota's number plate. As he went in search of the truck, he had a lump in his throat and a bad feeling in his stomach. As he reached the truck, his phone started to ring.
'Hello sweetheart, I'm just leaving the airport now.'
'You okay, darling, you see your friend?'
'Yes, I've seen him, he's not coming to Pattaya yet. I'll tell you all about it when I get home.'
'I wait at pool with Suk and Tom. No racing, darling.'
'No, I won't race.'

An hour into the drive, Bob was feeling great. Mooka was holding his hand and had her head resting on his shoulder.
'You, handsome man.' She whispered in his ear.
'Thank you, I know you do not speak much English, but I will teach you.'
Mooka said something to Nan, to which Nan first replied, then spoke to Bob.
'Mooka say she very happy you are here. She say if you want to sleep, you can. We drive through the night.'
'Look, Nan, if you get tired, stop at a hotel, I don't mind paying for a room. It's been a long drive for you.'
'Ka, thank you. It very long. I see how I feel later. I will stop and we can eat. If I feel too tired to drive, we find hotel.'
Mooka put her hand on Bob's thigh. The hotel idea was becoming more attractive by the second.

After a much quicker drive home than his journey to the airport, Tony parked the truck, and as he walked towards the complex, he could see Pooki sitting next to the pool with Tom and Suk. This was something they would do occasionally in the evening.
'Over here, darling.' Pooki called out, and Tony walked over. Tom stood up.
'Here you are, mate, get this down you.' Tom pulled out a bottle of Leo from his cooler bag and passed it to Tony.
'Cheers, Tom, I need this.' Tony took a long swig.

'Your friend not come with you, darling?'
'No, the soppy bastard has gone off to Chiang Mai with two women he thinks are sisters. Strangers that he's met for the first time today. Let me rephrase that. He's gone off with a woman and a ladyboy.'
'Darling, you always think women are ladyboys.' Pooki was laughing.
'Okay, I admit I sometimes get it wrong. But this one was taller than me.' Tony thought it best not to mention brushing his hand along Nan's thigh for confirmation.
'Some women are tall.' Pointed out, Suk.
'Hang on a minute.' Tony pulled his phone out and found the photo he had taken of Nan. Passing the phone to Pooki, he asked.
'Well, am I wrong?' Pooki looked, then passed the phone to Suk.
'Let's have a look,' asked Tom. Suk showed him the photo.
'It's hard to say with this photo, both are very attractive though. Is that your mate, Bob?'
'Yes, that's him. The girl next to him is his internet date, Mooka. It turns out she hardly speaks a word of English.'
'Well, how's he been communicating with her then?'
'Exactly, Tom. The one I think is a ladyboy, Nan, she speaks good English. I'm guessing she's the one who's been doing all the internet chatting. She is a ladyboy, isn't she?' Tony turned to Pooki for confirmation.
'Ka, I think you right, darling.' Pooki said something in Thai to Suk, which resulted in them both roaring with laughter.
'Share the joke,' asked Tom. Suk explained.
'Tony say she ladyboy. Ladyboy a man, so she a he.' The two girls started to laugh again.
'Honestly, you two laugh at the silliest things. So, Tony, you couldn't persuade him to come here first?'
'No, unfortunately, I got to the airport a bit late, so, by the time I got there, they'd already got to him and he'd promised to go and see the family first.'
'I thought you were cutting it a bit fine to get to the airport for four o'clock.' Remarked Tom. Pooki gave Tony a "told you so" look, which he completely ignored.
'I left in plenty of time, Tom. It didn't help that I sat in traffic on Sukhumvit for over an hour.'

'Precisely, always want to give yourself a bit of extra time, that road is notorious for hold-ups.' Tony didn't comment; he knew he was on a loser.

'So, what did your friend Bob say about the ladyboy? He must have realised they couldn't possibly be sisters.'

'He doesn't know.'

'What, you didn't say anything to him about it?' Tony could feel the three pairs of eyes staring right at him.

'Well … I didn't get a chance, to be honest. I mean, I could hardly say in front of them, oh Bob, by the way, they can't be sisters as Nan is a man, could I?'

'You should have got him on his own, Tony.'

'I didn't get a chance,' he lied.

'That's one hell of a drive to Chiang Mai from Bangkok.'

'Yes, it is.' Tony didn't have a clue where Chiang Mai was, but he had gathered by now that it was a long way from Bangkok.

'How long would that take to drive, Tom?'

'Whoa, hard to say. At least ten hours, I'd have thought, more like twelve with the traffic.'

'Something doesn't add up here. That Nan said she drove down from Chiang Mai, if we gave her the benefit of the doubt and said they did it in eleven hours with stops. That means they must have left home around 5 am, maybe earlier. She drove all the way to Bangkok. Waited for, Bob, and is now driving maybe eleven hours back.'

'Why they not stay in a hotel in Bangkok tonight, darling?'

'That my sweetheart is what's worrying me. Why were they so keen to get him away from me? Common sense would tell you that's too far to drive in one day.'

'Have you got his phone number?' Asked Tom.

'Yes, I made sure he got a Thai SIM card.'

'Darling, why you not call him, see he okay or not.'

'I don't know, I don't want to pester him.'

'You're not pestering him, Tony. Look, you're obviously worried about him. Just ring and ask how the journey is going. It will give you peace of mind.'

'I don't know, Tom. They've only been going for a couple of hours. Plus, he said he'd ring me in the morning.'

'You'll sleep better if you speak to him tonight.' Pointed out, Tom.

'Yes, you're right, sod it.' Tony picked up his phone and called Bob's number. After about two minutes, he hung up.
'Shit ... There's no answer?'

Bob's phone was ringing, but he'd put the phone in his travel bag that was in the boot of the car. Nan had the radio on, so there was no chance he would hear it.
Looking out of the window, he saw a sign for Nakhon Sawan, which meant nothing to him. Mooka was asleep, leaning against him.
'How are you doing, Nan?'
'Ka, I feel okay, maybe stop soon, get some gasoline and have something to eat.'
'Sounds good. I'll give you some money for gasoline and food. It's very kind of you to pick me up.'
'No problem, Mooka, my sister, I do anything for her.'
'Yes, she is lovely. You have a boyfriend, Nan?'
'Ka, many.' Nan started to laugh.
'Well, why doesn't that surprise me? You're beautiful like Mooka.'
'Khob Khun ka.' Bob didn't have a clue what that meant, but guessed it was some form of thank you.
The only concern Bob had was that Nan drove very fast. He wasn't sure if this was normal in Thailand. He remembered Tony telling him you took your life in your hands every time you ventured out on the roads.
'This is a very nice car.'
'Ka, present from my ex-boyfriend.'
'Really? Wow, that was generous of him.'
'He big liar, tell me he leave his wife and bring me to Germany. It not happen.'
'Oh, I'm sorry to hear that, Nan.'
'It okay, he scared I show wife photos of him and me together. So, he buy me car to keep quiet.'
'Okay, well, you came out of it alright then?'
'Ka, but I still send photos to wife after I get car. She get very angry with him and kick him out. He not happy man. He come looking for me, say he going kill me. I ready for him, but he never show.' Nan leaned over and opened her handbag up. Suddenly she was waving a gun around.

'He want to kill me, he in for big shock.' Nan started to laugh. Bob didn't know how to respond to that one. He'd had his own experience of a woman scorned when his ex, Janice, threw a rock through his window that time. But that sounded mild compared to Nan's way of dealing with man trouble. He decided to keep quiet. However, he did start to think that he didn't want to get on the wrong side of this Nan.

'Try his number again, Tony.'
'Something's not right here, Tom. I knew it, I bloody knew it.' Tony rang Bob's phone again.
'No, he's not picking up. Do you think I should call the police? I have the car's number plate details. I took a photo of it.'
'You took a photo of the number plate?'
'I did, there was no way I could remember a Thai number plate, it's all googly gook to me.'
'Me too. Listen, Tony, I know you're concerned about your friend, but I think it's a tad early to be calling the police. I mean, what would you say? My friend won't answer his phone. He's been missing for two hours.'
'Three hours, alright, Tom, I get your point.' Pooki and Suk strolled back from the shop outside the complex with some more cold beers.
'You try ring friend, darling?'
'Just now, still no answer.'
'Maybe he sleep in car?'
'I don't know, even if he's asleep, he should hear his phone. It has that annoying Benny Hill tune.' That comment meant nothing to Pooki and Suk.
'Have a couple more beers, Tony. Go to bed and I'm sure he'll answer the phone in the morning.'
'Maybe battery finish.' Suk had thought of an explanation as to why Tony's friend hadn't answered the phone.
'Yes, maybe that could be it, thanks, Suk.' Tony smiled, but inside he couldn't shake off the bad feelings he was experiencing.

Bob was just drifting off when Nan called out.
'We stop here, Khun Bob. Get gasoline, then eat.'

'Okay, sounds good.' He answered with a yawn. Nan had pulled into a large service station and stopped opposite a gasoline pump where a young female assistant stood ready.

'Can you open the boot please, Nan? My money is in my travel bag.' Nan reached down and flicked the boot release. Mooka groaned as Bob gently pushed her off his shoulder.

'Sorry, baby.' Bob tried to be as gentle as he could. Stepping out of the car, he felt the heat hit him again. Lifting the lid, he pulled out some Thai money from his travel bag but didn't check his phone. Climbing back into the rear of the car, he passed over some Thai money.

'Here, take this, Nan. Should cover the gasoline and food.' Bob handed over five thousand baht, about three thousand baht too much.

'Khob Khun ka.' Bob was surprised Nan hadn't turned the engine off as the young girl filled the tank. He guessed it was because of keeping the aircon running. A couple of minutes later, Nan paid for the gasoline. After she received the change, she drove towards the food outlets and parked.

Mooka was still half asleep, but not for much longer, for Nan turned around and shook her. After some groaning, she opened her eyes.

'Come on, sleepy head, we're going to eat.' Bob tried the gentler approach.

'Ka, you handsome man.' Mooka climbed out of the car, leaving Bob to wonder if that was the only English sentence she knew.'

Back in Pattaya, the two women had gone to bed, leaving Tony and Tom by the swimming pool.

'I suppose I'd better go up myself after this one.'

'I make you right, Tom. I'm beginning to feel half pissed.'

'Couple of lightweights, I thought you'd help me out with this.' Tony and Tom turned around simultaneously. Standing there in just a pair of shorts and flip flops, holding a bottle of brandy in one hand and a beer in the other was Barry.

'Bloody hell, Barry, how long have you been here?' Asked Tom.

'Oh, all of about thirty seconds.'

'I mean here at the complex.'

'We got dropped off about seven.'

'Where's Alan?' Tony looked around for Barry's partner in crime.

'He'll be here in a minute, you know him, he's got to tart himself up before we go to the bars.'
'He's as bad as a woman,' joked Tom.
'So, do you want a drop?' Barry waved the brandy bottle.
'I haven't got a glass.'
'Don't be a tart like Alan, Tom. Put a drop in your beer.' Barry walked over and put a generous measure in Tom's half-filled bottle.
'Tony?'
'Go on then, I don't want you talking about me.' Barry gave a similar measure to Tony and then poured one for himself.
'Christ, Barry, I feel ready for my bed, and there you are getting ready to go out.'
'Don't forget I'm on UK time, Tom. My body thinks it's about three in the afternoon.'
'What time did you fly in?' Inquired Tony.
'We landed about 4 pm.'
'Heathrow direct, Eva Air?'
'Yes, why?'
'You must have been on the same plane as my mate, Bob.'
'What's he look like?'
'A bit smaller than me, fair hair, my age.'
'No, doesn't ring any bells.'
'He was wearing jeans and a cream thick sweater.'
'We saw him, Barry. You said, look at that muppet dressed for winter.' The three men turned and saw Alan sitting down on a sunbed next to Barry.
'Hello, Alan, good to see you. So, you did see him then.'
'Yes, now you said what he was wearing, it could have been him. Is he not staying here with you?'
'Long story, to be honest, I'm very worried about him.' Tom stood up, he was feeling drunk and couldn't face hearing the Bob saga again.
'Right, on that note, I think I'll leave you to it and head up.' Tom made his excuses, said goodnight and headed up to his apartment.
'Tell us what's happened, mate.' Barry passed the brandy to Alan as they listened to Tony's worries.'

Back at the services, the two girls were eating some form of noodle dish. Bob had got himself a toasted sandwich after walking next door into a 7-11 outlet. Nan and Mooka were involved in a heated discussion as he walked back to their table.

'Everything okay?'

'Ka, everything good, Khun Bob.' Mooka spoke to Nan again, but she didn't reply.

'Don't forget, Nan. If you feel tired, we can stop at a hotel.'

'Ka, I don't think we make it home tonight. I drive some more, then stop.'

'I'll be guided by you, Nan. Stop when you've had enough driving.' Bob wondered if Nan and Mooka were arguing about Nan's decision to stop somewhere overnight, or her waving a gun around in front of him. After the girls stood up, Nan announced she was going to 7-11 to get some drinks.

'You want some water, Khun Bob?'

'Err ... I'm alright, I think.'

'Should drink plenty water. Very hot here in Thailand.'

'Yes, you're right. Okay then, I'll have some water, please.'

Nan spoke to Mooka, but Mooka didn't answer and looked the other way. Nan walked off, and Mooka turned to Bob. She had tears in her eyes. She hugged Bob.

'Sorry ka,' she whispered in his ear. Bob didn't have a clue what Mooka was apologising about.

'It's okay.' He couldn't think of anything else to say in reply. Nan returned carrying a bag; Bob noticed the dirty look she gave Mooka.

'Is everything okay between you two?' He asked.

'Ka, everything good, Khun Bob. Mooka just tired. We go now. The three of them trudged back to the car, Nan was speaking to Mooka in a firm voice. Bob didn't have a clue what was being said or going on. For the first time since he arrived at the airport, he wished he'd listened to his friend. As they reached the car, Bob could hear his phone ringing in the boot.'

'Can you open up the back please, Nan? That sounds like my phone ringing.'

Tony had gone through the whole story with Alan and Barry.

'So, as you can imagine, I'm very concerned.'

'It's a pity you got to the airport so late.' Tony let out a big sigh.

'It was, Barry. But I left here in plenty of time, there was an accident just as I was leaving Pattaya, and I got held up for over an hour. Bloody typical. Anyway, I wasn't that late; he'd only been in the arrivals lounge for about thirty minutes.'

'Enough time for those girls to get at him, by the sounds.' Remarked Alan.

'Yes, plus the fact he's smitten with this girl and can't see the wood through the trees.'

'Unfortunately, it sounds like he'll be another victim of letting his cock rule his head.'

'He's always been quite sensible up to this point. He's too trusting, that's his problem.'

'Why don't you try ringing him again?'

'It will be a waste of time.'

'Well, you won't know unless you try. Give it a go.' Barry picked Tony's phone up off the table and passed it over.

Tony called Bob's number and put the call on speaker so Alan and Barry could hear the ringing sound.

'See, nothing.'

'Hang on, Tony. Give it a minute.' The three men sat and listened. Just as he was going to cut the call, Bob answered.

'Hello, is that you, Tone?'

'Bloody hell, Bob. Why haven't you answered your bloody phone?'

'I put it in the boot of the car, I didn't hear it.'

'You know why they're called mobile phones, don't you? Mobile being the operative word here.'

'Sorry, Tone. I only saw you a few hours ago, what's up?'

Tony had to think for a minute; perhaps he'd read the whole situation wrong. Maybe the two girls were genuine.

'I was just wondering how the journey was going?'

'We're making good time, I think. Where are we, Nan?' Tony could hear Nan's voice faintly in the background.

'Apparently, we're between a place called Nakhon Sawan and Kamphaeng Phet.'

'Kamphaeng Phet? That's where Pooki comes from. Christ, you are making good time.',

'Well, Nan is the female equivalent of Michael Schumacher.'

'I see, as long as you're alright, Bob?'

'I'm fine,' he lied, knowing this wasn't strictly true. However, he didn't want to worry his friend.

'We're going to stop in a few hours, I think Nan is getting tired, it's been a long drive for her.'

'Good idea, in a way you'd have been better off staying in a hotel in Bangkok, then travelled fresh tomorrow.'

'Yes, in hindsight we should have done. Doesn't matter, we'll break the back of the journey tonight, then we won't have far to go in the morning.'

'Okay, Bob. Hey, keep your phone with you, okay?'

'Yes, Dad. I'll ring you tomorrow. See you.' Bob hung up. Tony turned to his two friends. Barry spoke up.

'Sounds like you've been doing a lot of worrying for nothing.'

'Well, I still think he's an idiot, doing what he's doing. Not keeping his mobile phone with him just confirms his idiot status.'

'Don't be too harsh on him, Tony. I can remember Alan and me dropping you off at your hotel when you first came here. We gave you some advice, you remember, Alan.'

'Oh yes, we said to you, don't go falling in love with the first girl you meet.'

'Well, technically, Pooki wasn't the first girl I met here.'

'Best not to get technical, Tony. You'd been here just over a week when you took Pooki to Koh Chang. A few days later, you told us you were getting married.'

'True, but I struck gold with Pooki.'

'You have mate, and good luck to you, you're living the dream.'

'Well, for a few more weeks, Barry. It will all change when that baby arrives.'

'That's true, but best we don't mention it.'

Tony looked at the two smirking buddies and knew they were winding him up.

'Well, you two, like Tom, my bed is calling.'

'Yes, go on, old boy, Alan and I are heading to the bars.' The three men shook hands, and Tony staggered off to his apartment.

'These youngsters have no staying power,' Joked Barry to his friend.

Bob checked his watch, it was gone midnight, and he guessed they'd been driving for around six hours. Nan was still driving at a high speed.

Mooka had gone back to sleep, and he was worried about Nan falling asleep behind the wheel. He leaned forward between the front seats to speak.
'How are you feeling, Nan?'
'I tired, Khun Bob. I stop soon, I know nice cheap hotel where we can stay.'
'Okay, sounds good. I must admit I'm feeling very tired myself.'
'Make sure you drink plenty, ka.'
'Mooka drank all that bottle of water.' Nan said something in Thai, and Bob thought she sounded angry.
'No worry, Khun Bob, you get water at hotel.' Nan seemed to go even faster, making Bob feel very frightened. As he watched the road, he realised they'd come off the main motorway and were driving along a smaller road. Not wanting to question her again, Bob sat back and held on. Mooka was snoring, and not for the first time, he wished he'd listened to Tony's advice.

'You okay, darling?' Tony was doing his best to be quiet, but was banging about in the darkness.
'Sorry, sweetheart, I'm looking for the bathroom light. Have I woken you up? I'm sorry. I've lost my bearings.'
'No problem, I awake, darling, our daughter is restless and keep kicking me. You drunk, darling?'
'No, just a bit merry. Here, I managed to speak to Bob at long last.'
'He okay?'
'Yes, still on his way to Chiang Mai.'
'That good darling.' Tony found the bathroom light and staggered in.'
'Alan and Barry are here; I just had a beer with them.'
'Ka, I see from balcony.'
'If baby come tonight darling, I drive to hospital.'
'Sorry, sweetheart, I will not drink like that again.'
'I don't mind, I glad you have friends you can drink and relax with.'
Tony climbed into bed and snuggled up beside his wife.
'I love you, sweetheart.'
'Ka, I know, I love you too.' The combination of the drink and the relief of hearing from Bob. Tony was asleep in seconds.

Bob's journey from hell was coming to an end. Nan pulled the car to a stop at a small hotel that seemed to be in the middle of nowhere.
'You go book room, Khun Bob. I wait here with Mooka.'
'Wouldn't it be better if you came with me?'
'No ka, better you book in alone, be cheaper that way. Get key then come back.'
'Shall I book two rooms?'
'No ka. Mooka and me will share bed with you. We here only few hours.' Bob thought this was all a bit odd, but he wasn't going to complain about sharing a bed with two beautiful women. Plus, Mr Thrifty kicked in, and if it meant saving some money, he was happy to do it. Making sure he had his small travel bag containing all the Thai money, he closed the car boot and headed towards the reception. The place looked old and very basic. A man was behind a small desk, his head resting on his arms, asleep.
Bob gently tapped the man on the shoulder, causing him to jump up.
'Sorry to disturb you. Can I book a room?' The man looked at Bob with suspicion. He was relieved when the man spoke English, albeit brokenly.
'How many?' Bob wasn't sure if he meant people or nights, so he plumped for people.
'Three.' The man grabbed a calculator, pressed some of the numbers and showed Bob.
'One thousand eight hundred baht, okay.' Bob wasn't sure what that was in English pounds, so he didn't realise he was paying for three nights. Opening his travel wallet, he passed over two thousand Baht.
'Passport.' Bob pulled his passport out and handed it over.
'Fill this.' The man thrust a form in front of Bob that was in Thai.
'Err, I not understand.'
'Name, address here.' Bob struggled with the form but did the best he could.
'All done.' The man looked at the form.
'Contact number.' Bob pulled out his phone; he wasn't sure if the man wanted his number. Looking at the phone, he couldn't remember what his new number was. Going into the contacts, he saw Tony's number, so he wrote that down.
'Sign book.' Bob signed his name, and the man checked the signature.
'Print name.' Bob printed his name.

'Pick up passport tomorrow.' The man handed over a key.
'Room 8, go out and it down that side.' The man pointed, and Bob nodded, but he didn't have a clue.
'Okay, thank you.' The man sat back down and rested his head on the desk again. Bob headed over towards the car.

Nan was sitting with the window down as Bob approached.
'Room 8, down there apparently.'
'I know, get in, we park outside room.' Bob climbed into the back, where Mooka seemed to be out for the count.
'She sleeps well, your sister.'
'She very tired, Khun Bob.' Nan started the car and slowly drove between the reception building and what Bob thought looked like chalets.
'This our room.' Nan stopped the car outside one of the chalet-type rooms, and Bob peered out and saw the number 8 on a door.
'You have key?'
'Yes.' Nan held her hand out.
'I open and you carry Mooka in.' Nan got out of the car, and Bob watched as she opened the door to the room and switched the lights on. Bob got out of his side and walked around to the other side and opened Mooka's door.
Lifting a dead weight wasn't easy and Bob was pleased when Nan came and gave him a hand.
'She is heavier than I thought,'
'Ka, she eat too much.' For the first time in a long while, Bob saw Nan smile.
'You should smile more often, Nan. Makes you look beautiful.'
'Ka, thank you, Khun Bob.' Holding Mooka's top half, Nan picked up her legs and they carried her into the room and laid her on the bed. Bob looked around, and the room was very sparse. There was a very basic bathroom, a small fridge, and a very old-looking television. The only godsend was that it had an air-conditioning unit, which Nan was in the process of switching on. Bob looked at Mooka, who didn't flinch when they carried her in.
'She's out for the count. I wish I could sleep like that.'
'Ka, she a good sleep. Bring your bags in, Khun Bob.' Nan passed him the car keys, and Bob trundled off to the car.

Tony suddenly sat up in bed; he was sweating profusely. The sudden movement disturbed Pooki, who turned her bedside light on and then struggled to sit up.

'You okay, darling?'

'No, I've just had a nightmare, that bloody Bob again. Christ, it's hot in here, switch the aircon on, can you, sweetheart?'

'It's already on, darling.' Pooki struggled off the bed, went to the bathroom and returned carrying a wet flannel. She started to wipe Tony down.

'You have bad dream, darling?'

'Yes, and I've not had one of those for years.'

'Tell me.' Tony was reluctant to say too much; he knew Pooki was very into dreams and their meanings. She once told him she'd dreamt about her grandmother, who died at ninety-eight years of age. Of course, when she won a small amount on the lottery the following week with the number 98, this did wonders for her, believing that dreams always had a meaning.

'I can't remember too much,' he lied.

'Was your friend Bob dead?'

'What … No. I dreamt he was in prison; I went to see him and he was dressed in a white suit. He kept saying to me, please get me out, please get me out. He was crying, and I just left him there. He kept shouting at me, it's all your fault I'm in here, you told me to come.'

'What next, darling?'

'Nothing, that's when I woke up. I need a drink.' Tony climbed out of bed, went to the kitchen and poured himself a big glass of water from the fridge. Downing it in one go, he looked at the time, it was 2 am. 'I need a shower.' Tony went into the bathroom while Pooki changed the sheet on the bed. She then walked over and stood by the bathroom door.

'You not think the drink give you nightmare?'

'Drink? No, I've drunk many times, sweetheart, beer doesn't give me nightmares.'

'Ka, but brandy?' Tony turned around and looked at his smiling wife.

'How on earth do you know I've drunk some brandy?'

'Not difficult, darling. Suk text me, say Tom sick in toilet, say he been drinking brandy.'

'Did he now? Well, I did have a small drop, but that wouldn't have caused me to have a nightmare.'
'Ka, I think so.' Tony was too tired to argue the point; he knew Pooki too well to know that anything he said would change her mind.

Bob struggled in with his suitcase and travel bag. Nan was in the bathroom and could hear the shower running. He was hot, sweaty and tired. Mooka was snoring and lying on her side on the edge of the bed. Opening his suitcase, he searched for a change of clothes and his toiletry bag. Sorting out a pair of shorts, pants and a vest, he waited patiently for Nan to free up the bathroom. He then remembered the perfume he'd bought in England for Mooka and Nan, so searched his case again. He had bought two bottles of the same Estee Lauder perfume as it was on offer when he was looking in town. Pulling one of the wrapped boxes out, he put it on the small bedside. The room was cooling down as the noisy air conditioner sent a stream of cool air out. The noise from the shower had stopped, and eventually, Nan came out with just a towel wrapped around her and carrying her clothes. Bob tried not to stare at this beautiful woman as she had just a small towel covering her. Her hair was still wet, and as she sat on the bed, he could see most of her long legs.
'You have shower, Khun Bob?'
'Err … Yes. That box is for you, Nan. I hope you like it?'
'For me, ka?'
'Yes, I wanted to get something for you and Mooka.'
Nan picked up the box and unwrapped it. She smiled as she opened the box and pulled out the perfume.
'I love it,' she said as she sprayed a drop on her wrist.
'Yes, it smells nice,' commented Bob.
'Right, I'll have a shower. Bob picked up his clean pants and toiletry bag and went into the bathroom. There was one towel hanging up. He had packed a towel but decided to save it for Mooka as he guessed she'd want to take a shower in the morning. Looking at the showerhead, he could see it had just a tap, no shower unit attached. "Typical, bloody cold shower," he mumbled to himself as he stripped off. Expecting the worst, he was pleasantly surprised when he stepped under the tepid water.

Five minutes later, he felt refreshed. He desperately needed some sleep, but wasn't sure how he would settle with two women on the same bed. Coming out of the bathroom in only his brief boxer shorts, he was surprised to see the lights out but the TV on. The sound had been turned down low, and Nan was watching what looked like the Thai news, propped up in the middle of the bed. This was a slight concern for Bob as he would be lying next to her rather than Mooka.
'I put bottle of green tea in fridge, Khun Bob. Honey lemon, very nice.'
'Thank you.' Bob opened the door of the rickety old fridge and pulled out a bottle, which he assumed was the green tea.
Taking a sip, he was surprised how nice it tasted.
'You're right, Nan, it's very refreshing.' Bob carried the bottle over and sat on the edge of the bed. Luckily, Nan had pulled the thin sheet over, but he wasn't sure if she still had the towel wrapped around her. Drinking the rest of the green tea, he then slid himself under the sheet and put his head on the pillow. Nan turned the TV off with the remote control, and Bob listened to the noise coming from the aircon unit mixed in with Mooka's snoring. He was starting to feel slightly groggy, but put it down to the jet lag.
After a few minutes, he could feel Nan turn on her side and was facing him. He could feel her breathing next to his ear. He felt uncomfortable with her being so close, but couldn't seem to move.
'Thank you for perfume, Khun Bob.'
'You're more than welcome, Nan.' It was then that he realised Nan was naked and felt a penis rubbing against his leg. Bob was horrified but was unable to do anything to fend the ladyboy off. Nan's arm was on his chest, his hand gently moved across until he had it resting on his nipple. After a few seconds, he started to slowly caress.
'I'm not sure this is a good idea, Nan.' Bob tried to protest, but physically he felt unable to do anything about it.
Nan didn't speak; he just continued to gently rub Bob's nipple. He slowly edged closer and started to nibble on his other nipple. By now, Bob, disgusted as he felt, couldn't stop getting fully aroused. He tried to roll onto his side, but he couldn't even manage that. Even opening his eyes for long was a struggle; he knew something was wrong with him.
'Nan, please stop, I don't feel too good.' Bob tried his best to protest, but Nan wasn't listening. He could feel him climbing on top and

straddling him. He felt silicon breasts on his chest as Nan slowly kissed his neck. He could hear Mooka's snores and wondered if everything was about to be ruined because of Nan's lustful behaviour.
'Nan, please, I can't move, something is wrong with me.'
'You not need to move, Khun Bob, just relax and enjoy. Bob felt helpless as Nan's tongue worked its way down to his crotch. It was then that Nan pulled his boxer shorts down and started to perform oral sex on him. As much as he felt sick that Nan, who he now knew was a man, was doing this to him. It had been such a long time since he had made love, so he couldn't stop the feeling of enjoyment. It wasn't long before he knew he would climax.
'Nan, stop, I'm going to cum if you don't.' Nan wasn't listening, in fact, after Bob's announcement, he sped up and as much as Bob tried not to, he couldn't stop the inevitable.
Nan sucked him dry, then sat up, wiping his mouth.
'You a bad boy, Khun Bob. You with my sister, but you make love to me. I think you need to be punished.'
Whatever Nan had drugged him with was now affecting his speech. Bob tried to protest, but he couldn't get the words out. He was now completely helpless and at the mercy of the psychopathic ladyboy. Nan climbed off the bed and rolled Bob over onto his front. As much as he had lost the power to move, he could still feel when his body was being touched, and it wasn't long before he could feel Nan's fingers prodding his backside.
'I think you virgin, Khun Bob. You have a tight ass, no worry, I can help you.' Bob could feel the pain as Nan tried to insert his penis into him.
'You very tense, Khun Bob. You need to relax. Bob could feel Nan's tongue probing his anus. After a short while, Nan stood up and walked into the bathroom, he came back with Bob's shower gel. Nan was well endowed and rubbed some gel around his manhood. He then climbed back on top of the helpless Bob.
'That's better, I think you like, you naughty man. What Mooka going to say when she finds out you like Ladyboy? She not going to like you anymore. She not want gay man, Khun Bob.' Nan slowly worked his penis in deep, causing untold pain to Bob.
'I can tell you enjoy, you sexy man.'
Bob was in agony as Nan started to thrust his penis in and out. Nan started grunting and calling out in Thai as he thrust his penis up to the

hilt. What seemed to go on for a very long time eventually came to a stop once Nan started screaming out with ecstasy. Breathing heavily, Nan stopped and slumped on top of Bob.
'I feel good, Khun Bob. Maybe I clean you and we can do again.'
Eventually, Nan climbed off and Bob could hear the shower running. It was around this time he fell into unconsciousness.

Tony woke to the smell of eggs and bacon. He sat up in bed and felt decidedly worse for wear. He could hear Pooki chatting to someone in the kitchen, so after using the bathroom and putting on some shorts, he ventured out to see who was there.
'Good afternoon,' Joked Tom on seeing his neighbour.
'Tom, come round to check on your friend, darling.' Tom was sitting at the kitchen table, holding a mug of tea.
'Hello Tom, well, I have good news, I managed to get hold of him in the end. He'd left his phone in the boot of the car.'
'I'm pleased to hear it; I was feeling a bit concerned about him as well.'
'Thanks, Tom. Well, I still think he's a wally, but it sounds like he's okay.'
'You sure you do not want some, Tom?' Pooki placed a large breakfast in front of Tony.
As much as he didn't fancy it, Tony didn't show it.
'Off your food, Tom?'
'Aye, just a tad. That brandy did me up like a kipper last night.'
'So, I heard, sick and bad were you?'
'Should never mix my drinks. I must admit I'm surprised you can eat that after the amount you tucked away last night.'
'I didn't have that much, Tom.' He lied.
'Nothing puts me off my food, in fact, I think the brandy did me some good.'
'Good? Tell Tom about your nightmare?' Pooki smiled at Tony.
'Tom doesn't want to hear about that.'
'I do, so you had a nightmare then?' Before Tony could speak Pooki got in.
'Ka, he wake up shouting and all sweaty. It the brandy, Tom. Give him nightmare.' Tom started laughing.
'What was it about?'

'I can't remember that much; I must have had Bob on my mind. For some reason, he was in some form of prison, dressed in white. Shouting at me, saying it was all my fault.'
'Strange dream. You think it means something?'
'Ka, it mean he not to drink brandy.' Tony ignored Pooki's little joke.
'No, I don't think it means anything. It was strange, though. It seemed so real. Anyway, it woke me up and I was in a bit of a sweat.'
'He very sweaty, Tom. Had to shower and I change sheet on bed.'
'Really, maybe Pooki's right, maybe the brandy didn't agree with you?'
'Possibly Tom.' Tony didn't want to give Pooki any more ammunition. 'When you next speak to your friend, ask him if he still wants the apartment, only I have someone who's inquired about it. I've told them I think it's let for the coming month, but obviously, I'd like confirmation.'
'Of course, Tom. I'll ring him later and find out for definite. It's a bit too early to be ringing him.'
'Not too early, darling, nearly lunchtime.' Tony looked at the clock on the wall and he could see it was ten minutes to twelve.
'Bugger me, I've never slept in so late. It must have been the broken sleep.'
'Brandy knock you out, darling. That why you sleepy.' Tony vowed never to let Pooki know he'd drunk brandy again.
'Yes, you're probably right, sweetheart.'
'Eat breakfast, darling, it get cold.' Tony forced a piece of bacon into his mouth and gave a forced smile to Tom.
'Right, enjoy your brunch, Tony. Let me know when you've spoken to your friend, Bob.'
'Will do, I'll eat this and then ring him. I'll give you a knock once I've spoken to him.'
'Right you are, I'm in the rest of the day. Thanks for the tea, Pooki.' Tom let himself out as Pooki walked over with the frying pan and tipped two fried tomatoes onto his already-heaving plate.
'I think I need to start eating a bit healthier, sweetheart. I shouldn't be eating a fry-up every morning. No wonder Bob said I'd put some weight on.'
'I like you this way, darling. I not want skinny man.'
'I know you do, but I need to be fit for the baby. All this fried food is not good for my heart.'

'Not problem for you, darling, you do plenty exercise.'
'Yes, but I should not be eating fry-ups every morning.'
'Ka, I cook smaller breakfast tomorrow. You want some toast, darling?'
Tony could see another battle coming up.
'Go on then, just a couple of slices.'

After the big blowout breakfast and a visit to the toilet, Tony made a cup of tea and sat out on the balcony. Picking up his phone, he called Bob's number. This time, there was no ringtone, just a message in Thai, followed by an English version.
'I'm sorry, but the number you are calling is currently unavailable.'
'Bloody hell, Bob.'
'What darling?' Pooki called from inside.
'I just called Bob's number and got a message saying he's currently unavailable.'
'Don't worry, darling. He most probably charging phone.'
'Why's he switched it off to do that? I never switch my phone off.'
'Try later darling, go and have swim, make you feel better.'
'Not after that breakfast, Christ, I would sink.' Tony stared at his phone.
'You'd have thought they'd be on their way to Chiang Mai by now?'
'Ka, maybe they are.'
'Yes, maybe.' Tony looked down at the pool area and saw Barry making himself comfortable on a sunbed.
'I'm just popping down to see Barry, sweetheart.'
'Okay, darling.' Pooki had her feet up on the sofa, watching TV.
Tony kissed her on the cheek and then went out, leaving his phone on the balcony table.

'Hiya Barry, I hope you've got plenty of sun cream on?'
'Factor thirty, mate.'
'Where's Alan?'
'Your guess is as good as mine. Last seen escorting a young lady along Walking Street.'
'How did you get on?'
'Oh, not too bad, you know me.'
'Yes, I do.'
'So, heard from your mate today?'

'No, nothing. And listen to this, his phone is currently unavailable?'
'Bloody hell, Tony. Give the guy a break. He most probably has his phone on charge.'
'That's what Pooki said.'

As Barry and Tony chatted, his phone started to ring out on the balcony. Pooki struggled to her feet and went outside to answer it.

'What are your plans for Christmas, Tony?'
'Nothing, as far as I'm aware. Pooki can't go far; she's uncomfortable a lot of the time. She doesn't like being bounced about in the truck, and I don't like her riding the scooter in her condition.'
'Alan and I will most probably have the day on the beach.'
'Sounds good. Much better than sitting on Brighton beach in December.'
'You're not wrong there, mate.' The conversation was interrupted by Pooki hollering down to Tony.
'Darling, come quick.' Thinking it was something to do with the baby, Tony sprinted back to his apartment. Not waiting for the lift, he ran up the stairs. By the time he'd got to his landing, he was breathless. Pooki stood by the door.
'What is it, sweetheart?' He gasped.
'Your phone rang, it was the police. Your friend Bob he in hospital. He in a bad way'
'Was it an accident?'
'No ka, he been drugged and robbed.'
'I knew it, I bloody knew something like this would happen.'
'There more, darling. He been attacked.' Pooki didn't want to tell her husband anymore about the attack. The policeman she spoke to gave her all the gory details. She couldn't face telling her husband the worst of it.
'How bad is he? What hospital is he in?'
'Sukhothai. Policeman say he bad but will be okay.'
'I need to go there, where is it?'
'Past my home. I come with you, darling.'
'No sweetheart, you can't go that sort of distance in the truck. Think of the baby. Did the police mention anything about Mooka or Nan?'
'No, just your friend. How will you find the hospital?'

'Tom has a printer; he can sort out a route to the hospital for me. I know how to get to your home, so I know most of the way.' Tony stared at his wife; he had tears in his eyes.
'I bet you any money you like this has something to do with those girls. I knew they were bad. Why didn't he just listen to me?'
'Not your fault, darling. You try help him. Come, I go see Tom with you.' As they were going out of the door, Tony's phone rang again. Pooki picked it up and looked at the number.
'It the police.'
'Well, answer it, then.' Pooki said hello and then chatted away in Thai. Tony picked up the odd word, including his name. The call went on for ten minutes. Tony noticed how Pooki had a worried look on her face. Eventually, she hung up.
'That was police, darling.'
'Yes, so I gathered. What did they want?'
'They ask if you can go to police station in Sukhothai before you go to hospital. And have spare clothes you can take to him.'
'Spare clothes? What for?'
'Your friend, they take everything.'
'What all his clothes as well.'
'Ka, everything. Only left passport, reception keep it. Cleaner, she lady who find Bob.'
'Where did the cleaner find, Bob?' Tony was struggling to piece together what had happened to his friend.
Cleaner go to hotel room, she see Bob on bed, he not look good. She call manager and he call police. Ambulance take him to hospital. Hospital check and find he been drugged.'
'What about his injuries, didn't you say he'd been attacked as well?'
'Ka, I not know injuries.' Pooki looked like she was about to cry.'
'Don't get upset, sweetheart, do you know the name of the hotel and where it is?'
'Ka, police tell me, it in Sukhothai too.'
'Okay, let's keep calm, you mustn't get stressed in your condition, sweetheart. Let's go and see Tom, he can print the directions to this hotel and hospital for me.' Tony went out of the apartment door, but Pooki didn't move. Tony went back in to check on her. He could see she was getting upset.
'I not tell you everything, darling. Police tell me, but I not want to say.'

'He's not dead, is he?'
'No ka. He not dead, he been attacked.'
'Yes, I know, you already told me, sweetheart.'
'I mean he been sex attacked. I not know English word for it.'
'Sex attacked?' Tony's thoughts immediately went to the ladyboy Nan.
'I think the word you're looking for is *raped*, sweetheart.'

*Chapter 8*

'That should do it.' Tom pulled some A4 sheets out of his printer. 'Right, that's the directions for you to go straight to the police station. This one is from the police station to the hospital, and this one is the directions from the hospital to the hotel in case you want to check it out. Last but not least, directions back to Pattaya.' Tom passed the paperwork over to Tony. Pooki was sitting out on the balcony talking to Suk.
'Thanks for this, Tom. It will help me immensely.'
'So, you don't know much about what happened?'
'Not really, although it's not hard to piece together what's happened.'
'Raped, you say? Is that the same as being buggered, I wonder?'
'I'm not sure, Tom. Raped, buggered, whatever you call it, He was sexually attacked against his will. I'd be grateful if you keep that to yourself. I'm hoping it might not be as bad as that; it could be a mix-up in the translation.'
'Let's hope so. Don't worry, I won't say anything, Tony. I just feel desperately sorry for him. Drugged, attacked and sexually assaulted, what a terrible ordeal for him. That pair he met at the airport involved, do you think?'
'I'd bet my life on it, Tom.'
'Sounds like you were right about the ladyboy then?'
'I knew something wasn't right with that Nan straight away.'
'Just a pity you didn't get a chance to warn poor Bob.'
'Yes.' That reminder from Tom didn't help Tony's mood.
'I'm so angry with myself. I could have stopped this from happening had I been firmer with him and warned him about that bloody ladyboy.'
'After what you told me last night, I don't think you are any part to blame. He'd made his mind up to go with them, and nothing you could say was going to change that outcome. Even telling him about the so-called sister being a ladyboy, I don't think would have helped.'
'I know you're right, but I can't get that feeling out of me that I could have done more.'
'Well, I don't think there was Tony. I think the most important thing now is to get yourself to the Sukhothai police station, tell the police what you know, and then go to the hospital to support him. Now, is there anything else I can do to help?'

Tony looked at Tom; he was of a similar build to Bob.
'There is something, Tom. The police have asked me to take some clothes up for him. Now, my clothes are going to swamp him. I don't suppose you have a spare T-shirt and shorts I could take up with me. I have some old underwear that I bought over from the UK but are now too tight, and a pair of flip flops.'
'No problem, Tony. I have plenty of spare T-shirts and shorts. Do you know what size feet he is?'
'I'm pretty certain he's a 9.'
'I have a pair of trainers I never wear, hang on a minute and I'll sort some stuff out for you.'
'Thanks, mate.' While Tom trundled off to the bedroom, Tony went out to see the girls on the balcony.
'You okay, darling?'
'Yes, I'm just waiting for Tom to sort out a few bits for Bob, then I'll hit the road.'
'You want Tom to go with you?' Suk volunteered her husband.
'No, I'll be fine, thanks, Suk. I don't know how long I will be up there, so I should go alone.'
'Give police the photos darling.'
'I will, don't worry. They're not getting away with this.' Pooki stood up.
'I make you sandwich.'
'I'm fine sweetheart. I can stop when I feel hungry. I just need to pack a bag with a change of clothes and a few toiletries.'
'Toiletries, darling?'
'Yes, toothbrush, deodorant, stuff like that.'
'I go do for you.' Pooki said something to Suk in Thai and wandered off back to their apartment.
'Here you are, Tony. Bob can keep the lot, although I wouldn't mind the rucksack back.' Tom stood holding a bag that looked full.'
'You sure, Tom. Seems a lot in here?'
'All stuff I never wear.'
'Thanks, mate, you've been a godsend.'
'Think nothing of it. You have a safe trip and ring me if you need help with anything.'
'Will do.' Suk walked in and hugged Tony.
'We look after Pooki, you don't need to worry.'

'Thanks, Suk.' After shaking hands with Tom, Tony headed back to see Pooki.

Twenty minutes later, they were standing by the truck.
'You got passport, darling?'
'Yes, just in case I get stopped by the police.'
'Money?'
'Yes, plus my credit card in case I need to stay in a hotel. Most importantly, I have Tom's instructions.' Tony looked at the one that would take him to the Sukhothai police station.
'563 kilometres, won't take long.'
'No racing, darling.'
'Don't worry, I'll go steady.' As they hugged, Suk came walking over carrying a plastic bag.
'Take with you, Tony.' Looking in the bag, it was half-full with some bottles of water, crisps and cakes.'
'Thanks, Suk. Okay, I'll ring you once I get there, sweetheart.' Tony gave her another hug and then climbed into the truck. The two women held hands as Tony started the engine. He waved and then drove off. Looking in the rear-view mirror, he could see them waving back. He settled back for the seven-hour drive.

After stopping twice for diesel and a toilet break, it was just coming up to 9 pm when, thanks to Tom's pinpoint instructions, Tony parked up outside the Sukhothai police station. Pooki had written down the name of the policeman he needed to speak to, so armed with that, he walked in and was surprised at the number of people in there. Luckily, a man in uniform walked over to help. Tony did a wai then spoke.
'Sawadee khab,' do you speak English?' He asked.
'I speak a little,' replied the policeman. Tony pulled the piece of paper out containing the name Pooki had written down of the policeman in charge of Bob's case.
'My friend has been attacked; I need to see this policeman.' The man read the name.
'Write friend name down and your.' The man passed a small notebook over. Tony wrote the two names down in block capitals and passed the notebook back.
'Okay, you come here tomorrow morning.'

'Tomorrow morning?'
'Khab.'
'What time?' The policeman showed Tony his watch and pointed to the number eight.
'Okay, thank you.' Tony did another wai and went back to his truck. He phoned Pooki.
'Hello sweetheart, how are you?'
I okay, darling. Where are you?'
'I'm outside the police station. I've been in and spoke to a nice policeman. I showed him the name and he told me to come back tomorrow morning.'
'Okay, darling. What you do now?'
'I'm going to the hospital to see Bob, hopefully. Not sure if I can get to see him this time of night. According to Tom's directions, it's only 3 kilometres from here.'
'No racing.'
'I won't race, sweetheart.'
'Ring me, won't you.'
'Yes, I'll ring you after I've seen Bob, okay.'
'I miss you, darling.'
'I miss you too. Don't go worrying, okay? I'm fine here, and once I've seen Bob, I'll book into a hotel for the night. Speak later.' Tony hung up and started the truck. Checking the directions, he drove off in search of the hospital.
Less than ten minutes later, Tony pulled up in the hospital car park. Even at 9.30 pm, it seemed quite full.
All the signs were written in Thai, which didn't help Tony. Looking around, he decided to head to the main building. Once inside, like the police station, he was surprised at the number of people milling about. His previous experience of speaking to nurses hadn't gone well, but he had no choice but to try. There seemed to be a main booking desk, so Tony joined the queue. After only a short wait, he was faced with a very nice, smiling lady.
Tony started with the polite wai and asked if she could speak English.
'One moment,' she replied. Picking up the phone, she spoke quickly to someone in Thai.
'Take seat, mister.' The lady pointed to a row of chairs. Tony walked over and sat down. A few minutes later, he saw a man in a hospital

uniform speak to the lady, who then pointed to him. The man walked over. Tony stood up and gave the man a wai, which the man returned.
'How can I help you, sir? Said the polite man.
'My best friend was brought here; I think this morning or early afternoon.'
'Your friend name?'
'Bob Bates, or I should say Robert Bates.'
Take a seat, I go and check for you.' Tony sat back down and watched the man walk off. A lady came and sat down next to him. She was carrying a little girl who seemed to be fascinated with Tony. Giving her a little wave, she started to smile at him.
'Sir, I take you to see a doctor who will speak with you.'
Tony gave the little girl another wave and then followed the man who headed out of the main building and across a small road to another smaller building. The man didn't speak to Tony, just occasionally glanced back to check he was still there.
Eventually, they reached what Tony thought was a ward.
'Take a seat, sir.' Tony sat down as the man disappeared through some swing doors. The one thing Tony thought was the same as a UK hospital was the smell. They all had that distinctive smell. Watching a lady mopping the floor, Tony didn't see the man come back, accompanied by a man who Tony thought looked Chinese.
'This is Doctor Channarong, he will help you. The man did a wai and walked off. Tony did a wai to the doctor.
'Hello Doctor, my name is Tony Fellows, I'm Robert Bates' best friend. I've travelled up from Pattaya to see him.'
'Well, I'm afraid you can't see him this evening, Mr Bates is still heavily sedated.'
'Okay, that's a pity, but of course, I understand. Do you think I will be able to see him tomorrow?'
'Yes, I think that will be possible.'
'Can you tell me how he is?'
'He is coming out of a drug-induced trauma, and we are still waiting for the lab report to see what drug was administered to him. I'm hoping tomorrow will see a big improvement.'
'What about his injuries?'
'I'm afraid I can't comment on Mr Bates' injuries, apart from they are not life-threatening.'

'I was told he was sexually assaulted.'
'As I said, I can't comment. Come tomorrow, sir. Visiting is between 2 pm and 6 pm.' Tony felt frustrated with his lack of progress, although he felt relieved that his friend was not suffering any life-threatening injuries.
Tony gave the doctor a Western handshake.
'Thank you for what you're doing for Mr Bates, and thank you for seeing me, doctor.'
'Not a problem. If you need a hotel, there is a very nice one just a bit further on from the hospital.'
'Thank you, doctor, but I have a hotel in mind.' Tony smiled and headed back to the truck.

Once inside and with the engine and air-con running, he phoned Pooki.'
'Hello sweetheart, you okay?'
'Ka, I just lay on bed watching TV. How your friend, Bob?'
'Well, I didn't get to see him, but I spoke to a very nice doctor who told me that he hasn't got any life-threatening injuries.'
'That good, darling.'
'It is. I should get to see him tomorrow, all being well. The doctor recommended a hotel near the hospital, so I will go there and get a room. I need to be at the police station by eight in the morning.'
'Have you eaten?'
'Just the crisps and cakes Suk got me.'
'Get something from a 7-11, darling.'
'I will. You get some sleep, sweetheart. I'll call you in the morning.'
'Okay, I love you, darling.'
'Love you too.' Tony hung up, and from the truck, he could see a 7-11 convenience store right opposite the hospital entrance. Walking over, he picked up a cheese and ham sandwich, which he got one of the staff to warm up. Getting some more water and a can of iced coffee, he paid and strolled back to the truck.
After eating the sandwich, he checked the directions to the hotel where Bob was found. He didn't mention his intentions to Pooki for fear of worrying her. According to Tom's printout, the hotel was about 12 kilometres away. Putting his seat belt on, he went to check it out.

Twenty minutes later, Tony pulled up outside a very old and shabby-looking building. He wouldn't have known this was a hotel as the sign was all in Thai. Although it was dimly lit, he could make out some outbuildings to the right of the main building. Locking the truck, he took a walk along the side of the building first. As he got closer, he could make out the individual chalet-type rooms. He could see a couple of the rooms were occupied, as one had a scooter outside and another had a car parked up alongside it.

Tony decided he wouldn't be staying here; the place made his skin crawl. Walking into the entrance, he could see a man behind what he assumed was the check-in desk, slumped back in a chair, fast asleep. Tony was about to wake him when he spotted a book lying open on top of the desk. Pulling out his reading glasses, he found Bob's name and signature straight away. He could see that room 8 had been entered in a little box next to his name, and the check-in time was 12.30 am. Looking behind the sleeping man, Tony could see some keys hanging up with large wooden key fobs with numbers on them. He zoomed in on the number 8. The man was snoring, so Tony chanced it. Creeping past the man, he gently lifted the key off the hook. He then silently made his way back outside. As he reached the door, he looked back, and the man was still fast asleep.

Tony's heart was racing as he made his way to Chalet 8. He'd never done anything like this before. He didn't know what he would find as he fiddled with the lock. He gently opened the door and went inside. Finding the light switch, he pressed it on. He could see straight away that the room had been cleaned, although there was no bedding or towels in the bathroom. Tony checked the mattress for stains but came across nothing unusual. Checking the drawers and under the bed, there was nothing to link Bob ever being in this room. Tony kept thinking to himself that if this were a crime scene, surely the room should have been left as it was found. Thinking he'd been watching too many crime dramas or perhaps he was in the wrong room, he turned the light off and crept out, locking the door and headed back to the reception. As he walked in, he could tell the man had moved. He was now asleep, using his arms as pillows, slouched across the desk. Tony once again silently walked over behind the man, dropped the key back on the hook and went back to stand in front of the desk.

Tony did what Bob had done less than 24 hours earlier: he tapped the man on his shoulder. Unbeknown to Tony, he got the same reaction. The man leapt in the air in a state of shock.
'Sawadee khab.' Said Tony to the man who looked like he'd seen a ghost.
The man took a few seconds to compose himself, then replied.
'Sawadee khab, mister. You want room?'
'No, I have come to collect my friend's belongings.'
'I not understand, mister.'
'My friend stayed here last night. He was attacked and ended up in the hospital. I've come to collect his belongings.'
'I think you mistake, Mister.' After a long drive and no luck at the police station or the hospital, Tony's patience was starting to wear thin. He grabbed the book.
'Don't play stupid with me. My friend, Bob Bates, see, here. He stayed here in room 8 last night with a woman and a ladyboy.'
'He come alone, mister. I not see anybody else. He book and pay for three nights.'
'Three nights?'
'Khab, but he was alone, mister.' Tony was confused. He pulled his phone out and found the photo he'd taken of the three of them at the airport.
'Is this the man?'
'Khab, that him. But you didn't see him with these two women?'
'No, I tell you, mister, he alone.'
'They must have been here; he couldn't have got here on his own. You took him to his room?'
'No, I give key. I not leave desk.'
'So how do you know they weren't waiting outside?'
'I not, but no reason to do that.' Tony looked at this little Thai man and wanted to punch him.
'You know what happened to my friend last night.'
'Yes, I sorry mister, I tell police, I not hear anything.'
'Well, you wouldn't, would you, I mean, I come in here and you're asleep, and it sounds like you're too bone idle to take a guest to his room.'
'Sorry, mister.'

'I'm not interested in your sorry, why's the room been cleaned?' The man looked at Tony and wondered how he knew what condition the room was in.
'We not clean room, mister. That is how it found.'
'You sure?'
'Khab, police ask same question. We not touch room.' Tony started to wonder if this Mooka and Nan had taken everything and cleaned the room so as not to leave any trace. He felt tired, and he knew he wouldn't get any further with this man, so he decided to drive back to the hotel near the hospital and get some sleep.
'Okay, well, thank you for nothing.'
'You want room, mister?'
'No, I don't want a bloody room, I wouldn't stay here if you paid me.' Tony turned and walked out; he didn't say goodbye or take a look back.

Forty-five minutes later, Tony was showered and lying on the bed in a very nice hotel room. He was glad he decided to take the doctor's recommendation. It had just gone midnight, and when he booked in, he ordered a 7 am alarm call. His mind still racing, he knew sleep wouldn't be easy. After plugging his mobile phone into charger, he walked over to the fridge and checked the contents. Taking a small bottle of beer out, he flipped the top off and sat back on the bed. It gave him time to reflect on his own life. He'd been so lucky meeting Pooki, as much as he didn't have the baby coming along in his plan, he wouldn't change anything. He knew that had he not been made redundant, he'd still be going to work at the forklift factory. Most probably still living in the expensive flat that he couldn't afford. The British weather, Tony shuddered for a second, then smiled. He knew he'd been very fortunate.
His thoughts went to poor Bob. He knew he wouldn't have dreamed of coming to Thailand had he not moved here. Tony let out a big sigh. He knew he'd made a big mistake not warning his best friend about Nan being a ladyboy. At the time, he was more interested in berating his friend about the amount of cash he was carrying around with him, rather than warning him about Mooka's alleged sister. Bob was bound to ask him if he knew about Nan. What would he answer? He decided to cross that bridge when he came to it.

Thinking back to his friend in the hotel room, he wondered what the hell had gone on?' They obviously drugged him; Tony hoped his friend was unconscious throughout the ordeal.

Sitting up, he decided not to keep second-guessing what went on. He'd wait to see the policeman in the morning and hopefully get some answers.

He swigged down the last of the beer, lay down and surprisingly fell asleep quite quickly.

The sound of his phone ringing brought Tony back to the land of the living. Checking his watch, it was nearly 7 am. Climbing out of bed, Tony knew who was ringing without looking.

'You okay, sweetheart?'

'Ka, I okay. What you doing, darling.'

'Well, I'm just about to take a shower, then go down and have some breakfast. I want to get to the police station at eight.'

'How much hotel?'

'Thousand baht.'

'Expensive, darling.' Tony smiled; he thought the hotel was very reasonable. The equivalent of around twenty pounds for a nice room with breakfast.

'Yes, a little bit, but I was too tired to look around for something cheaper. How are you feeling?'

'Ka, good. Baby moving a bit, but that good sign. I go market with Suk soon.'

'Is that wise in your condition? You make sure you go in their car, not on the scooter.'

'I will, darling. What's that noise?' The phone next to the bed started to ring.

'Hang on, that's my alarm call.' Tony walked over and picked the receiver up, he listened, but there was no one there.

'I asked for a 7 am alarm call. Right, sweetheart, I need to get on. I'll ring you later when I have some news, okay.'

'Ka, make sure you do, and no racing the truck.' Tony smiled as he hung up.

Just over an hour later, Tony parked up at the police station. Walking in, he was happy that there weren't so many people standing about.

Not quite sure what to do, he walked over to a window where a policeman was sitting.

'Sawadee khab.' Tony did a wai and then asked the man if he spoke English. He didn't, as he called out something in Thai. A young woman in uniform came over and came through a door to talk to Tony. Doing the Thai greeting and wai, he passed over the policeman's name Pooki had written.

'My friend was attacked and I've come to see the policeman in charge of the case.'

'Ka, take a seat, I tell him you here.' The woman walked off, and Tony made himself comfortable.

As he waited, the police station started to become busy. Tony wished he could understand more Thai; he was intrigued by some of the conversations. Checking his watch, it had gone nine, and he'd been waiting over an hour.

Eventually, the young woman returned and asked Tony to follow her. Going through a secure door, they went upstairs to a maze of desks. Along the back wall were some offices. She went to one of them and knocked. She opened the door and ushered Tony in.

'Sit down, please.' Said the policeman. Tony was relieved that the policeman spoke English.

'Good morning, thank you for seeing me.'

'No problem, I believe you are Mr Bates, friend.'

'I am, I'm Tony Fellows.'

'I'm police Sergeant Jandaeng.' The two men shook hands.

'Mr Bates said you would come.'

'Have you spoken to him?'

'Khab, I just come from hospital. He look better today. I take a statement, but I not sure he is fully aware what went on'

'I've not been able to see him yet. I have to go back during visiting hours.' The policeman opened a drawer and passed Tony a business-type card.

'Show staff this card, they let you see him.'

'Thank you.' Tony put the card in his wallet.

'Can you tell me what happened?'

'According to the statement, it look like he met two Thai women on the internet. They pick him up at Suvarnabhumi airport and say they will take him to meet family. Not far from here, they stop at hotel, there he must have been drugged and was assaulted. He was robbed of everything. He claim around two hundred and fifty thousand baht and two thousand UK pounds. A gold chain, a watch and all his clothes. I think he may be mistaken by the amount of money taken.

'No, that sounds about right. I met Mr Bates at the airport, and he had that amount of cash with him. I remember telling him off about the amount of money he had on him.'

'I see, you met him at the airport? Mr Bates never said?'

'Maybe he's still confused, after all, he's been drugged.'

'Could be, I go back this afternoon to see if he remembers anything else.'

'Anyway, by the time I arrived, he was already with the two women, I should say woman and ladyboy.'

'Interesting, he said, one of the women assaulted him. He has a nasty injury in his anus. I thought maybe he'd been attacked down there with an instrument.'

'No, one was a ladyboy for sure. Do you think you'll be able to find these two?'

'We will do our best. Unfortunately, the hotel where the attack happened has no security cameras, and the room was stripped bare.'

Tony decided not to mention his little visit to the said hotel. Instead, he played his trump card.

'Not sure if this will help, but I took photos of the three of them at the airport, and the number plate of the ladyboy's car.' Tony pulled his phone out and showed the policeman the photos. Sergeant Jandaeng looked and immediately broke into a smile. Jumping out from his seat, he stared at the photos.

After checking all the relevant pictures, the policeman turned to Tony. Can I take your phone and copy photos?'

'Yes, of course, anything that may help.'

'It help, I know this ladyboy.' Tony waited in the office while the sergeant went off to copy the photos from his phone. Eventually, he returned.

'I have removed the photos from your phone, I have them copied. It may endanger the case if you have the photo evidence.'

'Of course, like I said, I'm glad to help in any way in catching these two.'

An hour later, Tony returned to the truck. He couldn't wait to phone Pooki. He called her number. When she answered, he could hardly hear her through the background noise.
'Where are you, sweetheart?'
'I market with Suk.'
'Okay, I'm going to the hospital now to see Bob. I have some good news, but I will tell you later when you're home.'
'I not understand you.'
'I'll ring you later when you're back home.' He shouted.
'Okay, darling.' Typical, thought Tony. The first bit of positive news he had, and his wife couldn't hear him.
Wanting to tell someone, he called, Tom.
'Hi Tom, it's Tony.'
'Don't go worrying, mate, Suk's taken Pooki to the market.'
'Yes, I know. I just wanted to give you an update.'
'Okay, how is Bob?'
'I'm not a hundred per cent sure, Tom. According to the policeman who visited him this morning, he said he looks a lot better than he did yesterday.'
'That's great news, Tony. Have you seen him yourself?'
'Not yet, I'm just heading over there now.'
'Okay, well, I hope the clothes and trainers fit him.'
'I'm sure they'll be fine.' Tony was thinking that the clothes fitting was the last of his worries.
'Did the directions help?'
'They were spot on, Tom. Got me door to door.'
'Glad they helped.'
'Okay, Tom, I'll speak to you later.'
'Give my regards to Bob and tell him we wish him well.'
'Thanks, Tom.' Tony hung up and drove on to the hospital.

This time, he went straight to the ward Bob was in. As he walked into the entrance of the ward, he was stopped by a sour-faced nurse. She spoke to him in Thai.
'I'm sorry, I do not understand you. I come to visit my friend, Mr Bates.'
'Visiting not yet,' came a voice from behind him.

Tony opened his wallet and showed the card the policeman had given him. The two women looked at the card.
'Come,' said the nurse who spoke some English. Tony followed the nurse. The ward was big; Tony estimated that there were at least fifty beds in the ward. At one end, Tony could see the end of a bed that was partially hidden by curtains. As he approached, he saw his friend lying on the bed, a drip attached to his arm. He looked terrible, and Tony could feel his eyes welling up. The nurse opened the curtains a bit more, then walked off. Bob's eyes were closed, and Tony wasn't sure whether to wake him or not. He pulled a chair up and sat down, then gently put a hand on his arm.
Bob opened his eyes, and Tony could see the relief in his eyes as he recognised a familiar face.
'Tone,' he croaked.
'It's alright mate, I'm here now.' Bob tried to sit up.
'Stay there and rest, Bob. Tony leaned over, and the men hugged. Bob started to cry uncontrollably. Tony just hugged his best friend and did his best to comfort him.
'Don't worry, Bob, I won't let anything happen to you.'
'Don't leave me here, Tone. Please, I beg you, don't leave me here.'
'I won't leave you, Bob, I promise.' This seemed to calm his friend down a bit. Seeing Bob lying on the bed, wearing a white gown made him think of the nightmare he'd had. Shaking that feeling off, he looked for some tissues but couldn't find any. Seeing a nurse, he waved her over.
'You have tissues?' The nurse looked at Bob, then pointed to what looked like a little shop.
'Okay, thank you. Bob, I'm just going over to that shop. I'll get some tissues. Do you need anything?'
'I have not eaten since I came here, or drink.'
'Maybe you weren't allowed, Bob?'
'Can you ask? I'm hungry and thirsty.'
'Of course, I can. I'm just going to that shop, I'm not leaving the ward, mate.' Tony walked off and spoke to the nurse. He asked if Bob could eat and drink.'
'Ka,' replied the nurse who pointed to the shop again. Tony walked to the little shop and bought some tissues, biscuits, crisps, cakes and two

big bottles of water. Unlike the hospitals in the UK, here, you had to pay for everything.

Walking back to Bob's bed, he helped him sit up. He noticed Bob grimace with pain as he helped him up.

'Thanks, Tone, I'm bloody starving all of a sudden.'

'Well, that's a good sign, mate. Hopefully, you're on the mend.'

'I don't think I'll ever fully get over this, Tone. I thought I was going to die; in fact, I was certain I was going to die. That Nan had a gun.'

'Gun, bloody hell. Did you tell the police?'

'Yes, I think I told them about the gun. I'm not sure if I mentioned it or not, Tone. I can't remember.'

'It doesn't matter, the policeman said he'd come back later and talk to you again. You can tell him then. Can you face telling me what happened?'

'I'll try.' Before Bob even started telling Tony about his ordeal, he had tears in his eyes.

'I should have listened to you, Tone. I think you had your doubts about those two, but I stupidly ignored your warnings.'

'Well, there was something about them, I just couldn't put my finger on it.'

'That Nan was a man, Tone. One of those ladyboy types.'

'Yes, I had a feeling he was.'

'Did you know?' Tony was dreading this question.

'I wasn't a hundred per cent sure, Bob. I had my doubts, but he looked so beautiful, so I couldn't be certain.' Tony felt that he hadn't lied to his friend completely. He had been ninety-nine per cent sure Nan was a man, but not one hundred.

'I know, Tone, she had me fooled too, or I should say him.'

'So, what happened after you drove off from the airport?'

'All went well for a while, Mooka sort of fell asleep on my shoulder. That Nan drove like a maniac, he told me some story about an ex-boyfriend, and that's when he started waving a gun about, frightening the life out of me. Eventually, we stopped somewhere for petrol and to get something to eat. Thinking about it, I reckon that's where she first tried to drug me. She'd bought some drinks, Mooka whispered in my ear and said, I'm sorry. I didn't know what she was sorry about at the time, but I'm guessing now she knew what Nan's intentions were.'

'Was that the time you eventually answered your phone?'

'I think it was, Tone. Anyway, we got going again and the drink Nan had given me, Mooka drank it all. Within a short period, she was out for the count. I just thought she was tired. It had been a long day for her, so I didn't suspect anything else. I don't know how much further we went; Nan was still driving like a bat out of hell. Eventually, he said he knew a hotel and we ended up there.'

'Why didn't you book two rooms, Bob?'

'I was going too, but Nan said we're only going to be there for a few hours, so he said just book the one.'

'I went to that hotel last night; I checked your room. Everything was gone, even the towels and sheets.'

'They took everything of mine?'

'They did, sorry mate. What I didn't understand is why you booked for three nights?'

'Three nights? I didn't. I just booked one.' Tony was confused about this, but let it go.

'Doesn't matter, Bob. So, what happened next?'

'Well, Nan asked me to go and book a room on my own, I did think it was strange, but thought maybe it was a cheaper way of doing things. So, I went in and booked the room.'

'Was the guy asleep on the desk?'

'He was Tone, and not very helpful.'

'Don't worry, mate, I've already had a go at him. He should have taken you to the room, if he had, well, he would have then seen the other two.'

'He would have done. Oh well, doesn't matter now, does it?'

'So, what happened once you were in the room?'

'Mooka was so out of it that we had to carry her in. I know what you're thinking, Tone, but I just didn't realise she'd been drugged. I should have done; I can remember Nan getting the hump when I told her Mooka had drunk all the water. Plus, she didn't wake up as we carried her in.'

'You weren't to know, Bob. I don't think I would have guessed she'd been drugged. Why would you, I mean, you thought they were sisters.'

'Not for much longer, I didn't. Even when Nan came out of the bathroom with just a towel wrapped around, I didn't have a clue. I went in and had a shower, came out, and that's when Nan told me I had a drink in the fridge. Well, I think you know the rest.'

'I can guess.' Tony could understand Bob didn't want to tell him all the gory details.

'I thought he was going to kill me, Tone. What with having a gun and all that? I was helpless to stop him. I could feel everything, but I just couldn't move. That Nan is a bloody psychopath.'

'Well, hopefully, he'll be behind bars soon. I showed the policeman the photos I took at the airport of you with them and he recognized Nan straight away. He couldn't believe it when I showed him the number plate of his car.'

'You took a photo of the number plate?'

'I did, Bob. See all those years of watching those private detective shows have finally paid off.' For the first time since he arrived at the hospital, he saw Bob give a half smile.'

'You don't think he will come here to finish me off, do you?'

Tony could see his friend was still very frightened.

'Well, he'll have to get past me first, I told you, I'm not leaving you on your own.'

'Thanks, Tone.'

'How are you feeling, mate? I know it's a bit of a daft question.'

'Well, considering I was given a strong type of tranquillizer; I don't feel too bad now. It's just my arse, Tone. I have about a dozen stitches inside.'

'Christ mate, that must hurt.'

'Trust me, it does. Tone, please don't tell anybody. I don't want this getting back to people I know in the UK.'

'I understand mate. As far as anybody needs to know, you were just attacked and robbed.'

'Thanks, Tone. I don't think I could face anybody if I thought they knew what had happened to me.'

'You were mugged, Bob, that's all anybody needs to know.'

As the men chatted a nurse came up to the bed and informed Bob the police were here again and would like to speak to him.

'Can you stay here with me, Tone.'

'Of course, Bob.' Tony looked over and saw Sergeant Jandaeng who he'd met earlier that day, heading their way.

'Don't worry Bob, it's the guy who took your statement this morning and is in charge of your case.'

After saying hello, the sergeant asked how Bob was feeling.

'I'm feeling a lot better thank you. Still a bit of pain down here. Bob pointed to his groin.
'Yes, it does sound like you had sex with this ladyboy. I suggest you get an HIV test done when you return home.' Bob and Tony looked at each other.
'Now, thanks to your friend Mr Fellows we are making swift progress with this case. We have found and arrested the woman you knew as Mooka. Her real name is Ratana Chansungnoen.'
'That's quick work sergeant, well done.' Tony was impressed.
'Well it wasn't difficult; she gave herself up in this very hospital this morning.'
'She was here?' Croaked Bob.
'Khab, she's in another ward. She is also suffering from the after-effects of the same tranquillizer that you drank, Mr Bates.'
'Isn't it dangerous having her in the same building?' Asked Tony. 'I mean, she could come and look for Bob.'
'No, she can't do that. She handcuffed to the bed and she suffering from three bullet wounds.'
'Bullet wounds,' croaked Bob.
'Khab. She say the ladyboy you knew as Nan shot her.'
'Well, she did have a gun.' The sergeant looked at Bob.
'I think we need another statement from you, Mr Bates, you leave many things out.'
'I'm sorry sergeant, I wasn't fully awake this morning when you questioned me.'
'Don't worry, I understand. Now, I need to speak to Mr Fellows.'
'Come, let's get coffee.'
Tony followed the sergeant outside and he stopped at a mobile coffee vendor.
'Song café yen, khab,' the sergeant barked. The lady quickly poured two Iced coffees out. Tony went to pay, but the lady put her hand up. He guessed the sergeant was well known around these parts. Walking over to some concrete seating in the shade, Sergeant Jandaeng sat down and lit a cigarette.
Tony followed carrying the coffees.
'You come from Pattaya?'
'Yes, I've lived there just over a year now.'
'You married?'

'Yes, my wife is expecting our baby in just under a month.'
'Congratulations.' The sergeant looked genuinely pleased for Tony.
'I'm worried about your friend, Khun Tony.'
'So am I, it will take him a long time to get over this.'
'This ladyboy, he very dangerous man, very dangerous.'
'You think he will come here?'
'Maybe. That is why I am worried. He not worried who he shoots.'
'What do you think I should do?'
'If I were you, Khun Tony, I'd get your friend away from here as soon as possible.'
'I will, as soon as he is well enough.'
'He well enough, I speak with doctor. He need to pay his bill and get as far away from here as he can. Here, you better take this.' The sergeant handed over Bob's passport. Tony sat there stunned for a minute. He was shocked the police couldn't protect his friend from this ladyboy.
'Okay, well I don't have much of a choice. Where do I pay his hospital bill?'
'Drink your coffee, then I take you.'

Thirty minutes later, Tony arrived back at Bob's bed, armed with the rucksack of clothes. A nurse was in the process of removing the drip from Bob's arm.
'What's going on, Tone?'
'You've been discharged.'
'You are joking? Aren't you?'
'I wish I was, mate. I've just settled your hospital bill and I've got some antibiotics you need to take.'
'How much do I owe you?'
'Surprisingly not that much. It came to 16.000 baht. But that nice sergeant had a word and got it down to 10,000.
'How much is that in pound notes?'
'About two hundred pounds.'
'Why the sudden rush to get me out of here?'
'They think it's not safe for you here, mate. Not with a gun-toting ladyboy on the loose. Look, have a sort through these clothes, I'll come back and help you, I'm just nipping over to the shop.' Tony had spotted blood on the back of Bob's gown when he stood up. He couldn't believe the hospital thought he was fit enough to travel. While Bob

sorted through the clothes, Tony emerged holding a pack of lady's sanitary towels.

'Let's put one of these in your pants, Bob. Just to be on the safe side.'

After a painfully slow walk to the truck, Tony helped his friend into the passenger seat.

'Christ, I'm not sure how long I can stay sitting, Tone.'

'Let's see how you go, I just want to get us out of here, you never know if that Nan is lurking about.' That was enough to speed Bob up.

'Okay Tone, let's go.' Tony started the truck and he could tell straight away that Bob was in pain. A few hundred meters from the hospital, Tony stopped at a 7-11.

'I need to get a few bit's Bob. I'll get some drinks and snacks, you want anything?'

'I wouldn't mind a toasted sandwich, cheese and sausage if they've got it.'

'Okay, keep your door locked and your head down.' Bob did exactly that as he waited for Tony to return. Bob kept looking up, Tony seemed to be gone ages, but he smiled with relief when he saw his friend approaching the truck with a carrier bag.

'Sorry Bob, they were a bit slow with your sandwich.'

'It's alright, mate. You're here now.' Tony passed Bob his sandwich.

'Eat that, then take a pill.' Tony pulled a bottle of water out followed by a couple of blow-up neck collars from the bag.

'I'll blow these up for you, should help your bum a bit.'

'Thanks, Tone, that's a good idea.' Tony blew them up and then manoeuvred them under Bob's backside.

'That feels much better.'

'Good. Oh, by the way, the sergeant gave me your passport.'

'Thanks, Tone. What am I going to do, I only have these borrowed clothes to my name?'

'Well, you have plenty back in the UK, we'll have to work out how to send some money over. Don't go worrying about that now, I can look after you.'

'Where are we going now, Tone?'

'That is up to you, Bob. I can take you to Pattaya, you'll be safe there with Pooki and me.'

'I know that Tone, and I appreciate the offer. But can you take me to the airport? I want to see if I can get a flight back to the UK, I want to go home.'

'Of course, mate.' Tony didn't want his friend to go home, but after what he'd been through, he fully understood.

'I'll take you to the airport, see what we can do.'

'How long will it take us to get to Bangkok, Tone?'

'At least six hours I would say. Why don't you get in the back? You can most probably stretch out better and get some sleep.'

'Okay, I'll give it a try.'

About an hour into the journey, Tone could hear the odd snore coming from the back. He hunted in his door pocket and found his earphones. He managed to push them into his ears and his phone. He hadn't spoken to Pooki since the brief call he gave her as he was queuing up to pay Bob's hospital bill. He knew if he didn't call her soon, she would start to worry.

Dialling the number, she quickly answered.

'Hello darling, I've been worried about you.'

'Sorry, sweetheart, a lot has happened since I last spoke to you.' Tony tried to talk quietly.

'How your friend?'

'He's asleep on the back seat.'

'Are you coming home now, darling?'

'Not yet, I'm stopping at the airport. Bob wants to see if he can get a flight home.'

'He not need to go home; he can stay with us; I take care of him.'

'He knows that, sweetheart. Let's see what happens at the airport. I'll ring you again later.'

'No racing, darling.'

'I know.' Tony smiled as he cut the call. It was getting dark, so he put the headlights on.

After a couple of comfort stops, Tony parked the truck at Suvarnabhumi's short-term car park.

Helping Bob out of the truck, they slowly made their way into the terminal. Tony found the Eva Air booking desk and inquired about a flight home. The girl informed them that there were seats on tomorrow's 11.00 am flight to Heathrow.

'How much?' Asked Bob. The girl put the amount on her calculator.

'Two hundred pounds, Tone. What do you think? That's the fee to cancel my original flight home and transfer it to tomorrow morning's flight.'

'Look, Bob, I can pay for you. I can put it on my credit card.'

'Would you mate, I'd be ever so grateful, I will transfer the money to you as soon as I get back. Plus, a bit extra that you have forked out.'

'I know you're good for the money, Bob. It's up to you, mate. Are you well enough to travel? That's the main thing?'

'I think so. But where will we stay tonight?' Tony could see the worried look on Bob's face.

'I'll find us a hotel close by. Don't worry, mate, I'll stay with you until you get booked in tomorrow.'

'Thanks, Tone. You've been a bloody rock mate.'

'You'd have done the same for me, Bob. That's why you are and will always be my best friend. So, do you want me to book the flight?'

'Yes, please mate.'

Just after 11 pm, Bob and Tony were tucking into a late meal ordered from the room service menu.

'How are you doing, Bob?'

'I'm okay, Tone. It's a pity it didn't work out for me, but to be honest, I feel lucky to still be alive.'

'Well, you need to get home and put all this behind you.'

'It will take a while, that's for sure. Physically, it won't take long, I'm not sure about mentally.'

'Well, don't be too proud to get some help.'

'I won't, Tone, I promise. I'll have to explain to old Ted upstairs why I'm back so quickly. He's bound to have a tale to tell me about a short holiday.'

'Not that it will make you feel any better, but I woke up with a ladyboy beside me after my first night out here.'

'Never.'

'I did, mate. Got pissed and woke up in a strange hotel. I wouldn't have known if it wasn't for the fact that she rolled over as I was leaving the room, and it was all hanging out. And before you ask, no, I don't know.'

'Your secrets are safe with me, Tone.'
'You want a beer?'
'Why not? One won't hurt me. Cheers.' The long-term friends clinked the bottles.

After an early breakfast, Tony drove Bob back towards the airport. All Bob had with him was Tony's rucksack.
'Do you think I can claim on my insurance?'
'I'm not sure, Bob. Worth a try when you get home. I have the police sergeant's telephone number. He said he would call me if he had any news on the case.'
'Let's hope they catch that bloody nutcase, Nan, soon.'
'I'm sure they will, Bob. They've already captured the other one.'
'Yes, but I can't help but feel a bit sorry for her. God knows how she got mixed up with the bloody ladyboy.'
'Don't feel too sorry for her, Bob. She could have stopped it.'
'I know, mate.'

After parking the truck and a slow walk to the departure terminal, Tony waited as Bob booked in.
'Well, I'm certainly travelling home a lot lighter than when I came.'
'I'm really sorry this happened to you, mate.'
'It's not your fault, is it? You did your best to warn me. Thanks for the money, Tone, I'll send it to you as soon as I'm back.' Tony had got two hundred pounds exchanged for Bob so he could get a taxi home from the airport.
'No rush, get home and get better.'
'Right, I'd better go on through.' The two men looked at each other, both with tearful eyes.
'Safe trip home, mate.'
'Thanks, Tone.' After a hug, Tony stood and watched his best friend gingerly make his way through the crowd.

Back at the truck, he phoned Pooki.
'Hello sweetheart, I'm just leaving the airport now.'
'Your friend gone home, darling?'
'He has, I'll see you soon. Oh, don't worry, I won't race.'

After a late lunch, Tony was enjoying a cup of tea on the balcony. He couldn't get Bob out of his mind. He felt so sorry for him, and the thought of him arriving back at Heathrow on his own played on his mind. He looked at his watch; it was just coming up to 3 pm. He picked up the phone and called his daughter, Emily.
'Hiya, Dad, everything okay?'
'Yes, everything is good. Listen, I'm after your auntie Janice's number.'

After everything that had happened, Bob felt such a relief when the huge plane touched down at Heathrow. Adjusting his watch back to UK time, it had just gone 5 pm. Still, in a lot of pain, he knew the two blow-up neck collars had been a godsend, even though he received some funny looks when he sat on them.
Because he could only move slowly, he sat back and let the other passengers fight their way out first.
Eventually, he pulled the rucksack out from the overhead locker and ambled out. The December air of London hit him like a brick. Wearing only a thin shirt, shorts and trainers, Bob could see he was getting some funny looks. But by then, he was past caring. He just wanted to get out of the airport and get a taxi home. After a fairly easy transition through passport control, Bob slowly entered the arrivals lounge. Keeping his head down, he made his way towards the exit.
'You want a lift?' Bob recognised the voice straight away. He looked up and saw Janice standing there. She was holding a parka coat.
'You better put this on.'
'Christ Jan, how kind of you to meet me.' The sight of Janice made him cry with relief.
'I've always looked out for you, Bob. You've just been too blind to see it.' Janice hugged her ex-boyfriend.
'Come on, let's get you home.'

Around the time Bob landed at Heathrow, Police Sergeant Jandaeng was driving his police pickup truck. He'd turned off the main road and was heading to the hotel where Bob had been assaulted. As he approached the hotel car park, he could see a white Toyota parked up. He flashed his lights and slowly pulled up alongside it. The driver of the Toyota climbed out and walked around to the police sergeant's pickup. The policeman lowered his window.

'You're late,' said the woman.
'I'm a busy man, Nan.' The ladyboy passed over a thick envelope containing over 300,000 baht.'
'Don't spend it all at once, sergeant.'
'You don't need to worry about that. I suggest you go back to Cambodia for a while, you've overstayed your welcome.' The ladyboy winked and walked back to the Toyota.

## 2025

### Epilogue

Tony never heard another word about Bob's attackers. He did try Police Sergeant Jandaeng's number once, but the number came up unattainable. Bob never pursued an insurance claim and just wanted to forget about the whole episode. Whatever happened to Mooka and Nan remains a mystery to this day.

Ted, the retired policeman and Bob's upstairs neighbour, who kept him entertained with his endless supply of stories, passed away in 2013 at the age of 78. He never did get a computer.

Old Bert, who befriended Tony when he first arrived in Pattaya, passed away in 2014. The years of taking under-the-counter, herbal libido supplements finally took their toll. He died as he hoped he would. Making love to two young bar girls. He was 81 at the time of passing.

Alan and Barry are both now retired. Alan lives in Pattaya and is still frequenting the bars. His sidekick, Barry, unfortunately, suffers from heart problems and is no longer able to fly.

Tom and Suk have moved to a complex in Jomtien, but still keep in contact with Pooki and Tony.

Pooki's sister Jeab is still working in real estate, and her husband Peter, who is now in his eighties, is still plodding on.

Tony's ex, Susan, is now married to a retired school teacher. Ironically, her husband insisted on a prenuptial agreement.

For Bob, well after Janice picked him up from the airport, they slowly became close again. Bob took Tony's advice and saw a counsellor about what had happened to him in Thailand. Eventually, they pooled their money and bought an apartment in the lovely small town of Nerja on the Costa del Sol. Bob, who is now in his early seventies, never returned to Thailand. He still keeps in regular contact with Tony. He took up golf, and with Janice, they now enjoy the Mediterranean lifestyle. They tied the knot back in 2017.

As for Tony and Pooki, they are still blissfully happy. Their daughter Noi is now fifteen years old and the apple of her father's eye. She speaks Thai and English fluently. After three years of living at the family home in Kamphaeng Phet, they moved back to Jomtien. Pooki, who has just turned forty-seven, works as a receptionist at a condo complex close to the house they rent.

For Tony, well, like Bob, he is now in his early seventies. Still riding his bike, going to the gym and fishes most evenings with his friend Tom. He's never gone back to the UK, although he has plans to show his wife and daughter the country he came from in the near future.
If you ask him, he will still tell you he is living the dream ….

After all, I should know ☺

Any feedback on this book would be gladly received, good or bad.

trevorwhitehead58@gmail.com

Printed in Dunstable, United Kingdom